FROM RAGGED LONDON
TO THE GARDEN OF EDEN

From Ragged London to the Garden of Eden

Jean Jardine Miller

JM PUBLISHING

Library and Archives Canada Cataloguing in Publication

Jardine Miller, Jean
From Ragged London to the Garden of Eden / Jean Jardine Miller.

ISBN 978-0-9731376-9-9 (paperback)

I. Title.

PS8619.A735F76 2015   C813'.6   C2015-906907-6

Cover and text design: Design and Copy Consultation Services.
Cover illustration *Over London by Rail* etching by Gustave Doré 1872
Cover photography Can Stock Photo

Jardine Miller - publishing what is significant to today
Shelburne, Ontario L9V 2Y2 Canada

*In memory of the many "Home Children"
whose placements on Canadian farms were a
lot less fortunate than those of the fictitious
Tom and Annie Denton.*

CHAPTER ONE

"I'm jus' lookin' for coal an' wood for the fire," Tom told the boy, hoping he sounded like a mudlark and not like a schoolmaster's son. "So you can 'ave it, s' long as you give us yer coal."

"Well… don't want nobody saying Joe Spratt bilked yer, so you keep them rags and take them into the broker's – 'e should give you a few pennies for 'em. Good Irish lace that is, believe you me. 'Tain't yer everyday…"

Tom stuffed the rags into the front of his coat and looked hard at the plank of wood he'd found half buried in the mud. He'd dug it out thinking it would dry out and he could use it for firewood, propping it and gradually feeding it into the fireplace, then just as he spotted the nails, the boy had appeared out of nowhere and suggested the exchange. The boy's bag of coal would burn a lot longer than the wood, so Tom was quite ready to swap with him. He stood the plank up in the glutinous Thames-side mud and held open the battered satchel.

"Pour it in 'ere," he said, still eyeing the plank of wood.

"Fink I'm putting one over on you, don'tcher?" Joe Spratt said, tipping the muddy bits of coal into the satchel. "I ain't. Fing is, see, I takes the wood – good oak, that is – and sells it with the nails in to the marine shop. Worf more to them with the nails left in – sell 'em as is, they will, if they can get 'em out straight. Ain't no use trying to get them out straight wivout the tools, is it? Won't get paid much fer bent nails, you won't, and straight nails is gold nowadays wiv everybody wanting work done fast. Anyway, I gets paid immediate and can go an' get some eats and get on wiv me uvver business. Sellin' the coal round the courts an' alleys takes time but, if that's what yer want…"

He shrugged his shoulders and reached out to pull the plank out of the mud. Wondering what the boy's 'uvver business' was, Tom folded the flap of the satchel over the coal. "I don't," he said, squelching through the mud towards the wharf. "Go round selling it, I mean. I just need it for me fire at 'ome. Me ma's ill and needs to stay warm and we make matchboxes which 'ave to be dried or they won't pay us for 'em. Every bit of coal I find 'elps out. See, what money we don't 'ave to spend on coal, we can use to buy milk and bread."

"Sorry 'bout your ma – ain't got one meself, 'ave I? Not wot I remember, I don't. Well… 'least you got an 'ome," Joe Spratt said, looking a little envious. "Wiv a fireplace 'n all–" he caught himself and added, "Well, better be on me way, I 'ad. Maybe I'll see you again next ebb if I'm still down 'ere then. Gets around up and down the river, does Joe Spratt."

"I'll watch for you," Tom said as they reached the broken down end of Emmett Street Wharf that was used by scavengers to reach the river's muddy shore at low tide. Joe Spratt sprang up onto the embankment wall, throwing the plank up first then picking it up before darting away. "Ta ta."

Tom watched him go, wondering how he could run so fast in the wet broken down old boots he wore. Pulling over his head the laces of his own boots which were tied together to hang around his neck, then the satchel, he threw them onto the wharf and hoisted himself up beside them. Well, judging by Joe Spratt's actions, he thought, using the rags to wipe the mud off his feet before putting on his boots, it seemed that the regular mudlarks wouldn't resent his intrusion on their territory. He'd been half afraid of confrontation when he'd first had the idea of coming to the river, at low tide, to scavenge for bits of coal. Thankfully, nobody had come near him the first few times and, this morning, Joe Spratt had seemed almost friendly, and the now full satchel of coal would keep the room warm all day and all evening, too. It was a long walk down here and back again, but worth it – Annie and Harriet wouldn't have to work on the matchboxes with frozen fingers all morning and Ma and the baby wouldn't be shivering in the bed. He finished lacing up his boots, picked up the satchel and slung it over his shoulder, then crossed the wharf and hurried alongside the high dock wall to make his way to the High Street and through to the busy East India Dock Road, then across to Catherine Street and over to St. Leonard's Road.

Sleet had begun to fall by the time he reached the shabby row of yellow brick houses in the court where they had a room on the second floor of one of the middle houses. Just as it always did, an image of the house where they'd once lived in off Devons Road popped into his mind. He quickly dismissed it and ran up the stairs.

"Look how much I got," he cried, opening the door. "A full bag – how's that for good luck?"

"That's lovely, Tom," Annie smiled, looking up from the table where she was already busily assembling matchboxes and supervising four-year-old Harriet's pasting on of the sandpaper. "How did you manage to find so much?"

"I swapped a plank full of nails, with a boy I met, for the coal he'd found. Proper mudlark, he was," Tom pulled out the rags. "He said the lace on this rag was good lace once and I could sell it at a broker's shop…"

Annie looked doubtfully at the bundled rag. "I could wash the mud out and see what it looks like then. I wonder how a fine lady lost her petticoat in the river? It's not worth me washing these other bits, though. Just put them in the rag bag – we've nearly got enough to sell to the rag and bone man." She handed the matchbox she had finished to Harriet and stood up. "Here, I managed to get enough heat off the embers to make a bit of porridge. Me and Harriet's eaten ours. Ma didn't want any but, now we've got all that coal, we can have the fire burning early and see if she'll have some stew for dinner. Should be enough heat left to get a couple of small pieces burning now – it's been enough to keep your porridge warm. Bit of a luxury, but it's cold this morning."

Annie often performed miracles in the morning, somehow managing to coax the embers in the fireplace into giving off enough heat to get a few cinders burning again to simmer a small pot of porridge or heat water to re-use already used tea leaves. She got up and tipped the coal from the satchel, which she had once used to carry her night lessons back and forth to school, into the scuttle, picking out some small pieces to throw into the dead-looking embers, and then scraped the remaining porridge from the pot into a bowl for Tom.

"Thanks, Annie," he said, sitting down at the table, forgetting that he was still muddy.

"Better wash your hands, first. There's water ready for you in the bowl."

"There's poison in the river, Tom," piped up Harriet. "A bit of that mud could fall off your hands and into your porridge and you'd eat it and then you might die."

Tom rose again, went over to the washstand and rubbed the mud off his hands in the bowl of water there. He also picked up the clothes brush, once one of his father's prized possessions, and brushed some of the drying river mud from his sleeves and trousers.

"Now, you're safe to eat your breakfast," Harriet continued, as she watched him. "See my boxes – how neat they are? They're very good for some one who's only four, aren't they?"

Tom sat down and looked at the matchboxes. "I hope you're being careful with the sandpaper, like Annie tells you, so you don't make your fingers too sore."

Harriet nodded sagely and watched her brother eat his porridge. "Annie had to make bread and milk for the baby while you were gone. That's why there's not many boxes done yet."

"Ma had no milk at all for him again," Annie said, sitting back down and picking up a strip of wood to start making the next matchbox tray. "I ran out and caught the milk lady on her way along St. Leonard's and got the jug filled. There'll be enough to give him some for dinner and tea. Ma hardly woke up at all, Tom."

Earlier, before Tom had gone down to the coal wharf, Annie had run up to the matchbox factory with the big sack of matchboxes they'd made yesterday to get paid and to fetch the supplies for the day. Ma hadn't woken all the time he was helping Harriet wash her face and get dressed or when John woke up and Tom rocked him in his arms until Annie came back to look after him. Now, Tom looked across the room to the bed where their mother lay so still, the baby sleeping beside her.

Almost as if she had sensed him watching her, Ma opened her eyes.

"Isn't it time you were off to school, Tom?" she said in the weak voice that was all she was able to manage these days.

"I'm off in just a few minutes, Ma. There's still lots of time."

"You should see all the coal he got down at Limehouse Hole, Ma," Annie said, passing the matchbox she had just completed to Harriet. "We'll be able to put the stockpot on and have a hot dinner today.

"That's good of you, Tom, but it mustn't interfere with getting to school on time."

Tom felt uncomfortable as Annie looked away from him and then back to her work. He felt so dreadful still, about being the one to go to school while she spent the day making the matchboxes, to supplement Ma's annuity and provide enough money for them to manage on. He and Annie had both continued going to school after their father died but when Ma was unable to recover her strength after the baby was born, she had decided that Tom should go to school, because schooling was more important for a boy, and Annie must stay at home to look after Harriet and the baby while Ma worked on the matchboxes. At first, Ma had given Annie sums to do and grammar exercises. Then, as she became weaker, Annie had to take over the matchbox making and there was no longer time for lessons. She tried not to feel resentful, but Tom knew it must be hard for his sister to see him go off to school each morning leaving her to make matchboxes and look after the rest of the family. In a matter of months, nine-year-old Annie had changed from being his happy, laughing younger sister into a substitute mother to Harriet and John, and even to Tom, himself.

Tom finished his porridge, put the bowl on the washstand and went to get his school satchel from the corner where he'd left it after doing his night lessons the evening before. He crossed to the bed and bent to kiss his mother goodbye.

"Don't you worry about me, Ma. I'm off to school now and still have plenty of time to get there before the bell." He straightened and looked down at the baby who had wakened again, but was contentedly kicking his feet. "John's awake again, but he's quite happy. Annie fed him bread and milk."

"Annie's such a good girl," Ma whispered, sadly. "And you're a good boy. Now off you go."

Tom turned towards Annie as he went to the door. "I'll be back to help you at dinnertime." He paused and then said, "I wish we were going together like we used to."

"It's all right, Tom," she said. "Just as long as you remember what you learn so you can tell it to me when you get home. 'Bye."

"'Bye."

"'Bye, Tom," said Harriet, "until dinnertime." After Tom closed the door behind him, she turned to Annie and asked, "Why don't you go with him like you used to?"

"You know why, Harriet."

"'Cos Ma's too ill to look after me and John, and make the matchboxes?"

Annie put her finger to her lips. "Let's just get on with the pasting, Harriet," she said quietly.

"I could look after John, you know. I do when you're doing the washing and making dinner and suchlike."

"That's just for a short time, Harriet. School lasts for much longer and it costs money. I need the time to make the matchboxes so we can buy food and clothes, and medicine for Ma, and pay the pennies for Tom to go so that he can grow up and be a schoolmaster like Pa was."

"Will me and John be able to go to school when we're old enough?"

"Yes, I expect so."

"I'd be able to help you at dinner time and in the evening just like Tom does, wouldn't I?"

"Maybe Ma'll be better by then and she and me can make twice as many matchboxes and you and Tom won't have to hurry home to help us and you can play with your friends instead – just like I used to do."

"I don't have any friends –"

"But you will when you go to school. Now do you remember how to count to twelve?"

"Yes."

"Well, you count the matchboxes as we go and when we get to three lots of twelve, I want you to play with John over in the corner. I can tend to the fire and put the stockpot on the hob, then chop the potatoes and carrots and onions that Tom got cheap at the market last night, ready to make a nice stew for dinner. Then, you can lay the matchboxes out on the floor there for the paste to dry. Can you manage that?"

"I can do it all. I'm good at counting, aren't I?"

"Maybe good enough that you won't need to go to school."

Harriet smiled and shook her head, "I know you're joking."

Maybe, Annie thought. She hoped she was.

* * * *

She missed going to school. She missed the games in the playground with the other girls; walking with Tom and Pa to the girls' playground or, in earlier years, to the infant's school; waving goodbye as they continued on to the boys' schoolroom door, sitting at the kitchen table after tea with Tom as they did their night lessons; and so much more. That was at their old house, of course, which they'd had to leave after Pa died. Less than a year ago… just after Christmas, it had been. The weekly rent was more than the payments from the small annuity, which was all the income Ma was left with, so they had moved to this room, bringing what furniture would fit in a borrowed handcart. The rest had been sold because they had nowhere to store it. Ma said it would only be until she'd had the baby and was able to find some work which would provide them with enough money to rent a little house again.

After the money from the sale of their furniture had gone, Ma had started making the matchboxes with Annie and Tom helping her after school. It was just to tide them over, she said. But, after John's birth in April, Annie and Tom had started fetching the supplies and taking back the finished matchboxes, payment for which they spent on decaying vegetables and cheese, sometimes a piece of bacon or a loaf of bread, being sold off cheap in the market at the end of the day. When one of them fetched the weekly annuity payment from the Friendly Society office, they were able to buy a sack of oatmeal and a scuttle of coal as well as take the rent money to the landlord who lived in the front parlour of a house in the next road. The houses were quite new but already dilapidated due to rooms being divided up and rented to families who couldn't afford a whole house. At first, Ma would sit up in bed to make the matchboxes, saying she would probably feel better when the weather got warmer.

Summer came, but she didn't get better. By the time school broke up for the summer holidays, she was sitting up only to feed the baby and was unable to look after Harriet, who Tom and Annie had often found out in the street when they came home from school, usually having been hit or scratched – on one occasion very severely – by the street urchins who played there. With no school, and with help from Harriet who they taught to count and pile the finished matchboxes together ready for tying, Tom and Annie were able to make matchboxes all day. Since the matchboxes could be set to dry in the sunny window, they did not have to buy so much coal and could spend the money saved at the dairy in Grundy Street, where the cows were kept in the backyard. However, despite the milk and butter, Ma made little progress. The baby often had to be hand fed with milk from a bottle – the midwife had given it to them, after Tom had gone to her asking for help when they realized that John was crying because he was hungry – and well boiled oatmeal or bread and milk. Annie did not go back to school.

Now, it would soon be Christmas time again…

"There," said Harriet, "twelve, again. See, I've put them in lines – three lines. The ones on the floor were before I started counting." She stood up, carefully stepped around the matchboxes on the floor and went over to the bed. "John's gurgling and smiling but I think he needs changing. He smells…" She wrinkled her nose.

Annie changed the baby and set him on a blanket on the floor in a corner of the room, telling Harriet to play with him there so that they wouldn't disturb Ma. Then she took the bellows and blew on the embers, which had been kept smoulder-ing by the small pieces of coal, and added enough coal to provide heat to boil water to wash the baby's napkins, which she'd left soaking in a bucket. She chopped the vegetables, us-ing what water was left in the jug on the washstand to clean them, and put them in the stockpot with the miniscule remains of a previous stew. Then she carefully removed the pot of boil-ing water from hob and replaced it with the stockpot. Tipping the napkins into the pot and adding the sliver of soap she kept for the purpose, she took up the wash-stick to pummel them, throwing in the ragged petticoat Tom had found in the Thames mud.

"I'm going down to empty the bucket and get some more water, Harriet," she said when she had decided the napkins were clean enough and squeezed the water out of them. "I'll be back as quickly as I can, then we'll get back to work. Don't wake Ma up, now."

* * * *

Annie said that babies knew about nothing but feeling hun-gry, sleepy, comfortable or uncomfortable but Harriet was sure that John knew his sisters took care of him instead of his mother. She also thought that he knew that he didn't have a pa. Her own memory of her father was already growing dim. Some-times she found that she'd forgotten what he looked like but other times she could picture him quite clearly. This would mostly happen when she thought about him stepping over the scrubbed front door step at the house they used to live in, and telling Tom and Annie not to spoil their mother's handiwork as they all left for school in the mornings. This, of course, was when Ma was well – before Pa had died and before baby John was born. They'd all hop over the step and go off down the road to school. When she was old enough Harriet would go with them but children who were only three years old weren't allowed. Instead, she spent her days with Ma and that's why she had decided that John must know that it was she and Annie who took care of him. Of course, she couldn't remember being as little as John but she knew that Ma had always been there. John only slept with Ma, and spent the rest of the time watching her and Annie make matchboxes or being fed oatmeal or bread and milk by Annie, or milk in the bottle, or having Harriet play with him on the blanket in the corner of the room. He looked sad sometimes and that was how she knew that he missed having a mother to do all these things with him.

"One day, Ma will get better and she'll look after you just like she looked after me," she told the baby, who chuckled and hit her with his rattle. "It won't be quite the same because she'll have to make matchboxes and I don't think we'll ever go back to our proper house. Annie says we have to live here now because we can't afford to pay the rent at our real house. It was nice there. Ma and me would go next door to Janie's house sometimes and other times Janie and her Ma would come to our house. I wish Janie was still my friend. There aren't any nice children here – you'll find out when you're older. They punch and scratch you."

John looked startled. She wasn't sure if he understood her or if he just had wind. She sat him up and patted his back. He just smiled so she decided that he had understood and was smiling to tell her not to mind about the nasty children because when he was bigger, he'd be her friend. He threw the rattle down and plunged after it. Harriet moved it out of his reach and he pulled himself forward. She straightened out his dress to make it easier for him to move his legs but, grasping the rattle, he rolled over onto his back and began to chew it instead. Annie had told her that her that he was growing teeth and his gums were sore so that chewing on something brought relief. Harriet wondered where his gum ring was. Probably in the bed, she thought. She stood up and felt under the covers trying not to move them too much for fear of waking her mother. Thankfully, her searching fingers made contact with the rubber ring near the outside part of the bed and Ma wasn't disturbed at all. Slowly pulling the ring out, she glanced at Ma and thought she seemed dreadfully still. She had been coughing and making choking sounds earlier but now she lay perfectly still. It was a scary kind of stillness. She quickly sat down on the floor again and, gently taking the rattle, placed the gum ring in John's hands instead. He instantly put it in his mouth. Harriet wondered for a moment why she found Ma so scary. Perhaps she should try and wake her up after all… just to make sure she was still – well, still Ma. Somehow she didn't seem to be Ma any more. But Annie had said not to wake her…

Harriet manoeuvred the baby onto her lap and began to sing "Rock-a-bye-baby" but found herself crying when she reached the part about the wind blowing the baby and cradle down. She wished Annie would hurry back. She was only fetching water but the pail was heavy for a little girl to carry. Perhaps that was her coming up the stairs now – she must be resting the pail on each of the steps.

"Let me up, John," she said, gently moving him so that she could stand up." Annie's back. I'm going to open the door for her."

CHAPTER TWO

Tom ran up the stairs thinking about how nice the stew Annie had promised for dinner would be after his walk home from school in the icy rain. He reached the door and was about to open it when Annie stepped out, closing it again behind her.

"What's wrong?" he asked, seeing her frightened face.

"I think Ma's dead," she said. "I mean, she is dead. She's getting cold and not breathing."

"Are you sure? Let me–"

"No, I don't want to frighten Harriet," Annie said, blinking back the tears which she had been refusing to allow herself for the last hour and a half. "I went down to empty the slops after I'd washed the napkins and, when I came back up, I bent down to put the chamber pot back under the bed, then I stood up again and was going to ask her if she would like some milk to drink. I was telling her how I had set it on the window sill to stay cool, and I looked at her and just knew somehow… the way she was lying… so still… I thought it best to carry on with the matchboxes and let Harriet think she was still asleep. That was best, wasn't it?"

"Yes," said Tom. "I suppose so. Should I see if I can get the doctor to come?"

"I don't know. He'll have to be paid. Maybe it's best if you go over to Aunt Ella's and ask her what to do. And see if she can look after Harriet and John while – while whatever has to be done is done."

"She'll have a fit."

"I know but she won't mind having the baby or Harriet – at least, I don't think she will… I've been telling Harriet that you have to run an errand when you get in. Here, I'll take your satchel for you." He slid it over his head and handed it to her. "Go on, please. It's the best thing we can do."

He watched Annie rub her eyes with the back of her free hand and go back into the room, then he turned and slowly went back down the stairs. He knew she was right – they needed help. Maybe it would be better for all of them to go. No, Annie probably wouldn't want to leave Ma alone and he could get there faster on his own, which was probably why she had told him to go while she stayed with the little ones. Aunt Ella was the wife of Uncle Alfred, their late father's brother who was a solicitor's clerk and worked in an office in Bow. Tom had been there once, a long time ago with his father, and thought he could remember where it was – not much farther than his house, which was off Bow Common Lane near the cemetery. Aunt Ella wouldn't know what to do and she disliked children. She'd send him to Uncle Alfred, anyway, so he might as well go straight there. He set off across Chrisp Street to Guildford Road to cross the Limehouse Cut to Bow Common Lane.

Twenty minutes later, after running most of the way, Tom was having difficulty controlling his sobbing breath when he reached the door of the solicitor's office. He stood for a moment and waited for his heart to stop pounding.

"Tom. Is that you, Tom?"

He spun round and found his uncle coming up behind him, half hidden by a large umbrella. He must have come out of one of the alleys he'd passed as he ran along the Bow Road. He tried to speak and found, to his mortification, that he couldn't get the words out – only shuddering sobs.

"What's wrong, Tom? What are you doing here?" Alfred Denton put an arm around his nephew's shoulders and guided him into the solicitors' chambers. "Come along in. Two of the partners are in chancery and the other's with banking clients so there's just young Mr. Martin and he won't object. Now sit down, my boy, and calm yourself. Here, wipe your face and blow your nose. I'll put a little bit more coal on the fire."

Tom hoisted himself onto the clerk's stool his uncle indicated, took the handkerchief he was holding out to him and did as he was told, thankful to be in the warm room.

"Now, my boy, what's brought you all the way over here when it's time you were on your way back to school for the afternoon?"

"It's Ma, Uncle Alfred." Tom's voice was a hoarse whisper but his breathing was beginning to return to normal. "Annie says she's dead. You know Annie's been looking after Harriet and the baby instead of going to school because Ma can't get up? Well…"

"No, I didn't, Tom. I didn't know things were as bad as that. Why didn't you come and tell me?"

"Ma sent Annie to see Aunt Ella after the baby was born. Annie told her that Ma was ill and didn't think she had enough milk for the baby. She told Annie that she must make sure that Ma ate lots of milk and butter and cheese to build herself up –

she didn't seem to understand that we didn't have the money. Ma was cross but said we must manage somehow without nobody's help if that's the way it was. So, we've been managing…"

"You mean, Ann – your ma's been ill ever since the baby was born?"

Tom nodded.

"That's some seven months ago. And why didn't you have the money for milk? She has an annuity…"

"It's not enough to bring up four children. That's what Ma told Annie and me. But it's all right – Annie and me've been making matchboxes – Annie, mostly, because Ma insists I go to school. And Harriet helps, too. So we buy food with the money, and milk, and Annie's almost weaned the baby now – gives him bread and milk, she does, and he's very healthy, but Ma… well, she isn't… I came home from school for dinner and Annie said I must come and get you to help us take care of whatever must be done when someone dies. We don't know what to do – we need the curate and the funeral undertaker and we have no money…"

Exhausted, Tom put his head in his arms on the desk in front of him and quietly sobbed. He was glad he'd decided to come to the chambers instead of going to his uncle's house. If Aunt Ella hadn't told him about Annie's visit all those months ago, it was hard to imagine her helping them now.

"You just wait there, Tom," his uncle said, "while I go along to young Mr. Martin's chamber and see if he can excuse me for the afternoon…"

Uncle Alfred was thoroughly alarmed now, Tom thought, as he wiped his eyes and blew his nose. Maybe he did care about them. Ma always said that Pa's brother and his wife thought they were a bit above her and that's why they never came to visit now that Pa was gone. You wouldn't catch them in Bromley's backstreets. Be afraid they'd catch something, she had said. He hoped Uncle Alfred would come straight back with him and not say they had to go to his house to fetch Aunt Ella. No, he couldn't imagine Aunt Ella walking all the way down Bow Common Lane… He wondered how Annie was managing. By now, she surely must have had to tell Harriet that Ma wasn't just sleeping. Perhaps they were crying together. He hoped the baby was sleeping – poor Annie would hardly be able to comfort Harriet and look after John… He had to get back to help her. And there were the matchboxes to get finished or they'd have no money at all. That brought his thoughts back to Ma.

She should have told them what to do, he thought, and immediately felt guilty about thinking such a critical thing. More importantly, what were they going to do without her to tell them what to do? He looked wildly around the little room in panic and almost fell off the stool in fright as the door opened and a boy came in.

"Ello," the boy said. "And 'oo are you?"

He was older than Tom by several years, although not much bigger, and dragged his left leg as he walked.

"I–I'm Tom," he stuttered. "I mean I'm Tom Denton. I–"

"You're Mr. Denton's nephew. I've 'eard about you. I'm Mr. Ernest John Smith, apprentice solicitor's clerk. You can call me Ernie, though."

"All right, Ernie. My uncle's gone in to talk to young Mr. Martin to see if he'll excuse him for the afternoon…"

"Leavin' me in charge of the clerks' room? Ooh, my! I ain't been left in charge before… 'Course there's only Mr. Martin in and 'e don't do no work unless 'e 'as to. Why's 'e want to be excused? Your uncle?"

"My mother has died. We need him to help us – me and my sisters and the baby do."

"I thought it was your pa that died. Right after I was bound to your uncle it was."

"He did – nearly a year ago now. And now my ma's died, too. I wish my uncle would come back – I need to get home to help Annie."

"Oo's Annie?"

"My sister. She's got the little ones to look after, and Ma… And there's the matchboxes to finish… I don't know what we're going to do…" Tom blinked back tears. He didn't want to cry again in front of this boy, but it was hard not to when he thought about his mother lying there in the bed.

"'Ere's Mr. Denton coming now," announced Ernest John Smith. He turned towards the short corridor as his apprentice master came back from the solicitors' chambers. "Young Tom 'ere 'as been telling me 'ow 'is mother 'as died. I'm sorry for your ber–bereavement, sir. You can trust me to look after the clerk's room while you're off to 'elp 'im."

"You carry on with the copying you were doing before you went home for your dinner, Ernest. I'll be back to look after the senior partners when they come. Come along, Tom. Young Mr. Martin's kindly excused me for a couple of hours. If we hurry, we can catch Dr. MacGhie before he starts his afternoon rounds."

Tom realized that the stool he was sitting on belonged to Ernest John Smith, and hurriedly got down and followed his uncle to the door. Dr. MacGhie was the hearty Scottish doctor they used to go to for various minor ailments before Pa died, but they hadn't been able to afford to go to a doctor since then. At least, that's what Ma said whenever he or Annie suggested they go and fetch him to see her – except once when she had let Annie carry Harriet to his charity surgery, which was Friday mornings, because Harriet was running a fever after the children in the court beat her black and blue.

"Ma says we've not got the money to pay the doctor," he said, hurrying along at his uncle's side.

"The doctor has to sign a death certificate before the funeral undertaker can look after the remains. I will take care of the expenses. I can't have her being buried as a pauper – whatever would your poor father think of me?"

Tom felt a chill go through him at the word "remains". Ma was "remains"... It didn't bear thinking about. He wondered how long it would take the doctor to come to them if he was already doing his rounds or, if he wasn't, perhaps, they would be asked to ride with him back over to Bromley. Or, maybe just Uncle Alfred would, if there wasn't room for him, too. But Uncle Alfred didn't know where they lived, did he? So they'd have to take him in the carriage to show them the way. He remembered Doctor MacGhie's horse and gig outside their house off Devons Road in the old days. Those days seemed as if they were somebody else's life now.

* * * *

Neither of them spoke again as they hurried back to Bow Common Lane hoping to get to the doctor's house before he left to visit his wealthier patients in their homes. Finally, reaching the house, they found the dispensing chemist busy with his compounds and scales. He sent his apprentice to find out if the doctor had left yet. Alfred knew the chemist well – his wife Ella was a regular customer for his wares. The apprentice returned, saying that the doctor said for them to go through to the surgery.

To Tom's relief, since the doctor had a patient to visit in Barking Road, they really did ride with him, and he was soon holding the horse, amid a number of admiring street urchins, while the two men went into the house and up the stairs, following his directions. It wasn't long before Dr. MacGhie come back down.

"I'm sorry, Tom," he said, taking the reins, "for your loss. Och, your ma was fair brave keeping things together despite all. It's a cruel shame she felt she had naebody tae turn to. Annie told me she was a mite poorly that time, in the summer when she came in to the Friday surgery with Harriet. I wish't I'd come over tae see her then but– well, I did not, not realizing the seriousness of the situation. Look, laddie, I don't know what's tae happen to you and your sisters and the baby now, but if it comes to ye havin' nowhere to go, there's a fellow countrywoman of mine over in Spitalfields can help a bright lad like you. So, ye can tell your uncle that he's to bring you to me if that's the case. All right, lad?"

Tom stared at him, not knowing what to say. The doctor stepped up into the gig.

"All right?" he asked again then, as Tom nodded, took a sixpence from his pocket, leaned over and handed it to him. "Lads always get a sixpence for holding my horse," he said and raising his hand in a wave, urged the horse out of the court.

Tom stood staring at the sixpence, then put it in his pocket and went into the house, ignoring the questions from the children in the street. As he slowly went up the stairs, the doctor's words, while still spinning in his mind, began to make sense. They were orphans. Even if they could earn enough money to pay the rent, the landlord would hardly let four children live there alone. Would Uncle Alfred take them to live with him? Aunt Ella didn't like children in her house. On the rare occasions when they had visited her, he and Annie had been told to play in the yard at the back of the house and to keep away from the flower beds. Harriet had been allowed in, but had to sit on Ma's knee. Perhaps that was true of Annie and himself when they were smaller. He couldn't remember. The baby, of course, hadn't been born then and had never been taken there. He knew the doctor had meant to be kind, but what did he actually mean?

He let himself into their room. Alfred was sitting at the table with Annie and Harriet. Annie was cradling the baby who was awake, but not crying. Both girls had obviously been crying, but were dry-eyed now, so he knew that Annie must have explained Ma's death to Harriet in his absence. There were, of course, matchboxes laid out by the fire to dry, matchboxes tied in bundles of twelve ready to be taken to the factory and matchboxes on the table.

"Come and sit down, Tom," his uncle said, looking distastefully at the baby's napkins drying on the washing line strung across the ceiling by the fire. "We have some arrangements to make."

Tom crossed to the remaining chair and sat down. He put the sixpence on the table.

"Dr. MacGhie gave me that for holding the horse. It can go towards the expenses."

"You keep the sixpence, Tom. I told you I would take care of everything. Now, Annie tells me she wants to stay with the– with your mother, but doesn't feel that it's fit for the little ones to be here. She says that Harriet is a very good little girl who does as she's told and will be no trouble to your Aunt Ella, so I think it's best for me to take them with me–" he looked a little nervous "–perhaps you, Tom, can come with us to find a hansom. We'll go by the Four Mills Bridge and you can ride with us and look after the baby in the cab while I go into the funeral undertaker's shop… Yes, that would be the best plan. Then you can walk back down here while I take them the rest of the way."

Tom nodded. He felt strange – sort of removed from everything. It was almost as if he was somebody else watching himself and his sisters and uncle as they sat here with Ma lying dead on the bed across the room.

"And, when you get back, Tom, you must stay with Ma while I go and find the curate or leave a message for him if he's busy with his duties," said Annie, earnestly. "I know it's a long time since she went to church but she used to when we first removed to this parish, and John was christened here. The curate is new since she ever did go, but somebody must pray for her soul now."

"Yes, my dear," Alfred agreed. "I'm sure there'll be a coffin that the undertaker's man can bring down and that Mrs. Crombie, who laid out your father, will come along with him, I expect. You must tell the curate that she will be buried beside your father. We don't want him to think she's going in a public grave – it's something he might think when he comes here," he explained, seeing Annie's confused expression. "You must tell him that your uncle is looking after the arrangements."

Tom came out of his reverie when he realized what his uncle meant. "It's all right. He knows us from school and we still go to the Sunday School when we can. He knows we used to live in St. Mary's parish and that Pa was the schoolmaster at the boy's school – he knows that we're not the poor, I mean that we didn't used to be the poor…"

"Yes, Tom," Alfred started to look nervous again. "Now, Annie, if you can make a bundle for the baby…"

"I already did, Uncle Alfred. And Harriet has her own bundle." Annie turned to her sister. "Now, remember everything I told you, Harriet. You are to do as Aunt Ella says and you show her how John likes his bread and milk so that she has no trouble feeding him. And–" she blinked back tears. "And, remember Ma was brave and we must be as brave as she was…" She stood up, still cradling the baby in one arm, and hugged Harriet, who slid out of her chair, with the other. "And– and– I'll see you soon."

Tom stood up and took John from her. "Do we have another blanket?" he asked.

Annie went to the end of the bed where a large bundle tied with rope was ready for Tom to put over his shoulder, a smaller bundle and a blanket. She picked up the blanket and, together, they wrapped it around the baby, then she helped Tom with the baby's bundle and fetched Harriet's cloak from the hook by the door. Once Harriet was ready to go, Annie handed her the smaller bundle and hugged and kissed her again, then kissed the baby who grinned up at her, showing his partly grown bottom teeth.

"Open the door for us, Harriet," said Tom and led the way to the door. "I'll be back as soon as I can, Annie."

When they were gone, Annie stood for a minute thinking about how out of his element (an expression her mother used to use) the poor solicitor's clerk was and wondered how he would manage after Tom left him and how surprised Aunt Ella would be when he arrived home with his baby nephew and little niece. Then, she sat down at the table, buried her face in her arms and cried.

CHAPTER THREE

Tom and Annie wrapped themselves in their blankets and lay down in front of the fireplace with its banked up embers. Annie blew out the stub of candle and they both watched the embers as they glowed in the dark.

Neither had mentioned the empty bed as they washed their faces and put on their nightshirts. They unrolled the tick mattress, as they usually did and settled to sleep by the dying fire. The bedsteads that used to grace the children's bedroom had been sold when they moved because there was only room for one bed and the table and chairs. Harriet and the baby slept with Ma and the older two children on the floor.

"I hope Harriet and John are sleeping," Annie said. "If they're good these next few days, maybe they'll be allowed to stay with Uncle Alfred and live in a nice house again. I shall miss them dreadfully, I know, and so will you, but they'll be safe there and Harriet won't have to paste matchboxes anymore."

She didn't really expect Tom to respond and didn't say anything more. Both children were afraid to voice their concern about what would happen to them. Annie had tied all the dried matchboxes by the time Tom returned, and was busily pasting more. Somehow the work helped to pass the time and stop her worrying about her little sister and brother. They would need the money, wouldn't they? So, best get on…

It had been teatime at the curate's house when she went to find him. His wife said he was taking tea with the Ladies' Visiting Society Committee and, after hearing Annie's request, she had insisted she come in and have a cup of tea and some bread and jam with her and her two small children. It had brought back memories of teatime when she and Tom were little and Annie found the bread and jam sticking in her throat as she tried not to cry. The curate's wife wanted her to stay and wait for her husband to come home but Annie said that she must get home help her brother with the matchboxes, at which the curate's wife had appeared puzzled.

Home again, she found that Mrs. Crombie, the undertaker's assistant, had arrived. Annie joined Tom at the table facing away from the bed where Mrs. Crombie was practising her craft. She kept talking about other deaths, bodies she'd laid out and orphaned children, and they concentrated on making matchboxes and trying not to hear her stories. By the time the curate arrived, the coffin had been delivered, placed across two chairs by the window and, Mrs. Crombie's administrations over, Ma had been placed in it. He was horrified that the children should be sitting with their mother's coffin all alone, and Tom explained about Uncle Alfred and his wife being their only relations, and how Harriet and John were with them, but he and Annie wanted to stay here. He didn't mention that they had nowhere else to go anyway because he was afraid that the curate might insist on taking them to an orphanage if he knew. Or, even worse – to the workhouse.

Annie thought about all that had happened and, still too worried to sleep, wondered when the funeral would be. Perhaps Uncle Alfred would come in the morning before he went to work or, maybe, at dinnertime, and tell them what he'd arranged.

"He will let us go to the funeral with him, won't he?" she asked Tom.

"He knows Ma let us go to Pa's funeral, so I don't know why he shouldn't take us," Tom replied. "It won't be a proper do – like Pa's, you know, with lots of people there. It's like Ma used to say, once you become poor, nobody wants to know you. He just told me to run along home after he'd been in to make the arrangements so we'll just have to wait and see when he comes."

They were silent again, each wishing for sleep in order to forget their problems for a while.

"Annie," Tom said, eventually, "Dr. MacGhie said something funny to me before he left."

"What d'you mean?"

"He said if it comes to us having nowhere to go, a fellow countrywoman of his – a Scottish lady, I suppose he meant – over in Spitalfields can help us. We must tell Uncle Alfred to bring us to him."

"D'you think she's an orphanage person?"

"I think he would have said so, if it was an orphanage. You have to be sponsored to go to an orphanage so he would have said she would sponsor us, not help us, wouldn't he?"

"Maybe it's someone looking for servants – there are people who have children for servants. But I don't want to be a servant – making the matchboxes is better than being a servant..."

"Nobody will rent a room to children so how can we carry on doing that? We'll be lucky if the landlord doesn't throw us out before the end of the week. Anyway, I don't think he meant to send us to be servants either. What he said was 'she can help a bright lad like you' and that doesn't sound like she's looking for servants. He'd have said 'reliable' or 'trustworthy' or something like that, wouldn't he? He's nice – Dr. MacGhie…"

"You mean, you think we can trust him and should tell Uncle Alfred what he said."

"It would be better than going to an orphanage, wouldn't it? Or, to the workhouse. If Uncle Alfred doesn't do something, the parish will put us in the workhouse. That's what they do. We'll run away if it comes to that, though, won't we?"

"Yes," Annie agreed. "I think it's best if we tell Uncle Alfred what the doctor said. He'll probably be glad that somebody's helping him because I don't think he knows what to do. He's a good man really and I'm sure he feels dreadful about not taking us in as a dead father's brother should. That's why I think that he'll, at least, persuade Aunt Ella to have the little ones, somehow…"

"When he comes tomorrow, we'll tell him. One of us will take the matchboxes up and get the supplies, then I'll go down to river and see if I can find some coal for the day. He's not likely to come then because he'll be off to work but, if he does, you must tell him that Dr. MacGhie said to bring us to him. He'll probably have lots of excuses about why we can't live with him and tell us that he's trying to find us places in an orphanage. So, he'll be relieved when we tell him Dr. MacGhie has a plan. I think, actually, he's more likely to come at dinnertime, though – not earlier, because there's an apprentice called Ernest John Smith who he can leave in charge while the solicitors are having their dinner and won't be needing his services. We can tell him then. All right, Annie?"

But Annie had, finally, fallen asleep. Tom snuggled down into his blanket, hoping Dr. MacGhie had meant Annie, too. If he had realized that Uncle Alfred was not intending to take him in, then he must have known that he wouldn't want Annie, either… Yes, he must have done. Reassured, Tom drowsily went over the events of the day in his mind and sleep soon claimed him.

* * * *

"In Canada, bright lads like you, Tom, have the opportunity to grow up and have their own farms with acres of land. Ye'll likely be placed in a farmer's home and treated as if ye were his own son – ye'll work on the farm and ye'll go to school during the winter months."

Tom nodded. He didn't really think that he wanted to be a farmer but he didn't want to disappoint Dr. MacGhie who seemed to be convinced that he should be.

The children had spent all of Saturday wondering what was going to happen. Their uncle did not appear. They thought perhaps they should walk up to Bow in the evening, but Tom decided that the funeral must have been arranged for the next day because Sunday was when poor people were buried, and it would be best to make bundles of their personal belongings and be ready for whatever happened after that. They continued to work on the matchboxes on Sunday morning but it was hard to concentrate. They put on their Sunday clothes – somewhat outgrown since there had been no money to replace them during the last year, but clean and pressed and, finally, at noon, their uncle came to fetch them.

Just as Annie had hoped, their uncle had managed to make his childless wife see that it was their duty to bring up his brother's younger children. He told them as the single mourning carriage brought them home from the cemetery. Tom didn't wait for him to get very far into explanations about the house being too small for more than two children but had told him what the doctor had said and, instead of taking them home, the undertaker's man was asked to take them to Doctor MacGhie's house instead.

Mrs. MacGhie, who had followed the little housemaid to the door, had not been too pleased at the disturbance on a Sunday afternoon, but the doctor, himself, ushered them into his library off the hall, and told the housemaid to bring in some tea and cake. He had then told them about the place where orphan children, and others whose destitute families wanted better prospects for them, were trained and taken to Canada where they were provided with homes. He even took down an atlas from one of the bookshelves and showed them where the ship would go down the great St. Lawrence River to the city of Quebec. Then, he pointed our the tracks of the longest railway in the world on which they would travel further west alongside the river and the first of five Great Lakes, which he said were like vast seas in the middle of the land, to a place called Belleville which was where the children stayed until families were chosen for them. At this point, Dr. MacGhie had turned to Alfred and told him how each applicant for a child must be upright and honest, attend church regularly and provide a testimonial from his minister. The children would have good homes in the country with fields and trees around them, he said, there would be no more slum courts for them – indeed, no more grimy London.

Now he was addressing Tom…

"First, ye'll be goin' tae Miss Macpherson's Home of Industry in Spitalfields and, there ye'll be stayin' until the summer. The snow makes travel difficult in Canada in the winter so that's when Miss Macpherson trains up the bairns she's chosen tae tak' over there the next summer. Every bairn has a job to do there – cooking and cleaning and getting everyone outfitted with all the clothes they'll need for the journey to Canada, but ye go to the schoolroom for part of the day and ye'll also learn the things that'll be of use tae you in Canada. And, Tom, ye'll be working with the rest of the lads, chopping wood and such. There's boot making, too. The lads learn to make the good, strong boots they'll be needing in Canada. Now, how does that sound?"

"C-Canada's an awfully long way away, isn't it, doctor?" asked Annie, hesitantly. "When will I ever see Harriet and John again?"

"Yes, Annie, it is a long way away but, do ye know what else Miss Macpherson does in the winter, besides train up more children tae tak' over there?" Annie shook her head. "Well, lass, during her trips in the summer – and the bonnie woman takes four or five parties over every summer – she visits the children she's placed before, or they visit her, and she brings back their letters and presents for their families and takes the time to tell them how well those children are doing. Right now, she's been back two weeks – comes back when snow starts falling there on her last trip of the year – and most of that two weeks she's been doing this visiting. Then, when she goes back tae Canada, she takes with her the letters and presents that have been left at the Home of Industry for the purpose, so your Uncle and Auntie can help Harriet, and the baby when he's older, tae write letters to ye."

That wasn't the same as seeing them, Annie thought, but she nodded and looked at the map again. She had missed Harriett and John already the last two days but knowing they were safe and warm just a mile or so away was much less frightening than if she were thousands of miles across the sea in one of those towns with the strange names. She looked more closely and read some of the names along the stretch where Dr. MacGhie had pointed to as he talked about the railway. Champlain, Three Rivers, some names that she couldn't read – she thought they must be French. Somebody, maybe Pa before he died, had once told her that the people in Quebec were French. Then there were Cornwall, Brockville – they were more easy to read – Kingston and Belleville, the place where Doctor MacGhie had said the home was. Further along the shore of the lake there was Port Hope, which sounded nice, and Toronto.

"Ye see that town there, Tom?" Doctor MacGhie pointed to a town a little further along from the lake and Annie moved back so that Tom could see better. "Well, that's Galt where Miss Macpherson is opening a new receiving centre especially for boys to learn about farming in Canada before they go to their new families. That's probably where ye'll be going because it's bright boys that she'll be needing there when she's getting things started."

"Not Annie?" Tom asked.

"Only boys will be going there but, that's not to say Annie won't be going tae a family nearby. It's an area where lots o' the families are Scottish and have taken in many of Miss Macpherson's children which is why she decided tae set up a separate facility in the area. Now it doesn't look so far from Belleville on the map, but it's a day's journey on the train – like journeying all the way from London to Manchester."

Neither Tom nor Annie were very sure about where Manchester was but nodded sagely because the doctor seemed to expect them to.

"It seems an awfully long way to go to find a new home," said Tom. "But, if other children are brave enough to do it, then Annie and me… well, we're brave enough, too."

"Well, that's settled then. Now, if we go and get your bundles and go along there, tae Spitalfields, they'll be finished their tea and it'll be time for the hymn singing and bible story they have of a Sunday evening."

"Now?" Tom asked.

Annie was too shocked to say anything.

"There's nae time like the present for making decisions," said Dr. MacGhie. "Your uncle will take care of what all else is in your rooms there. You just get your clothes and whatever else ye'll be needing and we'll have you in Miss Macpherson's care this very evening." He turned to their uncle, who was looking both surprised and relieved. "That all right with you, Alfred?"

"I'll certainly be glad not to have to leave the children in that dreadful room another day, Doctor," he said. "Are you sure this lady can take them at such short notice?"

"They're not the first children I've taken to her and they certainly won't be the last. There's a lot of children she has at the Home of Industry, but they don't all sleep on the premises. Many have homes to go to – poor homes but homes, nevertheless."

"But please, Doctor MacGhie, what about Harriet and the baby? Will we be able to see them?"

"It'll be several months before you'll be off to Canada, Annie. Ye'll be able to go to your uncle's house to see them, or he can bring them to visit ye right up until ye do go and, with Christmas coming very shortly, I'm sure your Uncle and Auntie will want to see ye altogether for that occasion, won't they?"

Annie wasn't so sure about that, but nodded, then looked at the map again.

"Now," the doctor continued, "you two children finish up that cake while I go out to the stable and tell the boy to get the gig ready for us."

CHAPTER FOUR

Darkness had fallen by the time they reached the huge old warehouse, which Dr. MacGhie said was the Home of Industry. He pointed it out when it loomed ahead of them as they drove up Commercial Street after the drive they'd taken through Stepney and Whitechapel. The children, seated on the bundles they had made of their belongings in the small space in the back of the gig, could see little of it until the doctor stopped around the corner and, calling for a boy to hold the horse, jumped down into the street. They climbed out and looked around. The doctor reached in and passed their bundles to them, then picked up his bag.

"Make sure you take everything in. This is, unfortunately, an area rife with thieves – we don't leave things where they can be taken."

Annie couldn't imagine anybody wanting to steal either her bundle of well-worn clothes nor the needles and thread, pen and ink and books that she had in her basket.

"Over there is where they have the Rag Fair," Dr. MacGhie said, nodding in the direction of what looked like open space. "Have ye heard of the Rag Fair?" The children shook their heads. "Well, it's a fair where clothes and even the dirtiest bits of rag are put out for sale and ye'll find most of the clothes that still look like clothes are being sold by the thieves that stole them. Come along now."

Annie wondered why Miss Macpherson had the children's home in such a dreadful place.

"I'll take your bundle, Annie," said Alfred, taking it from her. "You can't manage that and the basket, too."

They could hear voices singing *God Rest Ye Merry Gentlemen* as they approached the door, which became louder as they crossed an entrance hall with a staircase at one side and low burning gas lamps on the walls. Dr. MacGhie opened one of the doors, which led off the hall, and they entered a very large room which seemed to be brimming with children, all seated on the floor, and adults sitting on chairs behind them. Several of the children smiled and waved when they saw the doctor but everyone carried on singing. At the opposite end of the room from where the adults were sitting, there was a lady playing a piano and two others leading the singing. When she saw them, one of these ladies after a word with the other one, stepped around the children sitting on the floor and came towards them.

"And who have we here?" she asked, looking from Dr. MacGhie to the children.

"This is Tom Denton," Dr. MacGhie said. "And, this is his sister, Annie."

"Well, Tom and Annie, I'm Miss Shaw and I'm very pleased to see you here. Perhaps you'd like to take off your coats and, if you leave your bundles by the wall, Tom – yes, and your basket, Annie – then you can both sit down with the children and lend us your voices. We're practising all the carols we'll sing when we go a'wassailing in the next few weeks. We go around the neighbouring courts singing carols and bringing Christmas cheer," she said, turning to Alfred. "You are–?"

"Oh, I'm–" he was startled by the lady's cheerful manner and reference to wassailing "–I'm the children's uncle–"

"Perhaps you can come with me – Miss Macpherson wants me to take Dr. MacGhie up to the girl's dormitory where we have a young lady in bed with a chill who we'd like him to look at – so, I'll show you into our little clerks' room where Miss Macpherson will see you when I get back down. Now," she looked at the children on the floor and selected two of them, "Jennie… and Bert, I want you to sit with Tom and Annie, here, and afterwards you can show them where to go." She smiled at Tom and Annie. "Now, just join in, children – you do know the last verse, don't you?"

Annie nodded and dropped down on the floor beside the girl called Jennie. Tom stood for a moment as Miss Shaw indicated for his uncle to put Annie's bundle down beside his, then ushered the two men back the way they had come.

When the carol ended, the lady at the front, who Tom thought must be Miss Macpherson, said, "I think we'll have everybody standing for the next carol." She waited while they all noisily rose to their feet. "Who knows *The Holly and the Ivy*?"

There were cries of "I do!" and "I knows that one, miss" and "Me, me. I do!"

"Good. Now, for those of you who don't, this is a very old song about – well, who can tell me what it's about?"

Several children raised their hands.

"Johnny?"

"It's 'bout decorating the 'ouse wiv 'olly fer Christmas like the rich people does."

"You're almost right – but it's not only rich people who do so. Mr. Merry will be bringing lots of holly up from Hampton next week – enough for us to decorate the entire Beehive." Everybody cheered and she waited until the noise died down. "Long ago people used to bring boughs of holly and ivy plants indoors during the winter in the hope that they would all survive the winter cold just as the hardy holly and ivy in the ground do. And since the beginning of winter is not long before Christmas, an unknown poet many years ago, wrote a carol that combined the bringing in of the holly and the ivy with the birth of Our Lord. It's a very pretty carol. Now, we'll have Mrs. Lloyd play the first few bars –"

Tom thought Miss Macpherson's voice sounded a bit like Dr. MacGhie's and remembered the doctor calling her a "fellow countrywoman" on the day Ma died. He didn't really know what he meant at the time but now knew that he was right in thinking they must both came from Scotland. He wondered what the Beehive was – she must mean this place. Maybe it was the name for this room...

"We'll learn the chorus first. I'm going to sing each line and then I want to hear everybody sing it back to me... "Oh, the rising of the sun–"

"Oh, the rising of the sun–"

"And the running of the deer–"

"And the running of the deer–"

"The playing of the merry organ–"

"The playing of the merry organ–"

"Sweet singing of the choir."

"Sweet singing of the choir."

"Very good. Now all together –"

Tom and Annie both started to enjoy the singing as the chorus was sung, trailing off a little towards the end as some of the children forgot the newly learned lines. Miss Macpherson continued to teach the carol until Miss Shaw returned and took over from her and she went out into the entrance hall to join Uncle Alfred as Miss Shaw had told him she would. Tom and Annie exchanged glances, each wondering what would happen next.

Miss Shaw had everybody singing the carol by the time Miss Macpherson returned, girls and women singing some verses, the boys and the small number of men present singing others and everybody singing the first and last verses. Then, after the last verse was sung for the last time, Miss Macpherson stepped forward again.

"We have two precious little children with us tonight," she said, "who, just this afternoon, attended their mother's burial." A murmur ran through the crowd and many children looked at Tom and Annie. Annie felt tears spring to her eyes and the girl, Jennie, put her arm around her. "We are going to pray for them now and for their dear mother's soul, may she rest in peace, and, then, as you leave, we'll sing the hymn which the hymn writer, Henry Lyte, wrote just before he passed on to his Reward not many years ago. This hymn, *Abide with Me*, is also a prayer asking our Heavenly Father to remain with us through life, through our trials and through death. And we especially ask Him, tonight, to abide with Tom and Annie. You'll leave, as usual, during the last verse of the hymn, but all children living here in the Refuge, please remain in your places until we finish.

Tom had not heard the hymn before but most of the children seemed to know it quite well. He wondered if it had been taught to them because there were often deaths among their families. He blinked back tears, hoping the boys around them wouldn't notice.

Soon, the room was emptied save for a very large group of children, mostly boys, and Miss Macpherson.

"Now, before we go up for our cocoa, I want you each to personally welcome Tom and Annie and tell them your names. They already know Jennie and Bert, and I want you two children to stay down here so that, once I've personally welcomed them, you can show Tom and Annie where they'll be sleeping and where to put their bundles."

The children all solemnly shook hands with Tom and Annie, some of the older girls hugging them instead, before running off into the hall where they could be heard clattering up the stairs. Then Miss Macpherson came over to them.

"Now, Tom, I expect you know that I'm Miss Macpherson and I'm very happy that Dr. MacGhie brought you both here. He is taking your uncle back over to Bow now on his own way home."

She shook hands with Tom, then turned to Annie and took her hands.

"Now, I hear you've been a wonderful little mother to your brothers and sister these last months, Annie – cooking and washing, looking after the baby and, all the while, making matchboxes to earn money. Well, that, as I said, is wonderful and I'm sure Our Lord in Heaven is well pleased with you but, I would like – and I'm sure He would, too – to see you enjoy being a little girl again. Many of the children who come to us have also had to take on the responsibilities of adults and, always, the first thing we want is to ensure that they recover their childhood. So, will you promise me that you will try to enjoy being a child and learn to play children's games again while you're here?"

"Yes, miss," Annie whispered.

"Thank you, Annie. That's my name, too, you know. And we Annies must look after each other, mustn't we? If anything worries you, you must come and talk to me."

"Yes, miss."

"Now, Tom, after we've had our cocoa, all the boys come back down here and put up their hammocks for the night. I'm making Bert responsible for showing you what to do and he can show you where to put your things then take you up to the dining hall while, Jennie, I want you to take Annie up to the girls' dormitory and show her where to put her things, then take her up to the dining hall. Now we'd better all hurry or we'll be late for saying grace and our cocoa will get cold." She picked Annie's bundle up from the floor. "Who's is this?"

"Mine," said Annie.

"Perhaps Jennie can carry it and you can carry your basket and shawl. I see you've brought your books and I expect they make the basket heavy. Come along now, girls."

Annie shot Tom a scared look as she followed Miss Macpherson and Jennie from the room. He mouthed the words "Don't worry" and her scared expression relaxed into a tight little smile.

* * * *

"This way, Tom," said Bert as Tom picked up his bundle and coat. "See these cupboards over 'ere?" He began to limp towards the back of the room where the entire wall was lined with columns of two foot wide cupboards. Tom followed, realizing, for the first time, that the older boy was quite badly crippled. "Inside there's shelves and, on each one, you'll see an 'ammock rolled up so that there's space for your spare clothes and your coat. Now, we got to find an empty one – 'cept for the 'ammock, I mean. Pretty full we are at the moment but Miss Macpherson always finds room for them as needs it. More'n an 'undred 'ammocks there is on these shelves. Now, see, there's one for you – jus' push your bundle in. You can sort it out later." Tom stowed away his things on the shelf and Bert handed him a card and a stub of pencil which he'd taken from his pocket. "'Ere, write your name on this bit of card and when you've done, you jus' slide it into this slot. The first boys what come 'ere with Miss Macpherson made these shelves. 'Fore that, she 'ad refuges in different places for girls and boys, separate, like. Then she found this old ware'ouse, wiv gas and water all laid on – even got lavatories, it 'as 'cos it was a fever 'ospital once and she moved everyone in 'ere. You'll see the basement workrooms and the schoolroom and other rooms upstairs tomorrer – jus' now we 'ave to get up to the dining 'all and I ain't so quick on the stairs meself, so we'd better be going."

He continued telling Tom about the Refuge as they climbed the three flights of stairs to the top of the building. The children, chosen for emigration, were sent over to the farm at Hampton for a few weeks at a time, he said. He hadn't been there himself because, with his club foot, he wasn't eligible, was he? However, the children that went liked learning about farm life right enough. Some had never seen the countryside before. At each landing, he itemized the rooms that were on that floor, explaining that he looked after the smaller boys during the day, in their dormitory and playroom and was responsible for making sure they were where they were supposed to be at all times. Except for when he was in the schoolroom, he organized and helped them with all their work assignments and games. When he got better at reading and writing himself, he confided, he was going to be made assistant to the schoolmistress who taught the infant school classes. He already knew his scriptures well enough to tell them gospel stories.

From the top floor landing, they entered another large room with long tables at which all the children were sitting. At the end of one of them, a group of small boys immediately beckoned to them.

"'Ere, Bert, we saved you a seat," one of them called.

"'Ope you don't mind sitting with them young'uns," Bert said. "I don't really 'ave to at cocoa time, 'cos that's when we can sit where we want and nobody 'as responsiblilities – 'cept for being kind and well-mannered and them things, of course – but everyone's waiting for grace to be said, so it'd be quickest."

Tom nodded and followed him to the place on the end of the bench that the little boys had saved for them. Just as they got there, a youngish man stood up and asked them all to rise and then led them in a rather long grace which included a prayer for the two new children in their midst. Tom opened his eyes to see the curly haired little boy beside him squinting up at him, while keeping his head bowed, as if to ensure that Tom knew the man meant him. When they sat down, several of the older girls brought around jugs of hot cocoa, which they poured into the tin mugs already placed on the table in front of each child, and trays of rock cakes.

"My ma died, too." The curly haired boy told him. "'Ad the consumption, she did. 'Ad to stay in bed all the time or she'd cough up blood – lots of it. Then she died. "That what 'appened to your ma?"

"She had to stay in bed but she wasn't coughing up blood. She had my baby brother and didn't get recovered like they usually do…"

"Did 'e die, too?"

"What?"

"Your baby brother – did 'e die, too?"

"No. He's at my uncle's house with my little sister."

The boy nodded. "Oh. Don't want you and Annie, don't they? That's wot 'appened to me but, wiv us, it was the little ones wot got sent to the work'ouse – well would've if Miss Macpherson 'adn't took us in. Me bruvvers is big enough to bring in some earnin's, me pa says, but me and me sister is goin' to get adopted in Canada. Miss Macpherson says we'll 'ave a better life there. You know what adopted is? It's when you live with a new family. Are you goin' to Canada, too?"

"Well, we only just got here so I don't suppose it's been decided about yet. But I think so."

"Give over, 'Arry," broke in Bert. "The rest of us want to talk to Tom, too." Harry shrugged and took a bite of his cake. "Where you from then, Tom."

"Bromley."

"Thought you must be over there by Bow what wiv yer comin in wiv Dr. MacGhie. Lived down in Poplar, I did, when I was a little tyke but I don't remember it much – jus' that where we lived wasn't far from the river at Limehouse and me brothers would mudlark there. Moved to Wapping, we did, then me 'ole family got the fever 'cept me. Always say it was me club foot kept me safe but that's jus' me little jest. Don't really know why it spared me."

"It's like Miss Shaw said," piped up one of the boys on the opposite side of the table. "The Good Lord was savin' you for 'elpin' 'er look arter us lot, ain't that the trufe, fellers?"

"Right you are," several boys said at once.

Bert beamed.

"We've been living at the Poplar end of Bromley this year," Tom said. "We lived at the Bow end before my Pa died. I was going down to Limehouse Hole to dig up coal every ebb the last weeks 'fore Ma died so that Annie could use the money it saved from buying coal to get milk for Ma and the baby. We were making matchboxes to earn money so we had to have coal to burn so that we could dry them."

"Mudlarkin's miserable this time of the year," said Bert. "Freeze your toes off the mud does, don't it?" The little boys all began to clamour with stories of terrible things that happened around the docks until Bert held up his hands and they all quietened down. "Let's 'ave a bit of guiet now. Mr. Lewis'll be getting up and it'll be time for the lot of you to get to bed."

CHAPTER FIVE

On the other side of the room with the girl called Jennie and several other girls of about her own age, Annie saw Tom come in with Bert and go over to where the little boys were calling to them and wondered why they hadn't come to sit with the older children.

"Bert looks after the little tykes, see," Jennie explained, seeing Annie's puzzled expression. "I expect they wanted 'im to sit with them and, with the two of them bein' so long comin' up, it was probably for the best."

"Bert 'as a club foot, you see," put in a girl called Maggie. "Takes 'im a while to get up the stairs, it does."

Annie forgot about being separated from Tom as the girls questioned her and told her about life in the Refuge, while they ate their cake and drank their cocoa.

"There's no need to be ascared," Maggie said. "Miss Macpherson believes in teaching us wot she calls responsibility. It ain't like an orphanage or the work'ouse 'ere, it ain't. No rules for the sake of them, I mean. We 'ave to 'elp each uvver, we do 'ere an', I tell you somefink – you feels bloody awful when you let's someone down, much worse than if you'd been punished–" she stopped and looked around her. "What you all lookin' at me for? Ooh, I said a bad word, din't I? We ain't s'posed to swear, Annie, but sometimes I forgets meself, I do."

"The families in Canada wot take in Miss Macpherson's children are all God-fearin' good Christians, see," said Jennie. "So it's very important that we get rid of our bad 'abits or we won't get chosen to go. You got any bad 'abits, Annie?"

Annie thought about it. Did she? Was that what Miss Macpherson meant when she talked about the need for children to 'recover their childhood'?

"Never 'ad time to think about it, eh?" another girl said. "I expec' you was like me if you was lookin' arter everythink with a sick ma took to 'er bed. Not much time to think – 'cept about where the next meal was comin' from, ain't I right?"

"There was always a lot to do," Annie agreed, "but it wasn't always like that. Before Pa died, and Ma became so unwell, we used to sit, just like this, and have cocoa before we went to bed. It feels funny now, though, not pasting matchboxes together every minute between looking after the children, washing napkins, cooking stew, emptying slops and everything."

"There's no emptying slops 'ere, that's one good thing. There's WCs 'ere, with chains wot you pull to flush them slops away. It was an 'ospital, see. That's why it's got the gas on every floor, too. Makes you feel like a toff, it does, livin' 'ere."

Annie smiled.

"It does – 'specially for us middle-aged children. The older ones 'ave more duties to do 'cos they'll be goin' into service like, when they get to Canada. The little ones 'ave to 'ave some discipline so's people will adopt them. Us – well, we're too young for service and, most likely, too old to be adopted, so we got to learn to be useful... and nice so somebody'll like us and give us board in return for our 'elp around the farm. I don't know if I can learn to be nice and useful in time…"

"Where d'you get such ideas from, Kath?" asked Jennie. "If there ain't no family for you to go to right away, you get to stay at Marchmont – that's the name of the 'ome there, in Canada–" she added, for Annie's benefit "–until there is."

"Or until we're old enough to go into service."

"You ain't ascared, are you, Kath?" Jennie asked kindly. "There ain't nuffink to be ascared of. Children that ain't little or big get taken in, too – to 'elp around the farm in the summer and, in the winter, they 'ave to agree to send you to school…"

"I ain't ascared or nuffink but it won't be the same, will it? Livin' wiv a family but not bein' part of it. 'Ere we're sort of like a family, ain't we? But we're all of us not part of the family, either – all of us, I mean, not just me or you or you." She pointed to each of them, in turn. "See what I mean? I don't want that to change – I like being 'ere wiv the gas an' the taps bein' inside 'stead of out on the street, an' the lavatory an' everyfink… You seen the WC yet, Annie?"

"No…"

"You know wot a WC is?"

Annie nodded. She thought it was an indoor privy, but wasn't really certain.

"'Ave you been in one?"

She shook her head.

"'Ere, Kath, we ain't s'posed to talk about such fings at the table," protested Maggie. "It ain't good manners. Anyway, looks like we're s'posed to be finished. Mr. Lewis is getting up."

They all stood and thanked God for what they had received then waited as one of the lady helpers organized the children leaving the dining hall to go downstairs to the dormitories. Annie watched the man Maggie had called Mr. Lewis go up to her brother. He motioned the little boys off to their dormitory – at least that's what she supposed – and stood talking to him and Bert, moving his arms around as if he was explaining something. Maybe it was Mr. Lewis's job to ensure the older boys all put up their hammocks in the big room on the ground floor. She'd hoped to be able to see Tom before she went to bed but she was, obviously, expected to go down with the girls to the second floor dormitory which Jennie had shown her on their way up to the dining hall, instructing her to leave her bundle and basket on one of the beds along the wall. The room doubled as the girls' schoolroom during the day so the trundle beds lined all four walls head to toe and had shelves overhead to house the each girl's possessions.

When they got back down there, Jennie led Annie to the bed where they had left her belongings and they pulled out the lower bed so that the two beds were side by side.

"D'you 'ave a nightgown in your bundle?" Jennie asked and Annie nodded. "There's a rule that we wear nightgowns and not a chemise to bed. If you don't, Miss Barber'll give you one. She's in charge of the girls. She's the Canadian one. Learning 'ow to run an 'ome, she is, 'cos 'er bruvver's opening one in Canada, see. She'll be 'ere in a minute to send us to wash our faces and clean our teeth – the bathroom's down the passage. It's where the sinks are and the lavatory, as well as the bath. We 'ave to put our nightgowns on first, all ready for when she calls our turn. We're allowed to talk, read, play games – wotever we want – 'til it's time for prayers, then she'll turn the lamps off and we 'ave to go to sleep."

It was with a little trepidation that Annie followed Jennie to the bath-room when Miss Barber called their names and handed Annie a small cake of soap and a toothbrush, in a little hemp bag, and a towel. Jennie had already taken her own from the shelf over the bed. The splendours, which had been installed in the days when the building was used as a fever hospital, were like nothing Annie had seen before. There was a bath, which looked deep enough to drown in and a row of sinks with a looking glass stuck on the wall, which she supposed was there so that you could make sure you were clean. Then, there was the water closet that, when she pulled the chain as Jennie instructed, gushed water with a loud gurgle, startling her. Thankfully, it didn't overflow and make a puddle around her on the floor as she feared it would. Jennie also had to show her how to put paste, from a jar on one of the shelves in the bath-room, onto the toothbrush and brush her teeth with it.

"I'd never 'eard of such a thing before, neiver," Jennie said. "I think they give them to Miss Macpherson so they can say that the waifs an' strays in the Refuge brush their teeth and shame other people into buying brushes and the paste. We get new sorts of soap and ointments and tonics to try, then the factories wot make them can sell them to the 'ospitals, see, if they make us better or, at least, do us no 'arm. Modern hinventions, Miss Macpherson calls them. Food in tins, too. And sauce in bottles like wot you can put on your 'ot taters at a stand. If it don't kill us orf, then it's all right for people to buy, see?"

"What happens if it does kill someone?"

"Just a joke. We say that but, I expect they really give it us so people'll think they're nice. You know, like telling people that the Queen bought something to make them want it, too."

Annie didn't understand the connection. "Come on, or Miss Barber'll give us wot for – us taking so long in 'ere."

Jennie carried on the conversation in the dormitory, and Kath and Maggie, who shared the other bed, joined in. Annie had never heard of some of the things which the girls told her were donated to the Refuge by factory owners who Miss Macpherson and her helpers knew through the churches and missions which supported the Home of Industry. They were things that 'better off' people bought, not the poor, they said, who lived on plain cooking if they ever got anything cooked at all. Annie had thought her own family was 'better off ' before Pa died, but Ma made gravy from flour and dripping, flavoured with herbs from the little garden, made her own biscuits and had never bought peas in a tin, although Annie remembered seeing them in the grocer's shop where they went. Thinking about Ma brought tears to her eyes which she quickly blinked away.

"But it ain't all 'avin' fings wot the toffs buy, Annie," Maggie said, "we 'ave to work to pay our way in 'ere same as 'fore we was brung 'ere. An' we 'ave school – you bin to school?"

Annie nodded.

"'Course she's bin to school, silly," said Jennie. "You can tell by the way she talks – not like a toff, but proper, like she knows 'ow to read good. Ain't I right?"

"I used to go to school until last summer. Then Ma got too ill to look after my little sister, Harriet, and the baby. She said Tom was to go to school, because that's what Pa would've wanted, but she needed me at home. And she was making matchboxes and needed me to help her keep up or they'd drop her, and we needed the money."

"If you was going to school 'til last summer, you must know more about readin' an' writin' an' doin' sums than the rest of us. They'll likely make you a monitor. Wot about sewin' – you know 'ow to sew seams an' 'ems an' button'oles?"

"Not buttonholes. I used to help Ma sew shirts and frocks. And she showed me how to knit – I made woollen booties for John. I hope Aunt Ella knows how to wash them without shrinking them."

"Well, we 'ave to do lots of sewin' 'ere and knittin', too. Everyone gets a box wot the boys make, to take to Canada, and enough clothes to last out two years. Oh, and a satchel if you ain't got one. Boys make satchels, boots and coats and trousers, and girls do every thing else."

"We' ave sessions, see," put in Kate, "and change round every few weeks. I bin 'ere longest of us four so I done all the sessions now – makin' clothes, kitchen and dining 'all, cleanin' – like sweepin', dustin' an' polishin', wash'ouse, lookin' arter the tots – them's children under five. Last a month, they do – the sessions. All the boys get sent to 'Ampton for a spell on the farm. Talkin' about startin' a girls' 'ome there, too, they are. There'll be chicken and pigs and cows to look arter, and 'oein' and weedin' the vegetables. Boys 'ave to clean the barn and spread the manure on the fields. They learn about ploughin' an' them farm things, too. Girls don't do them things. 'Ere comes Miss Barber."

"Hallo there, Annie." Miss Barber had finished sending girls to the bath-room and come across the room to them and sat down on the bed, next to Annie. "I'm Miss Barber, as I imagine the girls have told you, and I'd like to properly welcome you to the Refuge. I didn't have much chance to talk to you before but I guess Jennie has been doing a good job of looking after you. I was a stranger here myself a month ago so I know how confusing everything is at first and, I know it's a sad time for you, so you mustn't hesitate to come to me if you can't manage." She smiled at the other three girls. "You couldn't be in better hands than these three girls so I'll let them carry on and I'll see you tomorrow."

Miss Barber stood up and moved on to another group of girls.

"She walks around an' talks to people until it's time for prayers," said Jennie. "She's nice – I 'ope all Canadians are as nice. Be terrible to go all that way to find out they ain't, wouldn't it?"

CHAPTER SIX

Tom and Annie quickly adapted to life at the Home of Industry, which Miss Macpherson fondly called the Beehive. They were both put in the cleaning workgroups for the December session and, although the boys' duties were different from the girls, they saw more of each other than they would have done had they been placed in the workrooms. While Harriet and John were not brought to visit them as Doctor MacGhie had suggested they might, they were able to walk the two miles over to their uncle's house in Bow and see their little sister and brother on Saturday afternoons. They had to be back before dark and, therefore were not able to spend a lot of time there, but it was enough to set Annie's mind at rest about their well being. Harriett said she'd rather be back with Ma and Annie and Tom. Annie supposed that death was hard for her to understand, and told her that she was a lucky little girl to live in Aunt Ella's lovely house with a pretty nursery where she could play with John all day instead of having to help make matchboxes. The baby would gurgle happily and put out his arms to Annie which reassured her that he still remembered her but she knew that, once she and Tom left for Canada, he would soon forget them, which made her feel sad. She would often find herself trying not to cry as she and Tom walked quickly back to Spitalfields in the darkening afternoon.

The weeks before Christmas were busy because free time was taken up with making Christmas presents on some evenings and carol singing in the courts on others. Annie found the courts frightening – far dirtier and more forbidding than the streets in Bromley where they had been living – but the rough people living in the crowded tenements seemed happy to listen to the singing and often joined in. Jennie said that they were used to evangelists visiting them and even the drunkards didn't mind somebody trying to save them because it was better than not being noticed at all. Her mother was a drunkard, Jennie confided, and she was thankful the evangelists were giving Jennie a chance for a better life.

Annie was glad she had put the petticoat Tom had found in the mud at Limehouse Hole into her bundle the night they came to the Refuge because she was able to make an apron for Harriet's Christmas present and a baby's frock for John from it. The apron she could manage by herself, but needed help with the frock. Fortunately, Miss Barber was able to find instructions for making a paper pattern and showed her how to measure and make outlines for the back, front and sleeves on a piece of newspaper, then use them to cut the shapes from the petticoat material. She also showed her how to cut the lace trim off so that she could ruffle it and sew it onto Harriet's apron. There was enough of the petticoat left to make a handkerchief each for their aunt and uncle. Tom made little cards with "Happy Christmas from Tom and Annie" written on them and, on Christmas Day after the service at the Refuge, they hurried to their uncle's house with the presents in Annie's basket. Annie was allowed to dress John in the baby frock and Tom helped Harriet into the apron and tied the bow. Their aunt said that Annie was a very good needlewoman and asked where the lace had come from. When Tom told her and Uncle Alfred about finding the petticoat in the mud at Limehouse Hole, a great debate began as to how it had come to be there. Had the poor woman fallen from a steamboat and drowned, her various articles of clothing being torn from her body by the river's current? Or, had she been assaulted and thrown off London Bridge? There was no way of knowing how far the petticoat had travelled. Aunt Ella said the lace was expensive and handmade – far more expensive than she would ever be able to afford and, even the lawn linen from which the garment was made would have been something which only a rich woman could afford to buy, and Harriet and John would only be allowed to wear their new finery on special occasions. When they had outgrown it, she would put it away to keep for when they were grown up and had children of their own. As for the handkerchiefs, she must hope that people wouldn't think they were putting on airs...

Tom privately thought his aunt put on airs anyway, but he was pleased that the Christmas presents had turned out to be so impressive. After dinner, to which Ella's Ma and Pa and spinster sister had also been invited, he and Annie said goodbye and hurried back to the Refuge. Poor people from all over Spitalfields and Whitechapel were expected for carol singing followed by ginger snaps, mincemeat tarts and mulled cider and all the Refuge children were needed to help ensure that a good time was had by all. During the long walk back along the Mile End Road, they talked about how they would be in Canada for next Christmas and wondered what it would be like having Christmas with a new family in a strange place. They still had not learned a lot about Canada because lessons in the schoolroom had, naturally, been about Christmas during the three weeks since they had arrived at the Refuge. Tom said they would learn about what Mr. Lewis called "the geography of Canada" in the boys' class after Christmas. Geography, he explained to Annie who had not been to school long enough to know, meant where places were and what the land was like. There were mountains, he'd heard, and great forests, bigger than Epping which was the only forest he'd ever seen – they had gone there twice by van on picnics in the old days – and lakes and marshes, much bigger than the Stratford Marsh, and miles of railways so that people could get from one place to another. Annie hoped that the girls would be taught the geography, too. All too often, she thought, schoolmistresses thought that girls only needed to be taught about the Bible and how to sew.

Annie did not have to wait long to find out, however, since it turned out that Miss Barber and Miss Macpherson, herself, taught both boys and girls about what life was like in Canada. Photographs of the Home in Belleville were passed around, and the children, used to the crowded streets of London, were astonished to see the large house, surrounded by trees and fields, which looked more like a picture of a lord's house they might see in a story book than a place where children like themselves would live. They found it hard to imagine being amid trees and fields instead of tenements and factories and warehouses. They were still trying to imagine life in Belleville in February when Miss Macpherson received the news that a fire had completely destroyed the house.

The terrible fire had happened during the night but everybody had managed to get safely away except one little boy, but it was freezing cold out in the snow and they had on only their nightshirts. Neighbours had taken them in and people from the town brought clothes and blankets because, by the time the fire engine arrived everything was burned. They were told the little boy's name was Robbie and they all bowed their heads as Mr. Lewis prayed for his soul. Annie found it hard to concentrate and imagined waking up in the dark night to find the room full of smoke, then being taken out into the snow without time to put on warm clothes. What if it happened when she and Tom were there and they burned to death and would never have the chance to come back to London to see Harriet and John again? She found herself crying and felt guilty when Jennie whispered that she mustn't worry for little Robbie was safe in heaven now because she could scarcely explain it wasn't Robbie she was crying for – that she was crying for herself when she was supposed to be praying for the soul of the dead little boy.

By the time that news came of subscriptions taken up to replace the Home with a new and better house, Annie had finally convinced herself that Harriet and John were safe with their uncle and she and Tom must look toward a new life in Canada. Miss Macpherson left for Canada at the beginning of March, taking Miss Reavell, the Refuge clerk with her. She told the children that they would ensure that everything was ready at the new house, as well as at the two Homes which were being prepared in Knowlton and Galt, for when they arrived in the summer. Tom was sent to Hampton soon after that and Annie was placed in the kitchen session for the month where learning to prepare and serve food to a large number of people left her little time to feel doubtful about what the summer would bring or to worry about how her brothers and sister were getting along. By May, she, too was at Hampton, at the new Girl's Home and found working on the farm much to her liking. Learning to milk cows reminded her, briefly, of the dairy in Grundy Street where she had gone to buy extra milk hoping it would build up Ma's strength. But only briefly – the memories of last year were receding and she was beginning to feel quite excited about boarding the ship for Canada.

* * * *

Most of the children had never been on a train before. Barely controlled excitement prevented too many regrets at leaving London as Mrs. Merry and Miss Bilbrough, who was going with them to help her sister, the lady in charge of the Home that had burnt down in the winter, led them onto the platform. They filed past the guard's van where their boxes were being loaded from the vans which had brought both children and luggage to the station and waved goodbye to the family members who had come to see them off. Both Tom and Annie had been surprised to see their Aunt Ella carrying John and their Uncle Alfred holding Harriet by the hand on the St. Pancras railway station concourse. Alfred had told them that he intended to ask the solicitors to let him leave early that day so that he could come along and see that they had everything they needed, but they hadn't expected their aunt and the children to ride on the omnibus all the way from Bow. Annie ran to hug her sister, then asked her aunt if she could hold her baby brother one last time while Harriet excitedly told them about the omnibus journey. John was fourteen months old now, and much bigger and heavier than in the days when Annie had fed him milk from the bottle given to her by the local midwife. Would she ever see him again? The excitement of travelling by train to Liverpool to board a steamship paled and she almost wished they weren't there to remind her of the great distance there would soon be between them. Baby John's face crumpled as he saw the tears running down Annie's cheeks and she quickly rubbed them off, nuzzling him until they were both smiling again.

"We bought you some sweeties," Harriet said, holding up two small bags of sweets. "They're for you to have on the train. Tom can hold yours for now, Annie. Aunt Ella says if you write a letter to me and John, she'll read it to me, so you'll do that, won't you Annie? Of course I can still read all the words you taught me and, soon, I'll be going to school and I'll learn more, won't I?"

Annie smiled, holding back the tears which were threatening to spill down her cheeks again, "Yes, you will and, of course I'll write to you. I'm going to write a letter on the ship – a bit every day. We'll have lots of time for writing letters on the ship and we have paper and lead-pencils, and the ship will bring them back when it returns and one of the helpers at the Beehive will deliver them. They're such nice ladies and gentlemen, aren't they?"

"Come along, Annie," Tom had said, taking her arm as their aunt reclaimed the baby. "Miss Macpherson wants us all back in line…"

Now they both stood on the platform ready to get on the train, the line growing shorter as each child boarded and Tom and Annie were soon waving to the little group on the other side of the barrier for the last time. Two third class carriages had been provided to the Refuge children and one of the older boys directed boys to one and girls to the other. Long wooden benches filled the carriage with a narrow aisle on one side. Mrs. Merry was in the girls' carriage and instructed them to take their blankets from their satchels, then stow the satchels under the bench. It was, after all almost bedtime and they could wrap the blankets around themselves and, in the meantime sitting on them would make the seats feel more comfortable, they were told, and they were going to be sitting in them for a long time. Since there were not as many girls, as there were boys, even including the very small boys who were in the charge of the oldest girls, other travellers occupied the seats at one end and the children were told to show consideration to their fellow travellers and not to make a noise.

Since she was quite alone in the world and there would be nobody to see her off, Maggie had offered to save a seat for Annie. The two had become good friends over the past few months, despite the session system being designed to prevent very close friendships being formed. This was in the interests of the children since many of them were leaving the people they loved behind which would be hard enough without having to face more tearful partings once they were in Canada.

"Got us one by the window, I did," Maggie said, waving Annie over. "Can't see much, it's so small, but it'll be nice to see somefink out there, won't it? So you sit there and we'll take turns 'avin' the window seat 'til it gets too dark to see. An' we can 'elp Jane an' Becky let them little ones see out, too."

The bench opposite had been taken by two of the older girls who had charge of eight of the smallest children. For a moment Annie half wished Harriet was one of them but told herself that her sister was happy with their uncle and aunt while these little girls had no relations to take them in.

"'Ere, let's get yer blanket out," Maggie continued, "and put yer satchel under." She undid the buckle on Annie's satchel and passed the blanket to her, then pushed the satchel alongside her own under the bench. They sat together and Annie wondered how many sweets were in the bag, which Tom had given her as they lined up to get on the train. She'd like to give one to Maggie but, if there weren't enough to hand out to the other girls, it really wouldn't be fair, especially for the little girls opposite them. She decided to wait and see if they had been given any of their own. Many of the people seeing the children off had been buying penny bags of sweets from the stalls at the station.

"Saw your uncle and them there, I did," said Maggie. "'Minded me a bit of me baby bruvver and little sister 'fore they got the plague." She thought for a minute. "I s'pose me sister must've bin a bit younger, though. I wouldn't've bin much older than your sister five years ago, would I? 'Course, I don't really know 'ow old I am, anyway, do I?"

"I told you before, Maggie," Annie said, taking her hand. "You're going to share my birthday, starting with our tenth birthday next week when we'll have birthday cake right on the ship. You know Mrs. Merry has it in one of food bins, candles and all. And, then, every year, we'll send each other a birthday card – wherever we are – for the rest of our lives."

Just then a bell rang and they could hear doors slamming, then a whistle blew and the train began to move. The children all looked at each other startled and one or two of the little ones began to cry. Soon, however, they became used to the motion and were taking it in turns to look out of the window to watch as the city streets began to disappear behind them to be replaced with trees and fields.

"Well," said Maggie, "we're really on our way now, we are, ain't we? Now, you stop the grizzling, Maisie, you 'ear me?" she added, as the frightened four-year-old opposite them continued to wail. "Come an' sit 'ere with me an' Annie an' you can look out the window. Then, we'll read your book to you. 'Least, Annie will. I still ain't so good wiv the reading, meself."

The children shifted along the benches as Maisie came to sit between Maggie and Annie while the Religious Tract Society children's books were being passed out. They helped Maisie and the other smaller children stand on the bench to see out of the window, as the train left the grimy city buildings behind and they could see only hills and valleys that they had never seen before. Most of the older children had seen farmland during their stay at the Hampton Homes, which they had reached by steamboat from London. Here, on the train despite the gathering twilight, they could see for miles across vast fields with not a house in sight

Maisie's book, which she begged Annie to read to her, was in rhyme and the rhythm of Annie's reading together with the gentle jolting of the train, as it sped through the countryside, soon caused little Maisie to fall asleep. Annie and Maggie began to read the book given to Annie. It was called Meg's Little Children and the first few pages reminded Annie so vividly of looking after Harriet and John and her mother's death that she found herself crying.

"Let's read mine instead," said Maggie diplomatically. "Yours is too sad. Mine's a Bible story – the one about Jesus making the dead little girl come alive again. I'll start–"

Maggie slowly began to read the story. She had not learned to read until she had been rescued from the streets and brought to the Refuge but had learned quickly, especially since becoming friends with Annie. Annie swallowed her tears and helped her friend with the words she didn't know. She soon took over, reading for the little children who were still awake on the opposite bench to hear as well. By the time she had finished, many were asleep and the train was well into the Midlands and, in no time at all it seemed the train slowed as it reached Rugby, which Mrs. Merry said was the halfway point of their journey. Those who were awake could get out of the train but must stay together on the platform. Everyone would have a chance to visit the toilets and get a drink of water at the pump if they wished. Later, there would be a short stop at a place called Crewe and, soon after that, they'd arrive at Liverpool. Before this year, Miss Macpherson had told them, the trains with third class carriages had stopped at every station and the journey had taken much longer, but now they would be there early in the morning and might even be able to board the ship if there were no delays in sailing since it was due to sail tomorrow. Often, however, there were delays and few ships sailed exactly when they were scheduled which was hard on emigrants because they had to spend money they could ill afford on lodgings, sometimes for several days.

"Not us," whispered Maggie to one of the girls who looked alarmed. "We'll be stoppin' at the Brethren in Christ's 'all, right near the docks, 'til it's time to get on the ship."

* * * *

It was while she was eating her bread and jam that Harriet came to the realisation that she might never see Tom and Annie again.

By the time they reached Bow again on the omnibus, it was past tea-time and John was fast asleep on Aunt Ella's lap. Uncle Alfred took him from her and carried him off the omnibus and through the streets to their house. Aunt Ella said Harriet was to have her tea while she put John to bed so she and Uncle Alfred were sitting at the table eating their bread and jam and chatting about the day's adventure when the realization suddenly dawned. She dropped her bread and began to cry.

"What is it, dear? What's wrong?" Uncle Alfred asked. "Blow your nose – have you got your handkerchief?" Harriet nodded. "Blow your nose and tell me what's wrong."

Harriet blew her nose. "If Tom and Annie ride in the train to that place..."

"Liverpool."

"...Liverpool, and then go on a ship across the sea to–to..."

"Canada."

"...to Canada, they'll never be able to come and visit us again. When will me and John ever see them again?"

"Look Harriet, we talked about this before. You knew they were going."

"Yes, but they were still here in London. Now they've gone." She began to cry again. "Why did they have to go? Why couldn't they have lived here with us?"

"Harriet, duckie, we've been through all this before. We don't have the room, and Auntie Ella is too delicate to cope with four children. She's managing you and John, mostly because you are such a good little girl."

"But Annie's good, too. Ma used to say that she was just like a little mother the way she looked after me and John." In truth, Harriet had mostly forgotten their life in the Bromley slum room but she knew Annie was good. She pushed her plate away and put her head on the table.

"Come along, Harriet, you know you don't do that at the tea table. Sit up now. One day, when you're grown up, perhaps you will go and see them or maybe they'll come home for a visit. We're told that there are opportunities in Canada for children to grow up and get good jobs and earn lots of money so who's to say one or other of them won't have the money to sail back to England for a visit."

Harriet wiped her eyes. "Do you really think so?" she asked.

"Well, I don't see why not. Now finish your bread and jam and drink your milk. It's past your bedtime but, if you eat up and then get ready for bed quickly, I'll come and read to you. We'll have to be quiet though so as not to wake John."

Later, after her uncle had read the story about the tea party in the Alice book, Harriet lay in bed wondering if Annie and Tom were still on the train. They had said they'd be sleeping on the train as it took a long time to get to the place where the ship was – she'd forgotten the name of it again. It began with the same letter as 'London' did. She wished she knew letters as well as she knew numbers, although she'd forgotten some of the numbers that Tom and Annie had taught her when she helped to make the matchboxes now because there were no matchboxes. She hadn't thought of the matchboxes for a long time. She tried to remember the events of that day when Uncle

Alfred had taken her and John to his house. Tom had come with them in the hansom, leaving Annie with the matchboxes and Ma... That was the last time she had seen either Ma or the matchboxes. The next thing she remembered was Aunt Ella insisting that she must be thoroughly washed in the tin bath she brought in from the scullery and filled with hot water boiled on the hob in the fireplace. She soaped her all over and washed her hair until her head ached. She had tried not to cry when her aunt kept talking about how it was necessary to scrub the filth of the slums off her, hoping that she wouldn't do it to John who Uncle Alfred was cradling on his lap on the other side of the fireplace. She had told them that Annie used the bowl to bathe the baby and begged them not to put him in the tin bath. He would surely drown. Uncle Alfred had gone to the scullery and fetched a tin bowl just like the one they had all used for washing themselves in as well as for washing clothes, vegetables and any number of things. He told her John would be safe in that, and not to worry. She couldn't remember much – just the much too big nightshirt Aunt Ella had put on her, saying that all her clothes must be washed before she could wear them again. Later she'd been told that Ma was now safely in heaven with Pa and that she and John would live here from now on. It was nice living here away from all those horrible children who scratched and kicked her if she went down the stairs without Annie or Tom, but she wished Tom and Annie weren't going off on the train and the ship...

CHAPTER SEVEN

As it happened, the party from the Refuge did board the *SS Prussian* the next afternoon. Miss Macpherson told Tom and the rest of the boys that they should take the fact that there were no delays as a sign of a propitious journey to come and thank the Lord in their prayers. The boys were not sure of the meaning of the word "propitious" but expected that one of the grown-ups would thank the Lord when evening prayers were said.

Tom had seen ocean-going steamships on the Thames at Limehouse but the iron ship, with its three masts and huge funnel, looked bigger than the entire court they had lived in at Bromley. Judging by the queues of people waiting to board, it looked as if it would be housing as many people as were packed into the houses there. He could see Annie ahead of him with the girls and little children. The boys were a much larger group, despite the fact that those under the age of five were with the girls' group, in the care of the thirteen and fourteen year olds, who must practise looking after them, since a farmer's wife in Canada most often needed a girl to help look after her children.

Further along the pier, he could see the gangplank where the cabin passengers were boarding the steam tug which would take them out to the ship. They, evidently, boarded first. He knew that they would have cabins that were like bedrooms instead of being allotted bunks on the steerage deck like the emigrants. One day, after he'd made his fortune in Canada, perhaps he'd travel cabin class when he returned to London to visit Harriet and John. He imagined himself dressed in a beaver coat, and wearing a top hat which he would doff to the ladies as he walked jauntily along the pier to board with the cabin passengers.

"Already got on, 'aven't they?" said a voice, waking Tom from his reverie.

"What?"

"The man wot's going to be the Gov'ner of Canada," said Will Jakes. "Fought that's wot you was lookin' down there for, didn't !?"

"No, I was just looking…" He wasn't about to admit to dreaming about being a cabin class passenger but Will, thankfully, continued before he could come up with anything.

"Well, that seaman over there, 'e told us. This bloke's going to be on board wiv us wot's going to be the new Gov'ner. Lord somefink–"

"Lord Duff'rin," Edmund Jenkins said. "Can't remember anyfink, you can't, Will Jakes. They 'ave a lord go over to look after fings fer the Queen, see? And now's the time fer changin' over, mus' be. Anyway, the lord and lady and the children and servants is all on the ship with us. Don't s'pose we'll see much of them though, eh? – bein' as we'll be down in steerage, like and the toffs'll be in cabins, won't they?"

Will and Edmund continued to argue about whether or not they'd see the lord's family on board while the queue of steerage passengers, at last, began to grow shorter as two more tug-boats began to ferry the emigrants across to board the ship.

The entire party from the Refuge was allotted an area together in the family section of steerage. Some of the older boys were disappointed at not being allowed to have hammocks in the men's area but Miss Bilbrough assured them that it was not because their ability to act responsibly was in doubt, but because they were needed to supervise the younger boys. She assigned the boys to the three berths in each bunk and told them to put their satchels at the foot of the berth and to ensure that all personal possessions, except for their blankets, were in the satchels at all times so that everybody had enough room. All the boys aged between nine and twelve were allowed to bunk together while those thirteen and older were each assigned two younger boys to supervise. Tom found himself placed in an upper bunk with Will and Edmund since they had all been together in the queue. The bunks had enough headroom for the occupants to sit up and all the children were told to sit facing the passageway between the two rows of berths, along the middle of which the seamen had lashed their boxes together, until everybody was accommodated and a head count made. Tom tried to see where his sister was. The girls, however, had been placed in bunks further along from the boys and, since he couldn't see her among the girls on the other side of the aisle, he decided that she must be on the same side as him. Even craning his neck, he could only see the girls' frocks as they sat on the edge of their bunks for the head count.

"Ain't much room, is there?" said Will. "'Ere, I fink it's only fair we take it in turns to 'ave the outside place. Agreed?"

"All right but we move ourselves and our mattresses, though," Tom agreed, "in case of sea sickness or worse…"

"Right you are," Edmund put in. "I ain't sleeping in someone else's soil."

"That's settled then. Fink we'll be allowed up on the deck when we get organized?"

"I expect so," said Tom. "When you see pictures of ships leaving the dock everyone's out there waving, so that must be what happens. The deck looked pretty small though, didn't it? Well, not small – but small for six hundred people to all fit on it."

"They got their own deck, them toffs in the cabins 'ave," Will said.

"Yeah, but I wasn't counting them. There's six hundred people in steerage, Miss Bilbrough said, and they've all got to fit on the deck we came across to get down the hatchway and there's lifeboats there taking up room, too."

They were quiet for a minute, each trying to imagine what six hundred people all together would look like. Finally, Edmund said, "Well, I s'pose there's enough room s'long as they all keep still." He craned his neck to look along the passageway. "There's people goin' up the 'atchway now. I wish Miss'd 'urry up wiv countin' us. Won't be werf goin' up there if we're stuck at the back wiv grownups in front of us, will it?"

"Yeah, but they might 'ave people to wave to on the shore. And 'cept for Miss Macpherson who we'll be seeing again in Canada she said, we only got them Brethren in Christ lot that give us our breakfast, and we don't even know them. Might as well stay down 'ere if we can't see nuffink."

"It's Mrs. Merry wot's doin' the counting an' she's coming along now."

Mrs. Merry finally gave the word for the children, except for the smallest boys and girls and the older girls who were needed to look after them, to go upon deck, assigning half a dozen of the oldest boys to be in charge.

"'Ere, Tom," Edmund said when they arrived on deck, "that there must be the lifeboat. If we squeeze along 'ere–" he ducked down on his hands and knees and crawled under the bow of the lifeboat "–and, 'ere we are – got our own little place 'ere, we 'ave."

Tom followed him, beckoning to Will, and found just enough room for the three of them to stand by the rail and look across the strip of water to the wharf. The sun must be getting low in the sky because the areas beyond the warehouses and other buildings of Albert Dock were shadowed and he wondered when they'd have supper. They'd had breakfast at the Brethren in Christ hall where they'd stayed last night, and bread and cheese, provided by the Brethren in Christ, which they'd brought to the docks with them, for dinner. Miss Bilbrough had said that there was no teatime on board the ship but that they'd be having supper instead like working men did. Today, they'd have mutton stew for supper once the ship was underway but it looked as if the preparations for leaving would take some time yet. The Brethren in Christ congregation was on the wharf with Miss Macpherson, who had only recently returned from Canada and would be catching the train to Glasgow next morning to make arrangements for taking some Scottish boys to Canada next month. They were singing a hymn called *Eternal Father, Strong to Save* which they'd sung at the hall this morning after breakfast. He could see the preacher energetically leading them. Somebody had written it, a few years ago, to pray that his friend would be kept safe on his journey across the ocean and, now, it was being sung at services on board ships all over the world. Other people, including the passengers on the ship began to join in and, soon, it seemed that everybody was singing, whether or not they knew the words.

When the ship began to roll as the moorings were released and the anchor raised – at least, that's what Tom surmised was happening – and the tugboats started to pull it towards the estuary, the singing stopped as people were taken by surprise. It was time to leave. Everybody began to wave and shout out their goodbyes and the Brethren in Christ began to sing again. Tom's stomach seemed to turn over but, hoping it didn't mean he was going to be sick, he joined in the shouting and waving. The ship moved slowly down the river. Then, there was a lot of noise and smoke and, soon, they could see the tugboats turning back to the wharf and the ship was proceeding under its own power into the estuary, towards the sea and then on to the coast of Ireland. Tom knew this because they had been told that they would stop at a place called Londonderry, which was in Ireland, to pick up the rest of the steerage passengers, before they actually began to cross the ocean. Lots of people seemed to want to go to Canada, he thought. There were many different accents among the steerage passengers thronging around on the other side of the lifeboat. Some of them were hard to understand. The three boys were quiet, each immersed in his own thoughts until soon looking at the sea, sky and passing coastline became a little monotonous and they began to wonder if it wasn't just about time for supper.

"'Ope nobody else finds this little spot," Edmund said, obviously pleased to have been the one who spotted it.

"Well, they ain't so far," Will told him. "Be nice to 'ave our own private bit of the deck, won't it, Tom?"

"We'd best not tell anyone or they'll want to come in," said Tom. "We'll check and make sure nobody's watching before we crawl out. You don't feel the movement of the ship as much as I thought you would, do you?"

"Can't really tell, can you? If you don't look at the wharfs, I mean."

"This ain't nuffink, yet," Edmund laughed. "Like being on me uncle's lighter on the Thames, this is. It's when we gets out to the sea that trouble starts. 'Ere I 'ope we do get to 'ave our supper 'fore we get to the sea. If we start to roll, they may not 'ave it."

"You fink they'd do that?" asked Will. "I'm starvin', I am. Let's go down an' see. I'll go first – you two watch me an' I'll beckon once I see that all's clear."

They crawled under the lifeboat's bow and found that most of the passengers had left the deck. Back in steerage the tables and benches, which had previously been tied down in the centre of the aisle between the berths, were set up ready for supper, the passenger's boxes remaining under the tables. The children were all sitting on the benches adjacent to their berths and bowls of mutton stew were being passed out.

"Didn't you 'ear me tell you to get on down?" asked John, one of the older boys put in charge of the children when they'd gone up on deck. He looked cross. "You're getting me in trouble with Miss, you are. Where were you?"

"Jus' on the deck with the rest of you," said Edmund quickly. "We was busy lookin' out to sea, we was. S'pose we didn't 'ear you. Sorry."

"Sorry, John," Tom and Will chimed in.

"Okay," said John. "Get along with you and don't let it 'appen again or you won't be allowed up on deck."

They found their places and quickly seated themselves, in front of the bowls of stew that had been placed ready for them, just in time for Mrs. Merry to lead them in grace.

CHAPTER EIGHT

The first stage of the journey, across the Irish Sea and around the north coast of Ireland to Londonderry, took place during the first evening out. By the time the ship moored in the river to await the boarding of the rest of the passengers early in the morning, most of the children were asleep. They were all very tired and slept well, despite the heat in the badly ventilated steerage cabin, without waking until the rolling of the ship as it steamed back down the estuary towards the Atlantic Ocean jostled them in their berths and the newly arrived passengers noisily settled their possessions in berths further along the steerage cabin.

To the children, used to dark and sooty London, the bright day, which greeted them when they were allowed to go up on deck after breakfast, was truly amazing. Annie and Maggie stared at each other. It was almost as if they had never seen each other clearly before.

"It's like being in fairyland," cried Annie.

"It is," Maggie laughed delightedly, spreading out her arms and doing a pirouette. "Makes you feel light and jus' like a fairy, dunnit?"

Some of the other girls followed her example.

"Girls are so stupid," said one of the boys in disgust. "Jus' wait and see 'ow like a fairy you feel when we get out into the Atlantic. That seaman – the one wiv the ginger 'air – 'e says to us to enjoy the weather while we can. 'E says them clouds way out there is where we're 'eaded and they're goin' to get blacker an' blacker an' the waves is goin' to come up. Be like that story in the Bible, it will, when them disciples got scared outer their wits an' woke Jesus up an' 'e stopped the storm. Only we ain't got 'im asleep on board 'ere, 'ave we?"

"'Course we 'ave," declared Maggie, stoutly, continuing to dance. "'E's everywhere, ain't 'e?"

"Well, 'e ain't goin' to stop this storm, 'e ain't."

"Maybe not," said Annie, "but he'll see us safely through it."

"Yeah, that's right," agreed Maggie. "So, you boys jus' scram an' leave us alone."

The girls carried on dancing and the boys moved off. Annie saw Tom and his bunk mates split off from the group and wondered where they were going. She thought they must have found themselves a secret hidey-hole because they had disappeared yesterday as well, when the ship was leaving Liverpool. She hoped it wasn't in a dangerous place and wished boys weren't so silly always showing off to each other.

"That's a lovely idea, girls," cried Mrs. Merry, bringing the younger children up the hatchway. "Would you little ones like to join in the dancing?"

Annie took little Maisie by the hand. "Pretend you're a fairy, Maisie. There's so much light here that we're pretending we're in fairyland."

"We ain't got no wings."

"Pretend, Maisie, pretend…"

The children danced around the deck until they were all out of breath and Mrs. Merry clapped her hands and beckoned them all towards her. It was time for Morning Prayers. Miss Bilbrough rounded up the boys, including Tom and his friends Will and Edmund, Annie was glad to see, and then invited the other steerage passengers to join them.

Singing hymns and listening to Bible stories outside in the sun reminded Annie of Sunday School picnics in the days before her father died and her mother became sick – in those days when they'd take food and outgrown clothes for the poor children, never dreaming that one day they too, would be poor children. Many of those children had made matchboxes instead of going to school, and Sunday was the only time they had to learn to read and write. At least, Annie told herself, she'd been able to go to school each day for four years before becoming a matchbox maker herself. The last few months at the Refuge had shown her how much better off she and Tom were than the many children for whom the schoolroom there was the first opportunity to learn about reading, writing and arithmetic.

After the service, they were divided into groups for what Miss Bilbrough and Mrs. Merry called 'educational' games and stayed on deck in the warm sun until it was time for dinner. Annie's group of six girls were given The Mansion of Happiness to play and Annie, getting ahead to begin with, soon landed on several vices in a row and had to miss turns while in prison and on the ducking stool, and was far behind when Maggie was first to reach the Mansion. She was glad Maggie had won because it made Maggie happy. After that, two of the mariners showed them how to play a game called deck quoits, which involved throwing rings made of rope over pins set up further along the deck.

It was that glorious first morning on the ship that came to mind when Annie thought of the journey to Canada in later years. After dinner the sea turned rough and the ship was rolling. It was difficult to walk about the steerage cabin and the children were no longer allowed to go up on deck. Soon, nobody was feeling very much like walking, anyhow, and the continual rolling was making them feel very sick, a situation which was to remain in place for several days.

Annie wasn't as badly affected as some of the children and helped to look after the little ones – cleaning up after them, washing them, emptying chamber pots as well as reading them stories and singing to them. The ladies from the Refuge were well used to their children becoming seasick and had brought along extra soap, towels and bowls, which Annie would queue to fill from the one tap in the washroom which piped in warm water. Sometimes she had to lie down herself until the nausea and dizziness passed. Then, propped up in her berth, she wrote about the first magical morning in her letters to Harriet and John, to Jennie Sparling, her first friend at the Refuge who had gone to live with an aunt in Sussex, and to Kath, who'd got her wish to stay at the Refuge for a bit longer. Dr. MacGhie had decided that her chest was too weak to stand the rigours of an ocean voyage just yet. She found that she really liked writing the letters – to the extent that she used up all her paper and had to ask for more.

Annie, and the other children who were not severely seasick, helped Mrs. Merry with the service on Sunday, reading from the book of Job because Mrs. Merry said this would help everybody to be patient for the time when *'this, too, shall pass'* and they'd all feel better again. Not very many people felt up to hymn-singing but the children who were well sang lustily to make up for the lack of voices.

Most of the travellers gave up trying to eat meals and lay dozing in their berths. With the ship rolling so much that water washed over the deck and poured down the hatchway at times, there was little else they could do. This lasted for five days and then the stormy weather began to clear and the sun came out again.

* * * *

By the time Annie's birthday arrived on the 20th, the sea was calm again and nearly everybody in steerage crowded out onto the deck where there was a service and hymn singing. At tea-time, the cake which, at Miss Bilbrough's instructions, had been stored in the ship's galley, was brought in with ten lighted candles on it and Annie's and Maggie's names written in red icing. A further surprise came when Tom and his friends, Will and Edmund, presented a puppet show, using a bench and their blankets to make the stage and curtains and puppets they had constructed from painted newspaper faces attached to stockings which they wore over their hands. Maggie cried and said it was the happiest day of her life.

The next day, Tom told Annie that the mariners said that they should soon see land – not Canada yet, but the island of Newfoundland. They should also watch for icebergs. None of the children were really sure about what icebergs looked like. It was hard to imagine something which they were told was a big block of ice. How big a block of ice? Soon icebergs were spotted in the distance but it wasn't until the next day that they drew close enough to one to see that it was as big as the ship, maybe bigger, and sparkled in the sun and, even, seemed to have fresh snow on its crown. They didn't look as if they were moving but, apparently, they had drifted down from the north where all the land was covered by ice and snow. Annie wondered how the captain managed to steer the ship past the drifting icebergs, during the night, without crashing into one.

As they drew closer to their new home, clouds began to hide the sun until they soon found themselves in gloomy fog and she hoped that there were no more icebergs. Miss Bilbrough said it was often foggy between Newfoundland and the Labrador coast and spread out a map so that they could see where they were approaching the estuary of the St. Lawrence River on their way to where they would land at Quebec. The fog cleared before the end of the day, leaving steam drifting up from the water. Amazingly, looking down into the clear water they could see small whales, which they were told were called belugas, darting about.

The next day the weather was beautiful and the children stayed on deck for the whole day watching the fishing boats on the river and seeing small settlements on the banks of the wide St. Lawrence. Off a place called Father Point, the ship dropped anchor for a short time to await the pilot who would guide them down the river. There was a lighthouse there, which the boys found intriguing, and a telegraph station from where Mrs. Merry telegraphed their imminent arrival to the receiving homes.

In the evening, a service was held to give thanks for their safe crossing of the mighty Atlantic Ocean and to ask the Lord for guidance as they took up their lives in this new land. Then, the children were told to stay in their berths and to make sure all their letters were finished so that they could be collected ready to be packaged together. They would be taken back to England when the ship returned there, to be delivered to the House of Industry and delivered to their families from there. After that, they must ensure they had all their possessions packed into their satchels ready for disembarkation in the morning. While all the children in steerage were confined to their berths, Lord and Lady Dufferin and some of the other first class passengers came down to talk to the emigrants about the great country of Canada and the opportunities for them there. Annie couldn't see them from her berth but she heard Lord Dufferin say that the more children they had the better because children were needed on the Canadian farms, which was followed by great hilarity among the emigrants. Annie wasn't sure what the laughter was all about but was glad to hear that children were so badly needed.

It was hard to sleep that night. The very idea of leaving the SS Prussian, which had been their home for what seemed – probably because of the storm and sickness, Annie thought – much longer than the ten days that they had been on board, had the same feeling of finality as the walk to St. Pancras had done the morning when they had left the Refuge.

* * * *

They anchored early in the morning but were not able to disembark until after the new Governor General's party had left the ship with many officials who had come aboard to escort them off. Cannons were fired and lines of soldiers were to be seen along the shore. Lord and Lady Dufferin and their children rode away into the town, in a carriage amid crowds of people who lined the way, and the emigrants were, at last, able to leave the ship.

Tom and many of the other boys were tremendously disappointed when they found themselves being ferried over to the other side of the river instead of following the Governor General. They had hoped to be able to see more of the troops they had watched from the ship. Instead, they were sent to a large shed to find their boxes which had been unloaded and piled on the floor and then to wait in long lines for the immigration inspectors to check their luggage and provide them with landing cards. Then a doctor and nurse inspected everybody. After all that, thankfully, they were herded outside to where a late breakfast, provided by the Immigration Society, was being served on trestle tables in the sun. On seeing their glum faces and hearing Edmund grumbling, the lady spooning scrambled eggs onto the tin plates handed out to them told them that this was where Wolfe had set up camp and laid siege to the city across the river and that it had been inhabited for centuries by Indian tribes. The boys' faces brightened at this news, especially the part she related about Wolfe's army firing cannons across the St. Lawrence.

"Climbed up the cliffs over there, they did," Will said, when they had all satisfied their hunger with the fresh bread and scrambled eggs, something which none of them had ever eaten in such quantities before. "'Auled up the cannons and slaughtered them Frenchies and won Canada for the Queen."

"No, we used to have a king then," said Tom. "We've been having kings – all called George, they were, except for William, the last one – for years and years until we got a queen again. Wish we could've gone to the fort. That's where Lord Dufferin went, they said – the mariners…"

"Them mariners 'ave a nice job, don't they?" put in Edmund, changing the subject. "I wouldn't mind bein' a mariner when I grow up, takin' emigrants over the ocean, I wouldn't. I wonder 'ow you get to be one."

"You have to apply to the steamship company, I expect. Anyway, it'll be years before you're old enough."

"If I'd've bin able to stay in London and got apprenticed to me uncle, I'd've only 'ad to be fourteen – couldn't, of course, 'cos me cousin was 'is apprentice – but wot I mean is that if you get apprenticed on the river at fourteen, maybe it's the same for going to sea. And I'm eleven now, so it's not so long, is it?"

"There was boys down below in the engine room, there was," said Will. "I expect that's all you get to do when you first start – shovel the coal…"

"Never mind. Miss Macpherson wants us all to be farmers, anyway, don't she? If them eggs is what you get fed 'ere, it don't seem like such a bad idea, does it? What d'you fink, Tom? Would you rather shovel coal or cows' shit?"

"Ssh. You'll get punished for –"

"Can't send me to sit in the corner 'cos there ain't one, is there? Goin' to be out 'ere all day 'til the train comes, we are."

"Well, watch the language anyway," Tom told him. "We don't want to be made to sit here all day instead of exploring, do we?"

"'E's right, Edmund," added Will. "They said we can get some proper exercise after breakfast. Prob'ly 'ave to run races and such, but maybe us three can sneak off and see what we can find…"

"Like wot?"

"Well… maybe stuff them Indians've left be'ind. Didn't only fight the French 'ere, that lady said. Before that, there was Indian battles, too. Them Frenchies even 'ad them Indians fighting for them. Scalped people, they did, in the night."

"Come off it, Will," said Tom. "That was over a hundred years ago. You'd have to start digging like an archaeologist to find things from hundreds of years ago."

"What's that?" asked Edmund.

"An archaeologist? It's a man who digs things up to put in museums."

"What's a museum?"

"It's a place where there's things that people used to have. My pa used to go to one – in Bloomsbury, he said it was. Said he'd take me when I was older, but that was before he died…" Tom trailed off thinking how he'd never get to see the museum now.

"Well," said Will, "I still think we should 'ave a butchers. Might even find somefink we can sell to a museum. Make ourselves a quid or two, we might. I mean, a dollar…"

"Don't expect they have museums here. It's not like the cities are big – like London."

"Pretty big over there…" Will said, nodding towards the opposite shore.

"Not like London, though, is it?"

Before Will could argue further, Mrs. Merry rang her bell and told everybody to congregate at the far side of the field and they'd hold their morning service. She invited the other emigrants to join them just as she had when they were on the ship.

After the service, as Will had predicted, they ran races and when it became too hot to run about, they all sat down in the shade under the trees to listen to chapter nine from Pilgrim's Progress, read by the children who were the best readers. Tom, of course, was one of these and had difficulty trying not to laugh when Will and Edmund made faces at him every time he said 'Beelzebub' until Miss Bilbrough caught them at it and sent them to sit at opposite sides of the group. Tom read on to where the pilgrims are beaten and put in a cage, then somebody else took over. He found it hard to listen to the story and wondered if any of the children really were. Most of the little ones had fallen asleep and many of the older ones were looking sleepy. The trial of Christian and Faithful before Lord Hategood couldn't really compete with the excitement of being newly landed in Canada. He looked across the river and wished, again, that they could have spent the time, until the train came, over there where the arrival of the new Governor General was still being celebrated.

Pointe-Lévy, for all its history, did not have walls and a citadel and those tower things, the name of which Tom couldn't remember. One day, when he had made his fortune, he'd come back here and explore the place. Maybe when he travelled back to England in a cabin instead of a steerage berth… Yes, he thought, there was opportunity here, in Canada, for a poor orphan to become a rich man. You could buy land, lots of it, for very little money and the family who took him in would have to pay him once he turned sixteen – four years from August – and he would save every penny of it until he had enough to buy his own land. Four years was a long time. He tried to remember the summer of four years ago. Harriet had been a baby then and Annie went to the infants' school. He and Pa would walk to the school with her and then walk on to the boys' school where Pa was the schoolmaster. He'd been proud of the fact that his Pa was the schoolmaster. It was beginning to be difficult, though, to remember Pa's face properly now. He wished he had a picture. Ma had once talked about saving some money and having their photograph taken but it was expensive and he supposed she had never managed to have enough money to spare to actually do so. He imagined a picture of Ma with Harriet on her knee, sitting beside Pa and the two of them flanked by Annie and himself. It would have been so nice to have had such a photograph. When he was rich he'd have his photograph taken – he and Annie – and they'd send it to Harriet and John so that they'd know what they looked like. He knew that, if he was already beginning to forget exactly what Pa looked like after a year and a half, then it wouldn't be long before his little sister and brother began to forget what he and Annie looked like. How long would it take to get rich, he wondered.

CHAPTER NINE

Tom didn't realize that he'd fallen asleep until he suddenly awoke to the sensation of movement around him and bells ringing. Everybody was getting up from the ground, some looking as bleary-eyed as he felt he did and others wide-awake. He must have looked confused because somebody hissed at him that they had to go and wee, then collect their sandwiches and get on the train. He slung his satchel over his shoulder and set off in the direction of the outhouses. Annie and Maggie were just ahead of him and stopped and waited for him.

"Did you fall asleep?" asked Annie.

He nodded.

"Annie and me did, too," volunteered Maggie, "but we woke up 'fore the train come in. Them silly boys you're always with are up there somewhere. You could stay wiv us 'til they separate the boys from the girls on the train…"

"Yes, do that, Tom," said Annie. "I hardly saw you on the ship – you were always with that Will and Edmund. I don't know why. They just get you into trouble."

"I wasn't in trouble when we were reading. It was just them pulling faces, but we can walk over together. Have to go to those smelly privies again…"

They all three wrinkled their noses.

"Actually, that's why we'd like you to stay with us," admitted Annie, exchanging glances with Maggie. "See, before – when we had to go after breakfast, some of the boys were opening the doors on us."

"Tryin' to see our knickers, they was," added Maggie. "Dunno wot they find so funny about seeing knickers. Told them to bugger off, I did, but they just said they'd tell on me for swearing."

Tom grinned. "All right. I'll stand on guard for you."

"You can hold our satchels, too. There's nowhere to put them down and it's awkward keeping them on."

The visit to the outhouses over, the children were told to form a queue beside one of the tables where breakfast had been eaten earlier. They were each handed a cheese sandwich, wrapped in a cloth, and an apple to put safely away in their satchels to eat during the journey, and then they filed onto the station platform. Surprisingly, boys and girls were not told to separate. Instead, Mrs. Merry read out names from a list and led the resulting group of children onto the train, settling them on benches together. Miss Bilbrough, then ushered the rest of the children into the adjacent seats. She put various older boys in charge of each bench and, with instructions that nobody was to move, hurried off to ensure that all the luggage had been loaded. Neither Will nor Edmund was in the section where he, Annie and Maggie were sitting. Since he'd only listened for his own name, he couldn't be sure which group they were in. Short of standing on his seat to look over the partitions, he had no way of finding out. He told Annie that he hoped they weren't in Mrs. Merry's group because rumour had it, those children would be leaving the train at a place called Richmond to go to the new home at Knowlton which was run by Miss Barber who'd been at the Beehive when he and Annie had first arrived there. Then, the boy in charge of their bench told him that Mrs. Merry's group were all girls, and Annie and Maggie began congratulating themselves on still being together.

"Do you think it's possible that there's a farm that needs a brother and sister and another girl?" Annie wondered aloud.

"No," said Tom, more sharply than he had meant to. "I mean, we don't even know if there'll be a farm that needs a brother and sister…"

"Miss Macpherson said she tries to keep families together. Or, at least, close by – so that they can see each other."

"But I ain't your family, am I?" put in Maggie. "So we just 'ave to 'ope for the best, don't we?"

"We'll practise your reading and writing," said Annie, "so that, at least, we can write letters to each other like Miss Macpherson said."

The conversation ended as Miss Bilbrough returned and checked all the benches, telling the children how proud she was that they'd been so good while she was away. Then, the train shook and shuddered, and whistles were heard and they were on their way.

* * * *

Marchmont, or the Marchmont Receiving Home to give it its full title, was a big, old, wooden house that appeared a bit lopsided because of the extra rooms that had been added to it. Except for the sheds and barn belonging to the property, it stood by itself in the middle of some fields and was reached by a rough lane that branched off the main road from the town.

At first sight, after the long walk from the train station, Annie had thought it looked like a lord's house or, at least, a rich man's home. Despite being told that this newly acquired building was in the country, she somehow imagined that it would be ugly, with small windows and… well, like an orphanage. Instead, looking out of windows at sky and trees and grass, was so nice that she half hoped it would be a long time before a place was found for her so that she could stay there. Since girls, and there were only eight of them left in the party, generally did not spend a great deal of time at Marchmont, they had small attic bedrooms instead of dormitories with just four to a room. The one which she shared with Maggie and two other girls looked out over the fields and it reminded Annie of the bedroom, with the window that looked out over Bow Common that she and Tom used to share before Pa died and they moved down to the rough court where they shared the threadbare hearth rug instead, at night.

The train journey had taken all night and most of the next day. A lot of the time had been spent on sidings, waiting for other trains to pass by before continuing. At Richmond, which they had reached relatively quickly, the children who Mrs. Merry had separated from the main group left the train. Miss Barber was there to take them to Knowlton and everybody waved wildly to her. All the small children were in the group, including four-year-old Maisie who had fallen asleep while Annie read to her on the train to Liverpool. There were applications to adopt them all in the area. Many of the oldest ones – girls who'd been in the dormitory at the Refuge and some who Annie had come to know better at Hampton – were going to be trained at the Knowlton Home for posts in the Eastern Township ships as the area was called. They all promised to write letters to each other but Annie felt sad as everybody waved goodbye and the train steamed on westwards. Miss Barber and her helpers had brought several loaves of bread, two whole cheeses and a basket of apples which served as breakfast next morning for those left on the train. They were advised to keep the apples for later in the day, though, as there wouldn't be anything else to eat until they reached the end of their journey.

The tired children ate a very late meal when they arrived at Marchmont and, after washing faces and hands, were sent to bed. Time enough tomorrow for everybody to bathe away the grime from the long journey, they were told.

The morning of the first day was spent having baths – girls, in a big tin hip bath in the scullery and boys under the outdoor shower by the barn. Then, under the guidance of Miss Moore, one of the instructors, the eight girls were taken to the washhouse and set to washing everybody's dirty clothes and hanging them out on the washing lines behind the house in the sunshine. The two Miss Bilbroughs – the one who had been on the ship with them and her sister who was in charge Marchmont – came out to inspect the washing and congratulated the girls on doing such a good job, telling them they could go and explore until the bell went for dinner. They were not needed to help prepare the meal today as only soup and bread and cheese was being served because many farmers and farmers' wives would be arriving during the afternoon to pick up the children who they were taking back to their farms and the women would be bringing along their contributions to a potluck supper for everybody.

The girls ventured, rather timidly, towards the field adjacent to the yard where they had hung out the washing. The two eldest said they'd prefer to sit in the shade of a huge old maple tree, since it was not likely they would have a chance to do nothing again as both had places to go to and would be off to their new homes the next day. Annie and the others followed a narrow path that went past the barn, and two cows and a horse in a paddock beside it, and continued across the field until they reached a line of trees which appeared to separate the property from the fields of a large farm beyond it. There were rows and rows of plants with long leaves.

"I wonder what they are," said Minnie, a girl who had only come to the Refuge in March, but was what Miss Macpherson had called a "quick study" and had become eligible for emigration in a very short time. She was rather too aware of her cleverness, though, and didn't usually like to admit that she didn't know something to the other girls. In this instance, it was acceptable not to know, but the other girls were a little surprised, nonetheless.

"We passed some like them on the train – lots of them," said Annie. "Whatever they are, they seem to grow them everywhere."

"We'll ask your bruvver when we get back," said Maggie. "Them boys got told wot crops they'd 'ave to plant and 'arvest when they was learning about it at 'Ampton. Let's go an' pick some of them big daisies to take back wiv us. Put them in jam jars, we can, to look nice for them visitors wot's coming to tea."

"Yes, let's."

"There's yellow ones, too. See – wiv the black eyes. An' them purple flowers that look like bells look pretty."

All six of them began picking flowers until they heard the distant bell and carefully carrying their bouquets ran swiftly back along the narrow path back to the house. Annie dropped some of her flowers as they reached the barn and Maggie helped her to pick them up.

"We know they've promised to keep you and Tom together or near to each other and that they're taking Tom to that uvver 'ome, so you must be going there, too, but d'you fink I'll get taken by one of them farmers wot's coming today?" Maggie asked as they continued on their way. It was a long question and she finished quickly, then drew a deep breath.

"I don't know," Annie said, shaking her head. She had been refusing to let herself think about parting from her friend but she knew they must face up to the fact that the time was drawing near. "Maybe they'll only want the big girls like Minnie and Jane…"

"Fink saying a prayer would 'elp?"

"We're not supposed to ask the Lord for selfish things…" said Annie, shaking her head doubtfully.

"It ain't selfish if I'm praying that you won't be left wivout me yet and you're praying that you won't be left wivout me…"

"Maybe if we just pray it silently – you know, like when we're told to silently ask God's forgiveness for bad things we've done–"

"–wot ain't no one else's business," Maggie finished. "You're right. That means it's coming from the 'eart Miss Lowe used to say to us, didn't she? We can keep praying it till they've gone and we're still 'ere, we can."

Annie nodded. "We'd better run the rest of the way. We're going to be late."

* * * *

Maggie was not selected by any of the visiting farmers. It turned out that Annie was right about their needing older girls and, at the end of the day, only the four ten year-olds remained. Annie and Maggie were told to get their sheets and pillows and to move their belongings into the larger of the two girl's rooms so that everybody would be together.

Tom's friend Will was, however, among the fifty boys who left to go to their new homes late that afternoon. Tom wasn't sure whether he envied Will for already having a home to go to or whether he felt sorry for him not being among the remaining boys who would travel on to the new receiving home at Galt, where they would work on the farm there for the summer before going to their new homes. He had heard that the Scottish boys whose emigration Miss Macpherson had arranged would be going to Blair Athol, the Galt home, but their own group would get there first and get the best places in the dormitory. He wondered when they would be moving on and where Annie would be going. Miss Macpherson had promised Uncle Alfred that they'd have situations as near to each other as it was possible to arrange but he had a constant fear that some farmer would find out how clever Annie had been at looking after Ma and Harriet and the baby and convince Miss Bilbrough that she was the girl he needed. In his imagination, Tom saw the farmer – whose wife had died, leaving him with babies to care for – taking Annie off in his cart, leaving Maggie and himself sadly waving goodbye to her. Well, it hadn't happened and it wasn't going to happen, he told himself crossly. Both he and Annie would be taking the train to Guelph or Berlin – he wasn't sure which, where you changed trains for Galt, and they'd be placed with nearby families where they would be able to see each other. The only worrying thing was that nearby seemed to have a different meaning in this country. When Will said that he'd been told that the place he was going to was nearby, the farmer's wife had said that they'd be travelling northwards for several hours but, if they left soon, the long summer evening would just about allow them to get there before darkness fell. Tom estimated this to mean that "nearby" was something like thirty miles away.

Tom's thoughts wondered. She was a nice lady. While her husband was providing information to Miss Bilbrough, she had talked to Will, and to Tom and Edmund who remained with their friend until he left. They had come to Canada twenty years ago and were definitely much better off than they would have done in if they'd stayed in Whitechapel. When the boys told her that the Refuge was in Spitalfields, she told them that they'd soon see for themselves how much nicer life was here than in the dirty, crowded courts and alleys of London's East End. Certainly winters were cold but it wasn't that nasty, damp cold you got in London. Houses were kept much warmer with pipes from the stove to heat every room. And, talking about rooms – why, in London, more likely than not, they'd lived with whole families and more in one room, if they'd had a home at all. In this country, she said patting Will on the shoulder, Will would have a cosy, little attic room all to himself to sleep in and he'd eat his meals in the big kitchen and have the parlour to sit in of a Sunday after service.

Tom had starting to feel almost homesick for London despite the negative comparison and felt quite relieved when the farmer came back and suggested the three boys run in and get Will's box to put into the cart. Now, Tom wondered if he'd ever see Will again and remembered, a little shamefully, how sharp he had been on the train when Annie and Maggie were wishing that they would find a home for all three of them. He should have helped Will more with his reading and writing, like Annie was doing with Maggie, then they could have written to each other.

"Wake up, Tom," cried Edmund, breaking in on Tom's thoughts. "We're s'posed to put the trestles in the barn, not stand around dreaming."

Tom took one end of a trestle as Edmund grasped the other. "I was just thinking about Will – he must be nearly there by now."

Many of the visitors had stayed until well into the evening and the boys were only now packing away the trestle tables that had been used to seat everybody for the potluck supper. The girls were busy covering the remaining food and taking it into the kitchen to be put away in the pantry until teatime tomorrow.

"Lucky bugger– begger," Edmund corrected himself, looking around to see if he'd been heard. "I liked them, didn't you? And the place sounded nice – just 'ope we're as lucky."

"I don't suppose there's too many people from Whitechapel got farms here."

They reached the storage area in the barn and stacked the trestle against the ones that other boys had already carried in.

"Not the people," Edmund said, as they made their way to fetch the other trestle from the table they were dismantling. "I mean I 'ope we're as lucky as Will wiv getting a proper 'ome –

I don't care about where they come from – mostly Scotch over at Galt, anyway, someone said. After comin' all this way, I just want a proper 'ome. I ain't never 'ad one – not a proper one, I ain't, and that place sounded like one, it did. Don't you fink so?"

"I expect he'll have to work pretty hard. Their boys have both died and their girl's getting married and going to live in the city – I don't know which city she meant. That's why they decided to get an orphan to live with them."

"It's sad, innit? Them making a success of their farm and 'aving nobody to carry it on – 'cept Will, maybe. That'd be good, wouldn't it – if it worked out like that?"

"It would," Tom agreed, "but I expect the daughter and her husband would have something to say about it."

"Well, anyway, like I said, I 'opes I'm as lucky. You, too. Come on, pick up your end."

They finished stacking the trestles and tabletops and went into the dining-room for milk and some of the left-over cake and biscuits before going to bed. Miss Bilbrough said grace and added a few words of thanks for the lovely afternoon they'd had with their visitors and asked the Good Lord to watch over the children who had gone to their new homes. Tom was only half listening. He was thinking about what Edmund had said about never having had a proper home. He hadn't known either Edmund or Will very well until they had shared the bunk on the ship and spent so much of the voyage on their private bit of deck by the lifeboat. There, he had learnt about the grim lives the two boys had led before being rescued by Miss Macpherson. Both had admitted to being by-blows of unknown fathers and had mostly lived on the streets or in the workhouse with their mothers at first, but not for long. Will remembered nothing of his mother, who had left him in the care of her own mother and never returned for him. His grandmother had done her best but had just dropped dead one day (at least, that's how Will told the story) and he and the other children, living in the damp and mouldy basement room, had been thrown out by the landlord to fend for themselves. Will had eventually become separated form his young uncles, aunts and cousins and managed to keep himself alive by begging and thieving in Whitechapel, going to the ragged school in the evenings where he could get warm and even learn to read and write a bit. Edmund's story was a little different in that he had lived with his mother and her two sisters until the three of them had died in the 1866 cholera outbreak. After that he lived with whoever among the families of his two uncles would take him in, mudlarking to earn his keep. His auntie, he told Tom and Will, upon hearing about Miss Macpherson and the boys she took to Canada, decided that this would be a good way to get rid of him for once and for all. A bit like Uncle Alfred getting rid of him and Annie, Tom thought. But they, of course, had been far luckier than Edmund having had a happy home for most of their lives. He hoped his friend would a get proper home when they moved on to Galt in the coming days.

CHAPTER TEN

Three days later, Mrs. Merry took the party of fifty boys, along with Annie and Maggie, on the train journey to Galt where she would be joining Mr. Merry. Her husband was working there with the first party of boys he'd brought out the month before. The train left from the station at Belleville at six in the morning and travelled along the edge of the huge lake, which the children thought looked more like the sea than what they thought a lake should look like, to the big city of Toronto. As they drew closer to the city, there seemed to be many more small towns and villages. As the train chugged into the city, the children all agreed that the dockland areas, which were all they could see, were much like London and they couldn't wait to get out into the countryside again. The week at Marchmont seemed to have given everybody a preference for fields and trees over city streets. They had to change trains at Toronto, where most of the passengers were disembarking, and wait to join other passengers, travelling on a train from the north, aboard yet another train, which would take all of them on to a place called Sarnia and the stations in between. Berlin was one of these. When their boxes had been unloaded onto the platform from the guard's van, which Mrs. Merry said they must learn to call a caboose, they sat on them to eat the bread and cheese that Mrs. Merry had brought with her in a big wicker basket, then sang songs until the train came. The platform was a temporary structure because the original station had been demolished and a huge, new one was being built. The train soon arrived to take them to the place called Berlin where yet another train would take them the short distance from Berlin to Galt, a journey which neither Annie and Maggie would complete.

The evening before, Miss Bilbrough had told the two girls that they would be travelling most of the way with Mrs. Merry and the boys but they would disembark at stations along the way. Maggie would be met at a place called Rockwood and taken by buggy to a nearby farm where a very nice church-going family needed a young girl to help the farmer's wife who had four small boys to look after in addition to three more who were old enough to help with the farm chores. The family's eldest child and only daughter had grown up and married and was about to start a family of her own. She had been well trained in all the household jobs she'd be required to do, Miss Bilbrough told her when Maggie gasped and gave Annie a frightened glance. At first they had been going to place Annie on the farm since it would be comparatively close to the area where Tom would be but another request had been received which allowed the two girls to go to homes much closer to each other than Miss Bilbrough had ever expected to be possible.

Annie's place was in a little village two stations before Rockwood on the Grand Trunk Railway. The placement was with a lady who owned a dry goods and general store and it would be the first time one of Miss Macpherson's girls had gone to live and work in a shop. She had originally asked for a boy, Annie was told, but on hearing about the schoolmaster's daughter who could read and write and do arithmetic very well, she had, by letter this very morning, agreed to 'see how things would work out with a girl'. She had nephews who could continue to look after chopping wood and such things, she said, and there was no reason why a girl could not be trained in the ways of commerce as she had been herself. Miss Bilbrough explained that this meant learning how to weigh out provisions such as flour, tea and sugar and cut dress lengths and ribbon. She would write the purchases and payments, as was the custom in rural shops, in the daybook – she would learn all about that. Annie must remember that there were one hundred cents in a dollar, twenty-five in a quarter, ten in a dime and five in a nickel as she had been taught but which would be a little difficult to get used to after the twelve pennies in a shilling to which she'd been accustomed all her life. And, Miss Bilbrough had smiled at this, she must learn to say store, not shop. They had great faith in her and knew she would be credit to Miss Macpherson.

The second train travelled through the villages of Parkdale, Weston, Malton, Brampton, Norval and reached the great viaduct, which Annie later learned was called the Iron Bridge, as they approached the village of Georgetown. Annie's heart began to thump. Her destination, the village of Limehouse was the station after Georgetown, and she would have to say good-bye to Tom and Maggie and Mrs. Merry, and start a new life. Maggie had insisted Annie sit beside the window because she'd get her turn after Annie's station. She looked out across the valley. They had crossed a number of these high viaducts across wide valleys but she thought this must be the highest one. They seemed to be a long way up from the ground. There was little to be seen but forest and limestone outcrops – at, least, Annie decided, these must be what they called them. They reached Georgetown, stopped while passengers climbed down from the train and luggage was unloaded onto the platform, then went on their way again, travelling through blasted out limestone rock to Limehouse.

Since it was a mixed passenger and freight train, Tom and Maggie were allowed to climb down onto the platform with Annie while the guard, or brakeman as they must learn to call him, was unloading packages, including Annie's box. The boys in the carriage – no, passenger car it was called here, as opposed to just a car which meant a wagon – admired the great limestone cliffs either side of the railway track. Mrs. Merry went to speak to the stationmaster.

"Annie, this is Mr. Pulford, the station agent," she said, walking back to the children. "He'll get his boy to bring a handcart over for your box. Miss Bryden's store is up on the 'rock', he says. You'll find out what that means very shortly," she added with a smile. "Now, you remember to write to us and we'll be over to see you when Miss Macpherson gets to Blair Athol. Come along, Tom and Maggie, the guard's about to wave his flag."

The three children hugged each other and Tom and Maggie climbed back up into the train, Tom surreptitiously rubbing tears from his eyes and Maggie weeping openly. The train moved on towards Acton and Rockwood, where Maggie would disembark and go to her new family, and then on to Berlin where the rest of the party would change trains for the short journey to Galt.

* * * *

Annie watched as the train left, immediately feeling very, very lonely. She knew that tears were running down her cheeks but couldn't move to brush them away with her sleeve.

"Well, young lady," Mr. Pulford said. "Better wipe them tears away afore young Jimmy gets over here with the cart. Miss Bryden's been telling us about the brave little orphan girl who's coming to live with her, so we don't want Jimmy telling people you're not so brave, do we now."

He patted Annie's shoulder and held out a clean handkerchief. She rubbed away the tears, adjusted the strap of her satchel and straightened her bonnet.

"Thank you, mister," she said, handing back the handkerchief. "It's just that it's very hard to say goodbye to your brother and your dearest friend both at once…"

"Of course it is. But don't you worry, they're only going to be a train-ride away, isn't that right?"

Annie nodded. "Yes, Maggie's going to Rockwood and we don't know where Tom's going to live but he'll be at Blair Athol for a while – that's the home. It's a farm at Galt. Do you know Galt?"

"Oh yes. It's not so very far away. Not now that we have the railways – not like in the olden days when you had to travel everywhere by horse and buggy. 'Tho it's not every one of them that stops here so you have to make sure you're on time. Now, you sound like you're a Londoner, young Annie. Is that right?"

"Oh yes,"

"Now, they tell me there's a place called Limehouse over there in London, too. That right?"

"Yes. It's nearby where we used to live. Is the village named after it?"

"No, no. It's called Limehouse because of the lime quarries. P'raps your Limehouse had quarries, too. This used to be called Fountain Green but they changed it to Limehouse when the post office opened… Now, here comes young Jimmy." He walked towards the boy who was trundling a handcart towards them, and Annie followed. "What took you so long, lad? Miss Bryden's going to be wondering where Annie's got to. She'd have heard the train come in. Now, this here is Annie."

"'Lo, Annie. I'm Jimmy – Jimmy McGuire. I often bring stock that Miss Bryden's ordered up to the store, so you'll be seeing a fair bit of me you will."

Annie smiled. Mr. Pulford picked up her box and placed it in the handcart.

"That's Miss Bryden's calico in the two long packages on top of the big tea chest there," he said, indicating the pile of goods that had been unloaded from the train. "You can take that up, too. And get straight back down here to get on with the rest of the deliveries. Now, off you both go. Nice meeting you, Annie."

"Nice meeting you," said Annie, "and thank you for being so kind."

Mr Pulford raised his cap, then headed towards his office.

Jimmy put the packages in the cart with Annie's box. "Come on, Annie, this way," he said leading her down a ramp from the station platform and onto the road. "Come all the way across the ocean, did you?" he asked and, not waiting for a reply, continued, "Only child I ever met come over the ocean by himself before is William that lives with the Grahams and he's a boy. My pa did, and ma and my brothers. Come from Derry, they did. That's in Ireland."

"I know," said Annie. "Our ship stopped there. That's where the Irish passengers got on, 'though I think some who got on at Liverpool were Irish, too. They talked like it."

"Like my pa talks, you mean. Plays it up a bit, he does. Most people around here are Scots, see?"

Annie wasn't sure that she *did* see, but nodded anyway. Jimmy looked to be a bit older than her, she thought, perhaps Tom's age. She blinked hard at the thought of Tom. She didn't want to cry again – not in front of Jimmy, but she felt awfully scared and alone. They were crossing the railway track on a boardwalk made for the purpose. The handcart rattled loudly and she had to concentrate on not tripping on the boards. When they reached the dusty road on the other side, Jimmy continued.

"Pa says the Irish in Derry come from Scotland anyway. Years ago, though. I guess that's why they talk different. Act different, too. What's it like on a ship all that time? We go up here. Bryden's Dry Goods is up the road a bit 'fore you get to McDonald's Hotel. So what's it like?"

"The first morning it seemed like a fairyland. It was so bright and beautiful," Annie said, assuming he meant the ship, not McDonald's Hotel. "Then we were all ill. The sea was very rough, you see. Then it got better and we got better. I wasn't very ill – not like some people, so I had to help a lot with the children that were. The weather was nice when we got closer to land again. There were icebergs. I didn't know they were so big. Like mountains in the sea, they are."

"I heard that at school. One day, I'll see them for myself – when I go to Ireland. Save all the money I get doing deliveries for Mr. Pulford, I do. It's in my savings bank at the post office.

'Course it'll take a long time before there's enough for the ticket."

"Why do you want to go to Ireland? People are better off here, aren't they? At least, that's what they say."

"I just want to see it. I'll come back again. This is my home. Pa says only the gentry can afford to live in Ireland. They own all the land there and you have to pay rent to them. Here, Pa made enough money with building the Grand Trunk to buy forty acres of a half lot on the seventh concession – it's mostly bush but he cleared enough to build a house and a barn and have room for some crops. Pa and my oldest brother work at the sawmill in the Glen, so they make a good living. Then the other two work in the Bescoby quarry. They're grown up, my brothers – two of them've got children not much younger than me. The after-thought, that's what I am, but Pa says that's lucky for me because they can afford for me to go to school all the year. 'Cept for the summer, I mean. So I'm to take the examination to go to the grammar school – high school, it's to be called now – down in Oakville when I'm finished Senior Fourth and be the educated one and have a profession – you know, like being a teacher or an accountant or something." He shrugged, then added, "You'll like the school here. We're getting a new teacher this year. He's a young man and he came to see us – look us over, I guess – last week before school ended for the summer. To introduce himself, like. Will you go all the year? You have to go for four months 'til you're twelve, it's the law now. It started last year."

"I don't know," said Annie, smiling. "I'll be happy to go whenever I'm allowed. I had to stop going when my Ma was ill, you see. And, in the Refuge, I mostly was teaching other children who'd never been to school, and I didn't learn any new things myself – except about Canada, of course."

"What's the Refuge?"

"It's where we were taken, my brother Tom and me, after Ma died. That's where we were until they brought us here–" Annie broke off. "What are they doing there?" she asked, pointing to a high cliff on their left, where men were clustered around what looked like some very large outdoor fireplaces in a wall of rock.

"That's the Farquar lime kilns," Jimmy told her. "Where they burn the lime. They're building a draw kiln over at Gowdy and Moore's kilns – it's the latest invention. It'll do the work of all three of these. They just built some further along the track at the new Dolly Varden Mine by Glen Lawson there. We went on a school trip to see them before they started using them. We turn just up here–" he stopped speaking to concentrate on pushing the cart up the steep incline, "and, here we are." He stopped, after they'd turned the corner, and Annie saw her new home for the first time.

The big shop window was rather dusty from the lime burning down the hill, she supposed. On the level ground in front of the window and the shop door, there were pails and brooms and various other household items, all of which were also very dusty. A sign above the window proclaimed Bryden's Dry Goods & Staples.

"It's not always as dusty as this," Jimmy said, following Annie's gaze. "There's not been much rain the last few weeks, so the dust from the quarries just blows around the village and there's nothing to keep it down. Cleaning it off'll probably be one of your jobs. Miss Bryden's not getting any younger, so it's hard for her to keep up with it. Joe and Doug Bryden come down and help her with the chores but they're needed for the haymaking right now. Their pa's Miss Bryden's brother. Their farm's up the fifth line at the top end of the sixth concession." He pushed the cart to the doorway, where the door stood open with a bamboo curtain to keep out the flies. "Here we are, Miss Bryden!" he called as they went in.

Coming in from the bright afternoon sunshine, Annie could see nothing when the bamboo curtain clattered behind her. Then, as her eyes became accustomed to the dimmer light in the store, she found herself surrounded by counters on three sides, goods for sale crowded onto the shelves behind them. Miss Bryden came hurrying from behind the counter opposite the door, around the barrels of flour and other provisions at the side of it.

"Well, my goodness me," she exclaimed, placing her hands on Annie's shoulders. "So this is Annie. You must be very thirsty. You run and get her a mug of my sweet apple cider from the jug on the cold slab in the pantry, Jimmy McGuire, before you unpack that cart. The poor lass must be parched. A long journey like that on a hot day like this! Oh, my! All the way from Belleville she's come–" she turned to the customer she'd been serving as she said this "–from that Miss Macpherson's orphanage where the Grahams got young William. That's what gave me the idea, then I talked to the Reverend about it and he told me as he had to give his undertaking that I was a good church-going Christian which, of course he was happy to give… but never mind about all that now, I should be getting your tea weighed up, shouldn't I? Now you just sit you down there,

Annie lass. Here comes Jimmy with that cup of sweet apple cider."

Annie found herself sitting on a crate drinking the cider while Jimmy unpacked the rolls of dress material from the cart. He placed them on the counter of what Annie could see was the drapery section of the shop, the area opposite being for basins and bowls and various other kitchen implements and the counter where Miss Bryden was weighing tea must be the 'staples' area. There was an iron stove in the middle for keeping the place warm in the winter. The stovepipe ran up from the stove and through the ceiling.

"Like me to take Annie's box up, Miss Bryden?" Jimmy asked, lifting the box from the cart.

"You can take it up the stairs and leave it on the landing, young Jimmy, and you can have a sip of sweet apple cider before you go back to the station. Now, I have all this down, Mary-Ann, so you can put it in your basket. You tell your ma that the figs'll be coming in on Monday by cart from Burlington. It'll be late – last delivery. It's the lad that carts your brother's local deliveries on his return journey." She put the last of the purchases into the girl's basket. "There you go now."

Mary-Ann, Annie could see now as she turned towards the door, was a girl of about fifteen.

"Welcome to Limehouse," she said and smiled. "I'm sure you'll like it here with Miss Bryden. She's one of my favourite people."

"Go along with you, Mary-Ann," Miss Bryden said, coming out from behind the counter. "Used to say that when she was little and hoping to get a fruit drop or a humbug, but she's a young lady now – too old for begging fruit drops."

Mary-Ann laughed. "She makes wonderful sweet apple cider, too. Don't you agree, Annie?"

"Yes. It's very nice and I really was thirsty."

"See you later, then"

"Oh yes, I hope so. Goodbye."

Annie stood up as Mary-Ann disappeared through the bamboo curtain. "Can I take my mug into your scullery?"

Jimmy's boots could be heard clattering on the stairs.

"Here comes Jimmy. I'll just close the shop door so that the bell will tinkle if someone comes in while we go in the back there."

"This way, Annie," said Jimmy, overhearing them. He led her through the little sitting room behind the store to the scullery beyond it. "I'm just going to quickly have my cider and get back to the station. Just put your mug in the washing basin there and pump a bit of water into it to rinse it out. Sticky things attract ants and wasps in this hot weather." Annie did as he said while he went to the pantry. He poured some cider into a mug and drank it quickly. "That's me on my way, then," he said handing her the empty cup to rinse. "I'll be at church with my ma tomorrow so I'll see you then. 'Bye now. Thanks for the cider," he added to Miss Bryden who arrived at the scullery door as he went back into the store to get his handcart.

"You're welcome. See you later, Jimmy. Now, Annie lass, I expect you're very tired and hungry after your long journey but we won't be closing for another hour. I don't have soups and stews cooking on the stove in this hot weather, but you can help yourself to bread and cheese or cold chicken and milk – it's all on the stone slab in the pantry. Then you can go up and lie down. I'll show you your room between customers."

"No, I'm all right," said Annie. "I mean I'm not tired. I can wait until you close the shop–" The bell over the door tinkled as somebody came into the store. "Can I come into the shop–store, I mean, and help you? I'll leave my satchel here on this chair. Is that all right?"

"Yes of course, lass, if you're sure you're not too tired."

Jimmy, trundling the cart back down to the station, thought about how scary it must be for a girl to have to come to a strange place where she knew nobody. He'd been a bit envious of his pal, William, when he first came to the village. He thought it must have been an exciting adventure to travel without your family but he had been younger then and William had straightened him out. It certainly wasn't an adventure when you're an orphan with nobody to call family, William had told him, and it wasn't exciting to be leaving the safety of Miss Macpherson's children's home for an unknown home in another country. It was frightening, even if you did pretend to the other boys that nothing could scare you. William, of course, had only admitted this to him because they had become good friends. To everybody else, William was 'tough'. When the other boys at school called him names and tripped him up during his first days there, William had fought every one of them and almost been expelled. It was Jimmy who had gone to the teacher and explained what was happening. The teacher had wisely waited out events and the other boys soon learned that William was a better fighter then any of them. But Jimmy was the only person he spoke to of his life in London. He was as good a worker as he was a fighter so the Grahams treated him as one of the family and let him go to school. William had wisely put the old life behind him and was soon accepted by the village children. Jimmy thought that he would make a good friend for Annie and decided he'd run over to the farm and tell him about the new arrival as soon as he'd finished his chores at the station.

CHAPTER ELEVEN

Tom, meanwhile, had reached Berlin where Mrs. Merry and the boys waited for yet another train to take them to Galt. They had said goodbye to Maggie at Rockwood where a boy of about fourteen or fifteen was waiting with a buggy to take her to his father's farm. She had looked as forlorn as Annie at the parting and Tom felt almost as sorry to say goodbye to her as he had when they'd left Annie with the station agent at Limehouse. Tom was beginning to feel quite miserable himself. It had been a long day and they still had the short train journey – Mrs. Merry and another lady who had joined them on the platform said that it was only fourteen miles and would take no time at all – and then a ride by cart to Blair Athol. He would be glad to just lie down and go to sleep.

"See them blokes over there," whispered Edmund. "German, they are. Talk outer their froats, they do, Germans. It's why they call it Berlin, ain't it? 'Cos Germans live 'ere. Well, I jus' 'ope I don't end up on a German farm 'cos I got enough to do learnin' English readin' and writin'. I ain't goin' to learn German, too."

"I don't think you need to worry," Tom told him. "The farmers that want us apply through Miss Macpherson's Scotch friends so you just need to learn to understand the Scotch-Canadian way they talk. Won't be much different from the way Miss Macpherson talks herself. Mrs. Merry, too."

"Never knew why they talked funny, I didn't. Well, that's good, innit? Wiv all them Germans and the French people 'ere, it gets a bit worrying. 'Ope we get somefink to eat soon as we get there. Starvin', I am. This our train, d'you fink?"

An engine hauling two cars steamed out of a siding and into the station.

"This way, boys," shouted Mrs. Merry. "This is the Blair Athol Special just for us." She sent two of the biggest boys to help load the boxes and ushered the rest of the party onto the train and, soon, they were on the last leg of their journey.

As promised, it was a short journey and they soon arrived in Galt to be met by Mr. Merry, a helper at the farm, who he introduced to everybody as Mr. McDermott, and two of the boys who had come out with him in May. They had a van drawn by two big farm horses. Mr. Merry instructed the two boys to organize the loading of the luggage. Then he helped Mrs. Merry and the other lady, whose name Tom has somehow missed, up onto the seat at the front beside Mr. McDermott who then shook the reins and the two horses moved off along the road with Mr. Merry and the line of boys following. They soon left the small town behind them and were walking along a road with fields on either side until they reached a lane which led up to Blair Athol where Miss Reavell and several other ladies were waiting on the veranda of the big farmhouse.

While the ladies were greeting each other profusely, Mr. Merry matched boxes to boys and led them all over to a huge barn which had been converted to a dining hall on the ground level and a dormitory in what had once been the hay loft. They hoisted their boxes up the ladders and placed them on the floor beside the bunks Mr. Merry allotted to each of them. Leaving the boxes to be unpacked later, they climbed back down the ladders to sit at the two long dining tables. By this time, the savoury smells of the supper they were about to have were making the boys feel very hungry indeed. The bread and cheese eaten on the station platform at Toronto seemed to have been a long time ago now.

Everybody stood when Miss Reavell rang her bell. She said she'd keep them standing only long enough to say grace because she knew, from previous experience, that boys coming in from the long train journey were far too hungry to listen to welcoming speeches. Also, just for tonight, the church ladies who had cooked the roast pork dinner would bring in their plates to avoid such accidents as may befall tired and hungry boys. A chore roster had been set up and would start tomorrow after breakfast.

"She means she don't want us dropping' stuff, I s'pose," whispered Edmund.

"Ssh," said Tom, as Miss Reavell began to lead grace. They all joined in and then sat down to supper.

After supper came a wash at the pump in the yard as the sun went down behind the trees across the fields from the farm, followed by prayers and, then, they were all sent up to the dormitory to unpack their boxes and get ready for bed.

Tom slept surprisingly well considering that he lay for a long time wondering if Annie was all right and what her new home was like which led to thinking about Harriet and John far away in London, and on to Will and Maggie and other children who had gone to new homes over the last few days. Then, of course, he started wondering where his own new home would be and how long he would be staying at Blair Athol. But, sleep he did until he was woken by a bell ringing and found the dormitory bathed in sunlight pouring through the small windows, which had been put in when the barn was converted.

"Rise and shine, boys," called Mr. Merry from the top of the ladder, clanging the bell once more for good measure. "You all have five minutes to get dressed and out to the yard where you'll form a queue to wash your hands and faces at the pump and then assemble for morning prayers in the yard. Come along, all you sleepyheads. First group boys are breakfast monitors today, except Danny and Fred who are already down at the dairy barn doing the milking, so you get back into the dining hall as soon as prayers are over. We'll set up a roster with the new boys' after breakfast. Meantime, you'll do drill with Mr. McDermott until the breakfast is ready. It's time for the first haymaking so we need everybody strong in body as well as mind."

He went back down the ladder leaving them to get out of their nightshirts and into their clothes. Tom and Edmund both dressed quickly without speaking and were out into the yard among the first group of boys. It was a beautiful summer morning and, looking across the fields after washing at the pump, they could see the long grass rippling gently in the light breeze.

"Did you do haying at Hampton?" Tom asked Edmund, who had been at the refuge last summer and spent time at the farm. It had been planting time when Tom did his session there.

"Yeah – you 'ave to be fourteen to scythe, though. We 'ave to rake it into lines then turn it over each day to get it dry for stacking. We did drill first there at 'Ampton, too. Mr. Merry's a great one fer 'ealthy bodies, 'ealthy minds. Musta gone to one of them posh schools where they act like all the boys is soldiers. You know, marching around and that."

"Miss Reavell's lining us up for prayers. Better get over there."

* * * *

The regimen at Blair Athol was much like it had been during the month Tom had spent on the farm at Hampton except that there were no lessons. They did spend time in the schoolroom learning about when crops were planted and when they were harvested, and about the wildlife that threatened both crops and farm animals, but academic work was put off until after the harvest when the Canadian schools re-opened. The boys, by then, would all have been placed in their new homes and would attend the local school there. Meantime, they cut and stacked hay or weeded and hoed under the hot sun in the mornings, learned about Canadian rural life in the afternoons until the day cooled a little, then were allowed to play games until teatime. Tom became more convinced that he really did not want to become a farmer...

One day about two weeks after their arrival, he was feeling particularly miserable. Miss Macpherson would be arriving next week with the Scottish boys and they'd been told that some of his own party would be moving on to permanent homes to make room for the new boys. He wandered over to the pigsty during the afternoon free time and sat on the fence moodily watching the big sow, Henrietta, whose litter wriggled and squealed around her while she rested in the mud. Mr. Merry had told the boys that pigs were very clever animals and that the Three Little Pigs folk tale shows how capable they are of planning. Folk tales aside, Tom wondered how such a thing could be determined. Certainly, Henrietta was clever at keeping cool, but she couldn't pump water and must rely on people to pour water into the dirt for her to make the mud to keep herself and her family cool. He imagined Henrietta hopping over the fence and walking on her hind legs to the pump and laughed at himself.

"That took the cross look off your face, whatever it was you were thinking," said a voice beside him. He turned, startled, to see Herb Taylor beside him. Herb was an older boy who lived in the area. He had come out two years ago, with the first group of Miss Macpherson's boys to come to Canada, to a position at a nearby farm. He was sent over from the farm where he was placed, two or three days a week to help teach the newly arrived boys.

"I was thinking about what Mr. Merry said about how pigs were very clever and thought how funny it would be if Henrietta got up and pumped her water by herself," Tom said, feeling rather silly.

"Tom, isn't it?" Tom nodded and Herb continued, "I haven't got all your names straight yet, but I thought I remembered you, being as you're considered pretty clever yourself. Dunno, if you're as smart as Henrietta, mind you… Right, Henrietta?" The big sow stirred and grunted, setting the piglets squealing as they rearranged themselves around her. "So, what was the cross face about?"

Herb was older than the boys he knew but not a grown man yet, Tom thought, about sixteen or seventeen, perhaps. He had come here to a job on a farm and seemed to have pleased his master so much that he was let off work to come over here to help out. He'd be a good person to talk to, wouldn't he?

"You can tell me what's bothering you and it won't go no further," said Herb. "Any further," he corrected himself. "Trying to remember to speak like a young gent I am for when I go to the college in the city."

"You're going to go to a college in the city?"

"Well… not yet. I have another year at the high school first, but the church is already raising funds for me to go to Knox College – that's the Presbyterian college. I'm going to be a missionary, you see."

"You mean you don't have to be a farmer?"

"'Course not. You feel God's call, you do what He asks."

"Oh," said Tom. "I see…" He somehow doubted he would receive God's call.

"What… Oh, I understand, you thought that because they pay for you to come out here to work on the farms, that's what you must work at. Right?"

"Well…" said Tom, "I don't think God wants me to be a missionary, but I would like to be a schoolmaster like my pa was…"

"What happened to your pa?" asked Herb, sympathetically.

"He died from a fever he caught when he went to see the dying mother of some matchbox makers who came to his Sunday School class." Tom smiled, seeing an irony he hadn't thought about before. "So, we became matchbox makers, too."

Herb smiled, too. "And, even so, you still want to be a schoolmaster?"

"They sent us over here because it's healthier and you're not so likely to get the fever, didn't they? And they don't have ragged schools and Sunday schools for poor children to learn reading and writing and give their teachers the fever."

"Well, there is that," the older boy agreed, "so long as you don't do your school mastering in the city. How old are you, Tom?"

"Twelve next month."

"So, there's a year or two before you can go to grammar school – high school it's called now and it's like an academy in the old country, then there'll be three or four years there and best part of a year at the Normal School in Toronto. That's what you have to do to be a teacher. So you need to work summers on the farm to pay your way, see. You'll need money to pay your board in the city."

Tom considered this. "You mean, they'll let me. I don't have to be a farmer."

"Well, I can't promise, but the families who take in Miss Macpherson's boys are all good Christian souls and take their commitment very seriously. Aside from that, you can't work the land in the winter in this country so there's nothing to stop you from going to school, as long as you do your chores. We're talking mostly Scots from the old country in this area and they understand the importance of education. There'll be a common school nearby and if you do well in the senior class there and pass the exam, the schoolmaster will find a way for you to go to grammar school. I'm sure the family that takes you will be happy about it and proud of you. Just like the McTaggarts are proud I got the call to be a missionary. So, that's why you have to learn to be useful around the farm, not necessarily to be a farmer."

"I'm glad you came over," Tom grinned, feeling happier than he'd been in a long while, "to look at the pigs."

"Me, too," laughed Herb. "But the real reason I came over to see the pigs is because I hear you have a sister who's been placed in the village of Limehouse."

"My sister, Annie. Yes, I had a letter from her yesterday. She says it's nice there but, knowing Annie, she might just be saying that so I don't worry about her."

"Well, you're going to get to see about that for yourself."

"What d'you mean? Tell me."

"Well, Mr. McTaggart is sending me to buy this special fire-proof paint from a new factory in Limehouse. Now, he could post a letter of inquiry, then wait for the information, then post another letter with an order and a bank draft, then wait for it to be sent on the Grand Trunk, but not him. Mr. McTaggart wants me to take the buggy and drive over there to get his paint. So, when Mr. Merry heard that I won't be coming here the day after tomorrow because I'm driving the buggy all the way to Limehouse, guess what he suggested?"

"That I should go with you and see Annie?"

"That's right, young Tom. I'll be here to pick you up first thing and we should be there by noon. We'll stop and eat our breakfast about halfway so that Blaze and Star can have a rest. I'll be bringing plenty of bread and cheese and water for us but I expect Miss Reavell will insist you bring some food, too. Think you're up to a thirty mile buggy ride, then?"

"'Course I am. Will you teach me to drive the horses? I've never done that."

"Oh, we'll have plenty of time to do that. Well, soon be tea-time for you and I've got a five mile walk home, so I'd better be off. Remember to thank Mr. Merry, now."

"Oh, I will," said Tom. "And thank you, Herb. I can't believe I'll be seeing my sister again in just two days." He waved at Herb's departing figure, then jumped down off the fence, pulling Annie's letter out of his pocket as he did so.

It was the second letter she'd written to him. The first, she had begun the first evening of her arrival at Limehouse but not finished until the following Monday. She described the village and Bryden's Dry Goods and Staples, Miss Bryden, the church, the anniversary of the confederation picnic, and a boy named Jimmy. The new letter was about an older girl called Mary-Ann, the kilns and the woollen mill in the village, and the paint factory where Mr. McTaggart was sending them to buy his paint, or so Tom supposed since it was unlikely there were two paint factories. Annie was full of admiration for Mary-Ann whose father, she said, owned one of the local factories but she did not put on airs about being better off but was very nice to her and was going to teach her how to play the piano. He hoped that didn't mean that there were girls who weren't nice to her. Tom wasn't sure what the things about which girls giggled with each other were exactly, but he'd be happy to know that Annie was able to do this again.

The tea bell rang and he folded the letter back up, put it in his pocket and started towards the dining hall feeling a lot happier than he had been before Herb came over to talk to him. The trip to Limehouse would enable him to see that Annie really was in a good placement and not just painting a happy picture for his sake. And Herb's reassurance about placement on a farm not necessarily preventing him from being a school master like his father after all, made him feel almost eager to move on to his new home.

CHAPTER TWELVE

Annie got her wish to go to school when it opened again. Her early morning routine of blowing the embers in the stove into flame and cooking the porridge reminded her, at first, of the days in the shabby room in Bromley, albeit that the stove burned wood, not coal, and the porridge could be simmered on its surface instead of on a hob over an open fireplace. While the porridge was cooking in the back room, she'd sweep and dust the store, the back room and the scullery and set the breakfast table before Miss Bryden came downstairs. When summer became autumn and then winter, she'd also tend the stove in the store, with its stove pipe that warmed up Miss Bryden's room above the store, and bring in the wood for the day and stack some beside each stove. After breakfast, her books and dinner packed into her satchel, she would hurry off to walk the mile to school.

She was a little disconcerted at first to find herself the target of nasty remarks. She didn't mind being called the orphan girl because that was what she was but she was not a vagrant or a dirty urchin or a guttersnipe – in fact, she didn't think these country children even knew what a gutter was. Jimmy McGuire told her to ignore them. He said the Irish were called names, too. Back when his older brother Bernard had been at the school, there were fights between the Irish and the Scottish boys all the time with Bernard at the centre of them, but the Scots in the village were more tolerant of the Irish now, many of the younger adults having grown up together and got used to each other, Jimmy supposed. Even some of the children Annie had met during the summer, who she had thought liked her, were less friendly when school started. She missed her good friend of the summer, Mary-Ann, who had gone back to school for her final year at the Oakville Ladies Academy, where she boarded during the week. Since Annie was happy just to be able to go to school again and, because she had to hurry home after school to help Miss Bryden in the store, she didn't much mind the unfriendliness. It was only during dinnertime when the children sat in groups to eat their bread and cheese that she felt a little lonely. Unlike school in England, the distances the children walked to and from school were too great for many of them to go home for dinner during what they called the noon hour. This was an even shorter break,during the short days of winter when school finished early to ensure that the children who had the longest walks to get home were able to make their way through the snow in daylight. She counted Jimmy and a boy named William, who was also an orphan brought to Canada by Miss Macpherson, as her friends but they were both older than she was and in the senior class. While it was nice to have their company during the trek up Gibralter Hill to Limehouse, she was glad when, eventually, some of the girls started walking with her, too. By the time the Christmas holidays came around, the name-calling had stopped and she even had invitations to one or two birthday parties.

At Christmas time, too, Annie saw Tom again for the first time since the summer. After the first trip with Herb to the paint factory, there had been a second one when a couple more Galt farmers prevailed upon Herb to drive over to buy paint for their barns and, once again, Miss Reavell allowed Tom to ride with him. In October, however, Tom was placed with Sam Halliday, a Scottish farmer and his family living in Eden Mills, which was a lot nearer to Limehouse than Galt was, but there had not yet been time to arrange a visit. Early in the morning on the Sunday before Christmas Miss Bryden borrowed her brother's sleigh. As pre-arranged by letters back and forth between herself and the farmers' wives, she and Annie drove, first to Rockwood and picked up Maggie, then down to Eden Mills, where Tom was waiting at the end of the long laneway up to the farm where he lived, and then back to Limehouse with Tom driving the horses. They delivered the sleigh safely back to the Brydens, who took Miss Bryden to church, while the children walked there with the Bryden boys. After dinner, Annie was able to show Tom and Maggie around the village before Sam Halliday came to pick up Tom and Maggie for the return journey before darkness fell.

A few days later, a massive snowstorm blanketed the entire region and everybody was snowed in for days. It was the strangest Christmas Annie had ever known. She and Miss Bryden were supposed to go to the Bryden farm for Christmas dinner but, like everybody else in the village, they were snowed in. The snow fell continuously for two days and violent icy gales blew it up against the sides of the buildings so that it covered the lower windows. Annie brought in the day's wood from the dooryard on Christmas morning and had difficulty closing the door again. The wind blew swirling snow right into the scullery. Miss Bryden said that on no account was Annie to attempt to open either that door or the door to the store until the storm was over. The wood kept in the cellar for such emergencies would be enough to prevent them from freezing. The neighbourhood men and boys would dig a path to the store eventually and shovel the snow from the doorways. Access to the stores, the hotels and the post office had priority in the village; then the mills and the factories; then the church. She had to admit, however, she had rarely seen a worse storm than this one and it was unfortunate that it should happen on Christmas Day, preventing people from even getting along to the church let alone visiting family for Christmas dinner. Never mind, they would cut off a piece of salt pork and put it to roast with potatoes and carrots and onions and they had all the good Scottish shortbread and the mince tarts they had baked to take with them to the Bryden farm.

While Annie's first Christmas in Canada was a strange one, it brought the realization that she was happy here in the village, living with Miss Bryden, working in the store and going to school. Yes, she did still miss the old life – not the days after Pa died when they lived in the shabby room in Bromley and Ma became more and more sick until she died, but the years before that when they had a whole house, small as it was, and enough money for food and clothes and books to read. She still missed Harriet and John, but her little sister's letters, written by Aunt Ella and signed by Harriet in her sprawling infant's hand beside a large X for love, assured her that they were happy. It would be nice if she were able to see more of Tom. However, Miss Bryden had promised that she would be paid fifty cents a month once she'd learnt how to write up the account book properly, without missing anything, during the hours from when she came home from school until they closed the store for the day. Fifty cents a month meant she would be able to buy a train ticket to Rockwood now and again on a Sunday, and meet her brother there or walk the two and a half miles down to the farm. Maybe visit Maggie, too, since she'd have to go on the morning train and come back on the afternoon one. And, she'd be able to save money in the little carved wooden box which was Miss Bryden's Christmas gift and, one day, be able to send enough money to Miss Macpherson to pay back the cost of her fare so that they would be able to use it at the Refuge to pay for another orphan to come to Canada.

Annie enjoyed serving customers in the store and writing their purchases and payments in the account book. Miss Bryden dealt with those who took too long to pay and those who brought in farm produce to barter. She told Annie to watch and learn how it was done because, one day, when Annie was older, she was going to go for a visit back to the old country and leave her in charge of the store for many weeks. As time went on, Annie would often wonder if this would really happen or if it was just an old lady's dream, not that Miss Bryden was such an old lady. Annie, however, had noticed that people did talk about doing something one day but never actually did it.

By the time the snow began to melt that first year in Canada, Annie felt as if she'd always lived in the busy Ontario village. It was so different from life in London. Everybody knew her name because they all came into the store at one time or another for 'staples and dry goods'. School ended for the year in late May when the boys were needed to help plough the fields and sow the crops and the girls to spring-clean the homes and plant the vegetables. Doug, one of Miss Bryden's nephews, came down to dig over the back yard, then Annie was set to break up the lumps and hoe the earth thoroughly before planting the seeds which Miss Bryden had stored from last year's harvest. It was very different from the little vegetable patch that Pa had kept in the back yard of the house off Devons Road. Ma did preserve some of the gooseberries and currants that grew there and pickled the onions Pa grew. Food was bought mostly at the market, however. Here, the whole idea of the backyard vegetable garden was to grow enough potatoes, carrots, turnips, beets, squash and onions to store in the root cellar to last until planting time came round again. Lots of corn, peas, tomatoes, cucumbers, peppers and berries had to be grown and put up for use during the winter and following spring. Throughout the summer, it was Annie's job to water and weed the vegetables. Unlike last year, these were crops that she had sown herself and she watched in delight as they quickly sprouted and grew during the short growing season. Miss Bryden said you'd never know she had been raised in dirty old London. Why, she even looked like a strong, healthy country girl now!

* * * *

So time passed and four years after Annie arrived in Limehouse, her school days had come to an end, she could grow and preserve vegetables and fruit, turn her hand to just about any household chore and she could run Bryden's Staples and Dry Goods – as well as she did herself, Miss Bryden would tell people. In future, Miss Bryden had been telling Annie, as the weather became warmer and the snow melted away, she would be leaving her in charge of the store while she attended quilting bees and such things again. In fact, she declared happily, she would be able to do all the things she used to do before her pa died fifteen years ago. Annie was quite used to looking after the store for short periods of time when Miss Bryden went along to the grocery or the post office, or sometimes to deliver special orders of dress material or lace, which she felt merited her presence at the customer's residence rather than Annie's. When Miss Bryden went to Georgetown with her brother to go to the bank once a month, Annie would be left in charge of the store for most of the morning. She was quite confident that she could manage whole mornings or afternoons or, even all day if necessary. Hearing this, Miss Bryden told her that it was high time she was paid a living wage. Her fifty cents a month wage had been increased to eighty cents on her twelfth birthday, mainly because being twelve meant paying full fare on the train when she went to see Tom or Maggie, although Miss Bryden said she definitely earned every penny. This was different. With schooldays over and working all day, Annie must be paid a store clerk's wage from now on, less board and lodging, of course. So it was that, on the last day of June, Annie received her first three dollars a month wage. Strictly speaking she hadn't actually begun working what Miss Bryden called 'full time' because she had been learning double-entry bookkeeping at school for most of June, when many children could no longer attend and special subjects were taught to those who could. Miss Bryden had decided it was high time record keeping was brought up to date and Annie was to learn how to keep a proper ledger instead of putting everything in the daybook.

The next day was the anniversary of the Confederation of the Dominion – a very special day. Tom, who was almost sixteen now, attended the high school in Guelph. His master, or foster father as Sam Halliday preferred Tom to think of him, was happy for him to attend because Tom, the youngest entrant, had scored the highest marks of all applicants in Wellington County three years before and he was as proud of him as any real father would have been. This year, just before school closed for the summer, the headmaster had persuaded Tom to enter an essay he had written into a competition run by one of the town's newspapers and Tom had won the first prize. The essay was to be printed in the Guelph Weekly Mercury and the prize was being presented, after the parade, at the Anniversary festivities. Annie walked down to the station to get the morning train to Guelph. Tom and the Hallidays would be on the platform at Rockwood. She felt happy to be alive on this beautiful sunny morning. She would buy copies of the newspaper and send the page with Tom's story to Harriet and John, and one to Miss Macpherson. She'd send one to Dr. McGhie, too, and tell him how grateful she and Tom were for taking them to Miss Macpherson to be brought to Canada where they had both found happy lives with people who cared about them and who they cared about.

Maybe it would be best to send Dr. McGhie's copy to Miss Macpherson at Marchmont, Annie thought as she reached the station, and ask her to take it to him when she went back to England. She still travelled back and forth two or three times a year, always carrying letters for people. Annie sometimes dreamed of one day going with her and seeing Harriet and Baby John again, not that John was a baby now – he was the age Harriet had been when they last saw each other that day at St. Pancras.

"You're deep in thought this morning, Annie," said Mr. Pulford said, startling her. She hadn't noticed that she had reached his office. "Off to Rockwood to see your brother, are you?"

"No, Mr. Pulford. I need a return ticket to Guelph today." Annie handed him the dollar she had brought with her. "Tom and his whole family will be getting on at Rockwood and we're all going to see the Guelph parade and then – well, my brother won the Guelph Daily Mercury essay contest out of all the people in Wellington county and, I expect some from Halton county, too, don't you? But Tom was the winner and he'll be getting his prize after the parade from the proprietor of the newspaper – and the mayor's going to be there, too. Ten dollars it is, which he'll be putting into the savings bank for when he has to board in Toronto when he goes to the Normal School."

"Well, I hadn't heard about that. Was it in the paper?"

"It's going to be this afternoon in a special Confederation Anniversary edition. It's so exciting, isn't it?"

"I'll say," said Mr. Pulford handing her the ticket and her change, which she carefully folded into her handkerchief. "You watch out for pickpockets in the town there. I expect you want to buy treats for yourselves at the parade." Annie nodded. She was hoping there would be food stalls in Guelph like they had in London and she could buy something nice for everybody, maybe even ice cream, which she had heard about but never tasted. Then the telegraph clattered on the shelf behind Mr Pulford's counter. "That's the train coming through the junction," he said. "I'll have to get the signal up – don't want them passing through without stopping for you today of all days, do we? Now, you have a nice day in Guelph and just make sure you don't miss that afternoon train back. You don't want to be stranded there and miss the big firework display Mr. James is putting on out on the green."

He went off to the signal box and Annie walked along the platform.

"Hulloo-oo, Annie," cried a voice behind her. It was Betsy Graham – no, not Graham any more – Betsy Kruger. Betsy, one of Annie's friend William's foster sisters, had been married at Easter. George Kruger was waiting for Mr. Pulford to come back to the office to get their tickets.

Annie waited for Betsy.

"Are you going to Berlin?" she asked.

"Yes, it'll be the first time we've seen George's family since they came here for the wedding. Pa said we had no time for the holiday because of the haymaking – says, even if the government did make it an official holiday, farmers would still have to work, this time of the year. But he relented when William said Jimmy McGuire was coming to help because he'd be ahead as he wouldn't have to pay George for the day and Jimmy wouldn't cost him half of what George would. Old skinflint, he is. Don't you tell anyone I said so. Now, I know where you're off to. Jimmy told us about your brother winning the contest. Is it today's paper it'll be in?"

"Yes. I'm going to buy one to keep at the store to show people – Miss Bryden suggested I do that – so you can see it there on Monday. I have to buy a copy to send to my sister and little brother who live with my uncle in London, too. And some others."

"They'll probably give your brother a few copies, you know."

"I hadn't thought of that."

"Save you the money, that will. Here's the train, and here comes George with our tickets. I don't get to go on the train much, so this is a treat for me. You going to sit with us? I've never met your brother but William and Jimmy have told us about him."

The train drew up and the noise drowned out further conversation until they were seated and underway. Annie happily told Betsy and George about how Tom had been placed on the Halliday farm in Eden Mills and how he had scored the best marks in the high school examination and was going to be a schoolmaster just like their father had been before he died.

CHAPTER THIRTEEN

Tom, waiting at the Rockwood station, saw Annie at the open window of the train as soon as it slowed to stop at the platform. Followed by Sam and Susanna Halliday and their two children, he waved and started in the direction of the car she was in, relieved that she had received his letter in time to know that they were going to Guelph by train. Annie introduced everybody, explaining that Betsy and George were going to Berlin for the day to see George's family for the first time since they were married. Then, Betsy took over the conversation telling the story of how George had come to work for her father on their farm and they'd fallen in love and had been married after building their own little house down the lane from her family's house. This involved descriptions of the farm and the wedding and took the same length of time as the train did to reach Guelph. Tom was quite relieved to get down onto the platform and wave goodbye to the Krugers.

"Fair chatterbox your friend is, Annie," said Sam, putting Tom's thoughts into words.

"I'm sorry," said Annie. "I don't know her very well at all really, and they were the only other people boarding at Limehouse, so I couldn't not sit with them, could I?"

"He's just chaffing you, Annie," laughed Susanna. "It's nice to see a girl so happy with her life. But let's forget about her now. I'm so happy you were able to come with us. We were all afraid that Miss Bryden would need you in the store…"

"No, she says that, with people busy getting their work done in the morning so they can go to the picnic, there's not so many will come to the store that we need two people, even though it is Saturday, and she's happy for me to see Tom get his prize."

"That won't be until after the parade," said Tom. "Sam thought, at first, we should come by buggy so that we wouldn't have to leave so early and could work this morning but, like I told you in my letter, Susanna and I persuaded him to take a holiday and bring the children to town on the train as part of the treat. They've never been on the train before and there'll still be plenty of time when we get home this afternoon to turn the hay. It's light almost up to ten o'clock these evenings, after all."

"Well, Tom," said Sam, "you're the one who comes here to school, so you show us the way around. Country bumpkins the rest of us are. Myself, I only ever have time to come here to the market, then home again. So, Annie and you two, Malcolm and Elspeth, this here's called Market Square and over there, past where all the horses and carts are, is the Town Hall. Now, Tom can show you everything else."

"Can we see where you go to school first, Tom?" asked Malcolm, for whom Tom's train journey to school each day, was impressive, despite the two and a half mile walk to and from the station at Rockwood. Malcolm fully intended to go to that school, and ride on the train each day, when he was big enough.

"Well, I told you, Malcolm, we can only look at it. There won't be anybody there. It's mostly all closed up for the summer, anyway. Most of the boys are either working on the farm or learning about their fathers' trades in the summer. Some of the wealthier ones might be going for extra lessons but not today because the town has declared the anniversary of the confederation to be a holiday."

"I know but I want to see it so I'll know where it is – for when I go there when I'm big, like we said…"

"I want to see your school, too, Tom," put in Annie. "It can't be far because you've told us about everyone having to run to get there in time for the bell when the train's been late."

Having now travelled to high school for three years, Tom had forgotten that Annie had never been to Guelph either, or seen where he went to school. Just as in the days when Ma was ill and Annie had stayed at home while he went to school, he felt a little guilty that he had opportunities that she didn't. They had talked about it and she had told him she was quite happy to work at Miss Bryden's store and knew that it was quite impossible for her to go to high school. In Esquesing Township, it meant going to Oakville and boarding during the week as her friend Jimmy McGuire was doing, and Miss Bryden's objective in taking in an orphan was to have help in the store. In Limehouse, only girls whose family owned factories like Mary-Ann, the older girl who had taught her to play the piano, went to school after turning fourteen. Most finished their education long before that because they were needed at home to look after younger brothers and sisters. It was wonderful of Miss Bryden to have let her go every day the school was open for four years, except for the Saturday morning sessions when she was needed in the store. Tom just wished their parents hadn't died because he remembered Pa saying that Mr. Gladstone's Endowed Schools Act meant that Annie and Harriet would have the same education as Tom. John had yet to be born at the time.

"Well, we have lots of time," he said now. "We'll walk over to the school, then down and along by the river, then around to St. George's Square. Mr. Tytler said we should walk with the parade from there and we can see the new buildings that are going up there. It'll be a long walk – I think Elspeth will need a piggy back."

"No, I'm holding Ma's hand and Annie's hand. I can walk all the way, you'll see."

Watching her thrust her hand into Annie's, Tom was reminded once more of their past life when Harriet would do the same thing. "All right," he said and turned back to Malcolm. "Come along, Malcolm. We'll lead the way."

They made their way through the market and along streets lined with large houses, factories and foundries until they reached the Guelph High School. Tom explained that it had been built on the large corner lot back when the building of the railway had closed down the original grammar school. There was lots of room for expansion as more families came to live in the area. Mr. Tytler, the headmaster, already had plans to build a bigger school and make more places available because he said that, while the wealthy families were able to send their sons to school in Toronto, a good education must be available to all boys, and girls, too, and he was determined to make this possible.

Tom had the feeling that both Annie and Malcolm were a bit disappointed in the school, which really wasn't as grand as either of them had expected. He told them that there were plans for expansion because Mr. Tytler believed that many of the boys from both the town and the county who didn't pass the examination should be allowed to attend. Those whose fathers could afford it went to the academy, but most were denied any further education and he didn't think that was right for them or for the country. The country needed educated minds, he would say.

"It'll be much bigger when you're old enough to go," he told Malcolm. "There'll even be a gymnasium if Mr. Tytler has his way."

"What's that?" asked Malcolm.

"Place where you do physical education. You'll see." Tom wasn't really very sure how to explain the headmaster's theories about healthy bodies and healthy minds without it sounding like play to Sam, so he thought he'd better change the subject. "Let's walk back to Glasgow Street so we can get to where the Speed River joins our own Eramosa River, Malcolm – water that's travelled all the way from Rockwood and Eden Mills, just like we have."

Malcolm was suitably impressed. "We could have built a canoe and paddled like the Voyageurs," he said. He had learned about Canada's pioneers at school, and remained enthralled at the idea of travelling by canoe.

"I think that may have taken a bit more time than we had, son," laughed Sam. "Besides, I thought you liked going on the train. Here's me spending money on tickets and leaving the hay unturned…"

"I did like going on the train, Pa. It's great that you took us all on the train. I only meant…"

"I'm just teasing you, son."

"Oh."

"Come on, Tom's going to tell us all that goes on when the river gets to town."

"When the river gets to town–" Malcom started giggling. "That's funny."

They walked along streets lined with recently built fine houses and factories, following the curve of the river until they came within sight of the Grand Trunk Railway again. There, they found a shady place to sit in the grass and eat the bread and cheese Susanna had brought with her and, afterwards, walked back along to Market Square. Then, since it would soon be time for the parade to begin, they began to make their way along Wyndham Street to St. George's Square. People were gathering to watch the parade. Annie nudged Tom's arm as they passed an ice cream parlour where the big freezer had been set outside on a counter and the owner was turning the crank.

"I want to buy us all for ice cream on the way back to the station," she whispered to him.

"It'll cost quite a lot of money for the six of us," Tom whispered back.

"I got my first what Miss Bryden calls full time pay yesterday, and today's a day to celebrate."

"What's all the whispering about, you two?" asked Sam.

"Oh, just a surprise my sister's planning," Tom said and immediately added, "This is where the parade will start. I think I hear the band tuning up behind those buildings…"

"What surprise?" asked Elspeth.

Annie laughed. "If I tell you it won't be a surprise, will it?" Elspeth solemnly shook her head. "You'll see later on. You'll like it, I know."

"Come here, Elspeth," called her father, "let's put you up on my shoulders so that you can see the parade. Here come the pipers now, and the mayor and corporation in an open cart behind them."

* * * *

They watched the parade and walked along abreast of the tail end until they reached Exhibition Park where the parade dispersed and Tom led them over to the bandstand where the mayor was getting ready to give his welcome speech. There were stands selling lemonade and pies nearby and, further away, was the stadium where the Guelph's Maple Leafs played. Tom found himself getting nervous about receiving his prize in front of all these people. He tried to counteract his nervousness by talking about Canada's best baseball team – still the best, according to everybody in Guelph despite the fact that the Maple Leafs had been beaten by the London Tecumseh on the Queen's Birthday just a few weeks before.

The mayor welcomed everybody and presented prizes to people in the parade and Tom began to wonder if he had been forgotten. It was a relief when he saw Mr. Tytler, at last, beside the dais standing with Mr. Innes from the Mercury.

"I have to go now," he said.

"We'll be waiting here for you," said Sam, "so you'll know where to find us. Off you go." He gave him a pat on the back.

Annie hugged him. "Don't trip over your feet, now," she said.

He laughed and hugged her back. The little warning that their mother would give them when she knew a little confidence building was needed, did the trick. He found he was no longer nervous and strode confidently over to the headmaster.

Soon the mayor was saying, "And now I'll ask Mr. James Innes, of the Guelph Mercury and Advertiser, to come up here. He needs no introduction, I'm sure." He handed over the fireman's speaking-trumpet he was using to address the large crowd.

"Two months ago, we were exchanging ideas on how the Mercury should be involved in today's celebrations – other than in reporting, that is," the editor began.

A number of people laughed, although some didn't appear to understand the allusion.

He continued, "Somebody said, 'Why don't we run an essay contest with a prize for the best essay on Confederation and what it means to us as Canadians?' Well, I thought that was a capital idea." People cheered and clapped. "So we invited all our readers to send in their entries. Then, being on the Board of Education, I thought we should encourage entries from some of our high school boys and suggested this to my colleague, Mr. Tytler, who put it to his pupils. Now, I'm very gratified to find that the best essay was the work of one of Mr. Tytler's pupils." Everybody cheered again. "The biggest surprise was that this young man has only lived in Canada for four years – he was still far away in London and but seven years old when Canada became a dominion – yet he knew more about it than many of the other entrants. And he writes so well, I'd take him on as an apprentice reporter like a shot, except that Mr. Tytler tells me that he wants to be a teacher. Well, if he can teach boys to learn as well as he has learned in four short years in Canada, he'll be a great teacher. I was a school-teacher myself before I met the great George Brown in Toronto and went to work at The Globe, so who knows what this young writer will do in the future..." Everybody cheered again. "Now, I expect you all want to meet this young paragon, so I'll waste no more time – Mr. Tytler, bring Tom up to receive his prize."

"There you go, Tom," Mr. Tytler said, pushing Tom ahead of him up the steps of the dais.

Mr. Innes spoke into the speaking trumpet. "Ladies and gentlemen, boys and girls – the winner of the Guelph Mercury's Confederation Essay Contest – Mr. Tom Denton!"

Never having been called 'mister' before, Tom didn't immediately recognize his own name. It sounded like some grown up stranger, but he was nearly sixteen so it made sense for Mr. Innes to call him mister, not master. He finally stepped forward and clasped Mr. Innes's outstretched hand.

"Congratulations, Tom."

The crowd applauded loudly and Tom thanked them, Mr. Innes holding the speaking trumpet in front of him so that they could hear him over their shouts.

"Tom's essay is in today's Mercury and I'm sure that when you read it, you'll understand why we chose it as the winner. Here's your prize, Tom, and, if you pop into the office on your way to the station, I've instructed them to give you some copies of the paper to take home to give to your friends and family. Let's have one more round of applause and it's back to you, Mr. Mayor."

Mr. Melvin, the mayor, shook hands and congratulated Tom while the crowd applauded again, then Mr. Tytler led him back to where his family were waiting.

"I'm sure you're all very proud of Tom," Mr. Tytler said. "I know I am and so is the whole school."

Tom quickly introduced his foster family to the headmaster, then said, "And this is my sister, Annie, the best sister a fellow could ever have."

"Well, I'm very glad to meet you, Annie. And I'm sure you think Tom's the best brother, too."

Annie smiled, shyly. "I'm just so very happy for him, sir," she said.

"Well, Tom," Mr. Tytler said, turning to Tom. "You make sure they all have a good time and don't forget to go in and pick up your copies of the paper. You know where the Mercury's office is?"

"Yes, sir. We have hay to turn, so we won't be staying long."

"It's a shame you're not staying for the baseball game, but I expect these two youngsters enjoyed seeing the parade. Right?" he said, addressing Malcolm and Elspeth who both solemnly nodded. "Well, there are some ladies over by the children's races who are going to be serving free strawberries and cream – just for children – so you must make time to go over there before you leave. Now, I must be on my way. Glad to have met you Mr. and Mrs. Halliday and you keep up the good work, Tom."

They all said goodbye as he strode away. Then Tom broke the seal and opened the envelope he had been given. Inside was a certificate, announcing him as the winner of the 1876

Mercury Essay Contest, and five two dollar Canadian Bank of Commerce banknotes.

"Not often you see that much money at one time," Sam said and they all looked at the banknotes with admiration.

"You must be careful you don't lose them," Susanna said, anxiously. "Perhaps you should let Sam put them in his leather pouch until we get home just in case a pickpocket removes them from your pocket. Annie can put the envelope with the certificate in her basket, but I think that pouch on Sam's belt is the safest place for the money."

Tom and Annie agreed that she was right and Sam placed it carefully in the pouch on his belt where he carried his own money.

"That's what you should make for Tom's birthday present next month," he said to Susanna as he did so. "You still have some of that skin, don't you?"

"Yes, that's what I was thinking, too, but I wasn't about to tell him, silly."

"Sixteen, he'll be. That's getting too old for surprises."

"Can we go to the races now, Pa?" asked Malcolm. "Maybe I can win a race and get a prize, too."

"We still have a fair bit of time before the train comes at three o'clock," said Sam. "so we'll go over and see which races they're having first."

Malcolm was second in the running race for eight-year-old boys and was given a prize of a bright new nickel. Tom made sure that they left the park with enough time to stop at the ice-cream parlour on the way back to the station and Annie happily bought them all penny licks. Sam said there wasn't time to have the nickel dishes of ice cream that she wanted to buy, and that penny licks would do them fine. Then he told her that the difference in the price for six people was almost half the price of a return ticket for her to come and see Tom so it was better she save it and visit them instead. Susanna added that she'd rather see Annie on a Sunday than have a dish of ice cream, and the penny licks were best for the children anyway seeing that they'd already eaten strawberries and cream.

Tom said he'd make the detour along MacDonell Street to the Mercury office by himself if they wanted to go straight to the station but everybody agreed that they'd like to see what a newspaper office looked like. As it turned out, Tom was told to take as many copies as he liked from the pile by the door so all he saw was the porter's room and the rest of them saw only the outside of the building, but they agreed that it was a very handsome place.

Finally, aboard the train home, they examined the newspaper article about Tom and the essay contest. Annie started to read the essay but Tom told her to wait until she got home because they needed to arrange about sending copies to people. Annie said she'd look after that as it would be easier for her to get them posted quickly. Tom counted out three copies for himself and put the rest in Annie's basket and she handed him his envelope with the certificate inside. Susanna offered to carry Tom's things in her basket to prevent them getting creased to which he agreed.

Soon the whistle went and the train began to slow down to stop at the Rockwood platform.

"Why can't you come with us, Annie?" asked Elspeth. "Pa or Tom could take you home in the buggy."

"They don't have time, Elspeth," Annie told the little girl. "You all have a lot of work to do and besides, I'm expected back before the evening – besides I've already paid for my ticket. I'll see you again soon. I promise."

The train came to a stop and Sam picked Elspeth up to jump down to the platform with her. Malcolm scrambled down by himself, his mother steadying him as he landed on the platform. Tom gave Annie a quick hug.

"I'll write as soon as I get some time off," he said.

"It's all right. I know it's a busy time on the farm. I'll let you know when I get replies about your essay. I know everybody will be proud of you – 'though not as proud as me."

Tom laughed and jumped down onto the platform as the conductor's whistle sounded. He slammed the door and they all waved as Annie leaned out of the window to wave back, holding onto her bonnet as the train gathered speed.

CHAPTER FOURTEEN

Lying in his attic bedroom that night, listening to the sounds of frogs calling through the open window, Tom thought about how lucky he was to have been placed with Sam Halliday four years ago. He often wondered if it had been a matter of luck or something contrived by Herb Taylor, the boy who had told him that there were farmers who were quite happy for the orphans placed with them to go to school. He suspected that Herb had told Mr. Merry about their conversation that day when he'd invited him to travel to Limehouse with him to visit Annie while he bought the paint, and that Mr. Merry had found the placement or, at least thought of Tom, because of the tip from Herb, when the request came in from Sam.

He smiled at the memory of his twelve-year-old self arriving at Sam's Eden Mills farm in the Blair Athol buggy and Mr. Merry telling him that the village got its name because the surrounding countryside was thought to be much like the original Garden of Eden. While he knew it was not what Mr. Merry meant, in his own mind, the phrase had conjured up visions of irresistible apples and serpents and resulted in his never feeling quite comfortable around the small apple orchard at the back of Sam's farmhouse. Serpent connections were further complicated by stories of native spirits in the area, which had once been the hunting grounds of the Neutral Indians. Sam had several arrow heads in his possession which he had found while ploughing his fields. Tom had never found one himself but many of the boys at school told of finding them, as well as the occasional stone axe. The spirit stories centred on the river valley where the trail passed the farmhouse and crossed the river a quarter of a mile to the west which was Tom's route to and from school during the first year he lived on the Halliday farm. The thoughts of serpents and spirits had been forgotten when he began walking the other way to get to the Rockwood Grand Trunk station to board the train for Guelph each day and, serpents and spirits aside, he'd come to love living here on the farm.

The moon was overhead and its light was shining in at the dormer window lighting the room almost as if it were day-time. It wasn't a full moon he knew, but it was very bright. He sat up startled as his door opened softly. Malcolm slid into the room and closed the door again.

"Malcolm," he almost yelped. "What are you doing awake at this hour? You frightened the life out of me."

"The light woke me up and it's scary. Don't you think it's scary?"

"It's just moonlight. What's scary about moonlight? It's beautiful."

"If it's not scary, why are you awake?"

"I just had a lot to think about. Let's take you back to bed."

"No. I want to get in your bed. It's lonely in the moonlight."

"Is Elspeth sleeping?"

"Yes, it's darker where her bed is."

"Ssh," Tom hushed him. "You'll have your Pa up here wondering what's going on if you talk so loudly. And he won't be pleased at being woken."

The attic was divided into two bedrooms reached by a narrow staircase with a gate across the top to prevent the children falling down the stairs in the night. Consequently, they tended to come into Tom rather than calling down to their parents if they awoke.

"Can I stay here for a little while? Just until I get sleepy," begged Malcolm. "Please."

"Okay," said Tom knowing, from experiences in the past, that this was the fastest way to solve the dilemma.

"Tell me a story about when you were a boy in London," Malcolm said, squeezing into the narrow bed beside Tom.

"I think you've heard them all."

"Well, tell me the one about when your pa took you and Annie on that underground train to the animal place."

"You must know it better than I do, Malcolm, after the number of times I've told you."

"But now I've been on a train, too. Was being on the underground train the same as being on the train to Guelph?"

"Not really. It was much noisier because of being in the tunnel."

"Our train was pretty noisy, too. But we didn't really go very far, did we?" He didn't wait for Tom to answer. "One day I want to get on a train and go all the way to the city. Maybe Pa and me can come and visit you when you go there to learn to be a teacher. But that's still quite a long time, isn't it?"

"Yes, I still have lots of things to learn at the high school before I can take the examination. Now, you're going to be very tired in the morning if you don't go to sleep, so close your eyes and I'll tell you the story."

He didn't get very far before Malcolm fell asleep. It had been a busy day for both the Halliday children. Tom carried the boy through to his own bed.

Back in his own room, he thought wistfully of the day he and Annie had travelled on the Metropolitan Railway with their father to visit the London Zoo. He had originally told Malcolm the story because he thought the little boy would like to hear about the animals, especially Jumbo, the elephant. Instead, it was the underground railway that had captured his imagination.

Sometimes Tom wished he hadn't turned his childhood memories into bedtime stories for Malcolm and, later for Elspeth, because they were beginning to sound like stories to him, too. The two children were almost exactly the same ages as his little sister and brother and, to some extent, they had taken the place of Harriet and John who were growing up without him back in London. He imagined them receiving his essay in the newspaper and Harriet explaining to little John how their big brother had won the contest. He wondered if she could read well enough now to read the essay to John. Perhaps Uncle Alfred would read it to both of them. Maybe he'd even feel proud of his nephew and wish he had kept Tom and Annie, although Tom was glad that he hadn't, all things considered. Life on Sam's farm was much better than living in Bow would have been. It would be nice to see Harriet and John again, though…

* * * *

It was just the next week when the fact came home to Tom that many orphan immigrants were not as fortunate in their placements as he and Annie had been.

It had been the previous summer that he had last seen Annie's friend Maggie, who had travelled with them on the train from Belleville when they had first arrived in Canada and then travelled westwards in the care of Mrs Merry. Maggie lived on a farm north of Rockwood. Several times, she had been allowed time off to walk down the lane from the Eramosa Gravel Road to the York Road to meet Annie at the railway station and had come down to the Halliday's farm with her to visit him. Sam would drive the two girls back up in the buggy, letting Maggie off at the laneway leading to the farm and taking Annie back down to the station. On a couple of occasions they had taken Annie all the way home to Limehouse, Sam saying that the horses, Moffat and Wamphrey – named for the traditional homeland of the Hallidays in Dumfriesshire, Scotland – needed some exercise. More recently, Tom had been allowed to use the buggy to pick Annie up or drop her off at the station, but Maggie had not been with them on any of these occasions.

Back around Easter time, Annie had confided that she was worried about Maggie. While not very good at writing, Maggie used to make a great effort to correspond with Annie but her letters, she said, had become very short and confusing over the last year. When Annie had written to say that she and Miss Bryden would pick her up in the sleigh the Sunday before Christmas as they had done the previous three years, Maggie had written back to say she couldn't come this year with no explanation. Maggie, of course, had only learned to read and write during the months she had spent at the Refuge in

Spitalfields and did not express herself very wells in words. She had been able to go to the school on the Eramosa Road at first because one of her duties was to take the family's six year-old twins and their seven-year-old brother there. Later, their mother decided she couldn't spare Maggie, and she would have to hurry back after taking the boys to school, then get back there again to fetch them at four o'clock.

Understanding Maggie's limitations, Annie had accepted the fact that Maggie couldn't come to dinner but, after hearing from her friend only once since the Christmas letter, she attempted to call on her one morning in April when most of the snow had melted, and the lane from Rockwood up to the Eramosa Gravel Road had became passable again. Two of the older brothers – hefty young men now – were filling potholes in the farm's laneway. They abruptly told her that Maggie was too busy to see her and Annie had no choice but to walk all the way back again. The next train wouldn't be coming through until after three so she had walked on to the Halliday's farm on the Indian trail, surprising Tom who had not been expecting her, just as he and the family were finishing their dinner. Susanna had immediately made her sit down and warmed up a bowl of stew and dumplings for her as she explained how worried she had become about not hearing from Maggie and how, since school was still closed for Easter, Miss Bryden had suggested she go over and call on her. Hearing how the boys had treated her, Sam said that there was no excuse for their rudeness, especially since they would have known perfectly well that she'd walked the three miles from the station only to have to walk three miles back again.

One morning the next week, Sam had driven up to have a word with Mrs. Poole, Maggie's mistress. He'd found her alone preparing dinner and was told that everybody, including Maggie, was out mending fences and generally cleaning up after the winter. Sam had expected the men to be so engaged, since he was taking time out from fence mending himself but it seemed odd that Maggie was out on the farm somewhere rather than helping in the kitchen. He told the woman how her sons had so shabbily turned Annie away and how Annie was concerned about Maggie's welfare. She said she'd tell Maggie to write to Annie but that she must have the dinner ready for when the men came in and couldn't stand around passing the time of day now. Sam had no choice but to leave. That evening he had told Tom that he was writing to Miss Bilbrough at Marchmont to suggest that somebody pay a visit to the farm as soon as possible because he was not at all satisfied with the encounter. The Pooles were said to be solid Church of Christ members like many of the families up there in Everton and he disliked casting doubt on people. Notwithstanding, something very odd was going on. Despite Maggie having been placed there for more than four years now, the Marchmont people would still be concerned for her welfare and would have her on their lists for visiting just as they did with Tom and Annie. It could well be, Sam had said, that Marchmont visitors had, on trying to see Maggie, received the same evasions as he and Annie.

Sam had received a reply explaining that Marchmont had been rebuilt after yet another fire and everybody was busy readying the new building to receive the first party of children, who were being accompanied by Miss Macpherson herself, within the next few weeks. Special attention would be paid to his request when they drew up their plans for visiting the children during the summer. In the meantime, Miss Bilbrough was writing to Mr. Poole, and to the workers at Blair Athol to ask that when somebody could be spared for the day, weather permitting, for a journey over to Everton from Galt be undertaken.

Late in the afternoon of the Saturday following the Confederation Day outing to Guelph, Elspeth came running out to the field where her father was bringing in the hay.

"Pa! Pa!" she shouted as she ran.

Sam stopped the horses, jumped down and shouted for Tom, who was pitching the previous load of hay into the barn, to come and take them. Tom dropped his pitchfork and hurried across the field to take the reins. He continued to guide the horses along the windrow, the hay piling up on the buckrake, then up the slope to the hayloft. Since there was no sign of Sam coming back out, he let the horses loose and herded them into the adjacent paddock, then continued pitching the hay into the barn. Soon Malcolm came hurrying out to the back end of the barn, telling Tom that visitors had come and his pa said Tom was to come and talk to them. Tom hung up the pitchfork and hurried to the farmhouse with Malcolm.

"It's the young lady who came to see you with that Mr. Merry last summer," said Malcolm.

"His daughter, you mean, Miss Merry?"

"Yes. There's another man with her this time. Ma sent Elspeth and me outside, then called me to go and get you. They all look very solemn like something dreadful has happened."

Tom knew immediately that it was something to do with Maggie and the Pooles.

"Tom," Sam said, as he came into the big farmhouse kitchen where Susanna had seated the visitors at the table with fresh lemonade to drink. "You remember Miss Merry, don't you from last year?" Tom nodded. "Came with her father, she did. Remember? And this is her brother, Mr. James Merry." Tom nodded again and shook hands with the young man. "I'm afraid they've some very bad news for us."

"It's Maggie, isn't it?"

"Yes, Tom," said Mary Merry. "We've only just been able to get over to visit the Poole farm as Miss Bilbrough told Mr. Halliday we would. Unfortunately, nobody from Blair Athol was able to do so before now. Everybody's been very busy writing up reports – because of the government enquiry last year on the children being brought to Canada. Anyway, now that my brother and I have arrived, we've been sent out to make all the visits in this area. Because of Mr. Halliday's letter, Maggie at the Poole farm was at the top of the list."

"What's happened to Maggie?" asked Tom. "Something's wrong, isn't it?"

"Yes, something's very wrong and we drove straight down here because it was Mr. Halliday who alerted us to the possiblility of there being a problem, and we know how worried you and your sister have been." She took his hand. "I'm afraid Maggie died last month, Tom. A terrible thing happened to her – probably some time before Christmas – and the Pooles did not contact Marchmont as they should have done and…

"You mean one of those boys made her pregnant, don't you?" cried Tom, suddenly understanding Maggie's refusal to see Annie and himself at Christmas time and subsequent lack of contact with Annie. He could imagine her humiliation…

"They blamed her and kept her hidden away, didn't they? Did they starve her? Is that why she died?"

Miss Merry was taken aback. "We don't know that, Tom," she said, startled. "At first, they told us that she had died of a fever and that they were going to write to Miss Bilbrough to let her know, but hadn't had the time. Eventually, Mrs. Poole broke down and told us the true story, although she didn't say it was one of her boys. What makes you think that?"

"I've heard of such things– no, not about Miss Macpherson's children. Things like this happen to orphans… Oh. Oh – how am I going to tell Annie?"

"It's all right, Tom. Mr. Halliday has agreed for us to take you over to see your sister and, perhaps, even stay for the night if Miss Bryden agrees. James and I are staying with friends of our parents in Norval tonight, so it's on our way and you can show us how to get there on the roads between the concessions instead of going up to the York Road."

"Malcolm can help me with the pitching, Tom" put in Sam. "There's only a couple more rows and we can get to the chopping after I come and fetch you home tomorrow morning. How's that sound?"

"The poor horses probably thought their workday was over when I put them in the paddock," Tom replied with a small chuckle. "Annie's going to be so upset. She'll think it's her fault – that she should have tried harder to see Maggie."

James Merry spoke for the first time since Tom had come in.

"There's nothing either of you could have done, Tom," he said. "It's possible that had we been able to check into the situation as soon as Miss Bilbrough received Mr. Halliday's letter,

Maggie's life might have been saved but, if she died last month, she must have already been in a very weak state by then."

"Miss Bilbrough will also think it's her fault," his sister added, "but it really wasn't possible for anybody to leave Belleville at that point and there was only my other brother at Blair Athol until my father arrived with the first group of boys in May. Of course, if they had known how serious it was, William and one of the farm hands would have come over… he, too, will blame himself once we tell him. It's a dreadful thing to have happened but it's not anybody's fault."

"Except the Poole family," said Tom. "How could they treat Maggie like that? I thought all the families who took in Miss Macpherson's children were good Christian families, with ministers to vouch for their characters."

"They are good Christians, Tom," said James Merry. "They say that Maggie was going to have a baby and refused to tell them who the father was. This was in February. She had been 'poorly' all winter but did all her chores until collapsing one morning. That was when Mrs. Poole realized what was wrong with her."

"Then, Mrs. Poole must have known it was one her boys," said Tom, "because Maggie never went anywhere, except to see Annie and to church with the Pooles. She never had the chance to know anybody else–" Tom stopped himself. James and Mary Merry were only a few years older than he was himself and had the responsibility of taking this story back to their parents who were now running Blair Athol. They could hardly tell them the Pooles' story and add that it was all lies because Tom Denton said so. He had no proof that the Poole boys had had their way with Maggie or that their parents deliberately allowed her and the baby she was carrying to starve to death. He only thought so because he had heard of such things happening, and he knew Maggie. "Maggie was a good girl," he said. "Somebody took advantage of her."

"Somebody took advantage of her," Miss Merry said kindly. "The Pooles say they put her to bed after the collapse and tried to get her to eat properly, but she wouldn't eat and grew weaker and weaker. They knew they should send her to Miss Bilbrough but she could hardly make the journey on her own, and I don't know what Miss Bilbrough would have done anyway – Marchmont was burnt to the ground and everybody was being put up by friends for the winter."

"Even if they did let her rest rather than work her to death, there was no reason for them not to let Annie see her," Tom said, dismissing the claims of the Pooles to have been kind and considerate. "They obviously didn't want Annie to find out what was wrong with her – or Sam, either, when he went up there and was told she was out with the boys mending the fences. That couldn't have been true! You do know that it could have been my sister, Annie, and not Maggie. Annie was going to be sent to that place. Miss Bryden wrote, just in time, to say that she'd take a girl instead of a boy. But for that, it would be my sister who was killed."

"No, we didn't know that, Tom. Mary and I were both at school in England at that time," said James. "Look I understand how you feel and I tend to agree with you about how this happened but we can't go around accusing the Pooles of 'killing' Maggie. They may not want to admit that it was one of their sons who– er, had his way with Maggie, if they even know that in the first place, and they may have been wrong not to have contacted Miss Bilbrough, but there is no evidence of ill-treatment. They say they treated Maggie no differently than they would have done had their own daughter been in the same situation which probably means letting her know she was a sinner but not actually being cruel. And, quite honestly Tom, I would imagine that they really would have – as you put it – kept her hidden away, but we can't berate ourselves over what's happened. And, you must remember that it was God's will that sent Annie to Miss Bryden instead of to the Pooles so she was never in any danger. For now, we have to get over to Limehouse and tell Annie what's happened. That's more important, isn't it?"

"I understand that Annie rather took Maggie under her wing and taught her how to read and write back in Spitalfields," his sister added. "She's going to need your sympathy, isn't she? Not being reminded that it could have been her."

"Miss Merry's right, Tom," said Sam, speaking for the first time. "First things first, lad. How about you get on your way and I'll be over after service tomorrow to fetch you. It'll be nice for Annie to have you go to kirk with her over there, won't it? Better run up and put your Sunday clothes in a bag to take with you."

Sam's common sense attitude gave Tom the sense of purpose he needed and he nodded gratefully. Ten minutes later he was in the buggy with Mary and James Merry, heading towards the Guelph Line on the Indian trail and waving to the Malcolm and Elspeth who had run to the end of their laneway to watch them drive away.

Maggie's death – or, more precisely, the manner of it – shocked Annie and it was many weeks before she began to feel joy in her own life again. The next Sunday afternoon, Miss Bryden borrowed her brother's buggy and she and Annie drove over to the church that Maggie had attended with the Pooles. With the help of an old man who evidently acted as a voluntary groundskeeper, they found the site of Maggie's grave in a distant corner of the churchyard. He was scything the grass and, when they explained who they were looking for, took them to the corner where the graves were marked, if at all, with rough home-made crosses. Somebody – probably Mrs. Poole or her married daughter, Miss Bryden said – had lettered Maggie's name in charcoal on one. Like the others, the letters would soon fade and the grave would become unidentifiable. Annie decided to find out how much a small stone would cost and save enough money to buy one with Maggie's name carved on it. At least, her dear friend had a grave, she thought. Had she died in London, in the same circumstances, she'd have been put in a pauper grave with all the other parish poor who'd died that week.

Like Tom, she remembered how she, herself, had been destined for the place at the Poole farm until Miss Bryden's letter had arrived at Marchmont agreeing to a girl being placed with her instead of a boy. She felt guilty for being alive when Maggie was dead and tearfully voiced this guilt. Miss Bryden, staunch Presbyterian that she was, became quite annoyed with her.

"The Good Lord knows what he's doing, Annie. He decided that you should come here with me – I was just his instrument – and he's going to be getting pretty upset with you if you carry on thinking she died in place of you," she said, as they sat on the back veranda podding the first crop of peas from the garden. "Maggie died for a purpose, known only to Him just now maybe, but one day it will become apparent. And, my lass, you can be assured she's in a far better place in Heaven than she was here on Earth. Now, let me finish these peas, and you run down to the mint patch and fetch a sprig of mint to cook with them."

CHAPTER FIFTEEN

Annie tried hard to believe that Maggie's death was pre-destined but continued to think she should have done more, though she had no idea what she could have done. She remembered that first evening at the Refuge when Maggie and the other girls told her about Miss Macpherson's non-rules. 'We 'ave to 'elp each uvver, we do 'ere,' she'd said, explaining the philosophy, 'an', I tell you somefink – you feels bloomin' awful when you let's someone down, much worse than if you'd been punished.' She had let Maggie down and she did feel 'bloomin' awful'. She should have persisted in seeing her that day after Easter when she'd taken the train and walked all the way to the Poole's farm, then let the boys scare her off. She should have done something much earlier than that. When Maggie wrote that letter breaking with the little tradition Miss Bryden had started of having Annie's brother and her best friend visit on the Sunday before Christmas – that's when she should have acted. If she had seen Maggie then, she would have known that something was terribly wrong. Well, of course she would – that was why Maggie had written that way. She was too ashamed to see them after what had happened to her. One of the first things a girl learnt at the Refuge was how sinful it was to allow a man to use her body. She didn't want them to know that one of those boys, and it had to have been one of those boys – and who else could it have been? – had used hers.

Maggie must have felt like a sinner. But she wasn't. She hadn't chosen to do this. It was forced on her. Annie wrote a long letter to Miss Macpherson telling her all this and politely suggested that the difference between being a sinner and being violated be explained to the girls so, if what happened to Maggie ever happened to them, they would know that it was all right to ask for help.

It wasn't until late September that she received a reply. Miss Macpherson had been on her way back to England before news of Maggie's death had reached Marchmont. Annie's letter, along with her earlier one including the copies of the newspaper with Tom's essay, had been held until her recent return. All the ladies had discussed what Annie had to say and were impressed by her introspection – Annie was not quite sure what this meant and had to look it up in the dictionary that she had won as prize one year at school. They would think immediately about a way to ensure that girls in the future would understand the difference between sinning and being violated. Annie must understand that it was because so many girls came into the Refuge, after already having experienced exposure to the sinful lives of street women, that an emphasis must be placed on such wickedness. What had happened to Maggie raised the difficult question of how to teach young girls understand the difference between sinning and being sinned against and the consequences of each. The letter ended with assurances that requests for the Lord's guidance of Annie in bearing the loss of her dear friend would be in the prayers of all the workers at Marchmont, as well as back home in London at the Refuge.

Annie told Miss Bryden what Miss Macpherson had said about teaching the girls about being taken advantage of through no fault of their own instead of only about the wickedness of the sinful use of their bodies. Miss Bryden's thought perhaps that was God's purpose for what happened to Maggie and that, maybe, many girls in the future would be better off for it. Annie couldn't believe that the Lord would have allowed Maggie to suffer so, but kept her thoughts to herself. She wrote again, enclosing letters about Maggie's death to Jennie and Kate, the girls who had been friends of Maggie's at the Refuge, which she asked Miss Macpherson to pass along to them when she was able to. Somehow this sharing of the sad news helped her to feel a little less unhappy herself and, by degrees, to feel more like her own practical, optimistic self again as summer became autumn and she and Miss Bryden canned and stored their garden harvest so that, in addition to the autumn months being a busy time in the store, there was little time to brood.

She talked to Jimmy McGuire about getting a grave marker made for Maggie. Jimmy wanted to apprentice to an architect or engineer when he finished at the high school and knew many of the Irish immigrants who had originally come to work on the building of the Grand Trunk Railway. When the work was finished they had developed their skills as builders and carpenters and now built many of the new homes and barns in the area as well as repairing the older ones. Jimmy found a stone mason who, in return for the modest sum that Tom and Annie paid him, carved a small limestone marker from a slab of limestone which one of Jimmy's brothers acquired at the quarry for no charge when he told his boss the story of Maggie's death. Their own contributions were augmented with donations from the Hallidays, Miss Bryden and the Merry family. Both Mr. and Mrs. Merry had come over from Galt to see Tom and Annie, after their daughter took the news of Maggie's death back to them, and Annie had told Mrs. Merry of her project to place a marker on the grave. When it was ready, Miss Bryden had prevailed upon the minister from their own church to come to the Everton cemetery after the service one Sunday at the end of September to sanctify the marker when they placed it on the grave. The nice little service there helped Annie to truly believe that Maggie and her baby were at peace.

* * * *

Harriet and John waved good-bye to Miss Macpherson as she hurried off in the direction of the Bow Common Road to make another call and deliver letters to another family of some children she had taken to Canada. She looked back and motioned them to go in out of the cold. Sleet was beginning to fall.

"Is she a lady postman?" asked John, as Harriet closed the door and they took the letters into the kitchen, where the Christmas decorations were still up, making it feel very cheery after standing at the open door looking out onto the bleak street.

"Whoever heard of a lady postman," Harriet scoffed.

"Well, she always brings letters for us and the man postmans don't bring letters for children, do they?"

"The postman *does* bring us letters, too. From Canada, but usually they're in the envelope with Aunt Ella's all on thin paper because you have to put more stamps on if it's heavy. Anyway, Miss Macpherson doesn't just bring letters. She brings us news, too."

"Yes, about Tomandannie way across the sea."

"It's not Tomandannie. I've explained it before – it's *Tom* who's our big brother, and *Annie* who's our big sister. And Miss Macpherson's the lady who found them homes to live in when our ma died and we came to live with Uncle Alfred and Aunt Ella..." Harriet sighed. It was hard for the little boy to understand that he had a brother and sister he didn't remember.

"She talks funny."

"That's because she's from Scotland. They all talk like that up there. At least, that's what Uncle Alfred said and he must be right because Dr. MacGhie sounds the same and he's from Scotland."

"What is a fromscotland? Where is it up?"

"It's not a fromscotland. They're *from Scotland* – they lived there before they came to London. Why must you always put words together? Aunt Ella will be back in a minute and we'll have to get tea so let's read our letter from Annie."

She read out the letter. Annie sounded very sad. Her friend had died. She wrote that Miss Macpherson was staying nearby and would be visiting her and Miss Bryden, so she was writing a quick letter for her to take when she sailed back. She said she had sent a little package of Christmas presents to them by packet ship which may or may not reach them before the letter but expected that Miss Macpherson would be too busy with Christmas activities at the Beehive to do her visiting until afterwards. Annie said that she would see Tom at Christmas as usual but it would be sad for them with Maggie not being there.

"Poor Annie," said Harriet. "She's very sad, isn't she?"

"Why did her friend die?" asked John.

"I don't know. Perhaps she got the fever."

"I thought they didn't have the fever there. Uncle Alfred said that when everybody was getting it – he said he was glad he only had you and me and Aunt Ella to worry about catching it with Tomandannie being safely where there wasn't any fever."

"Well, I don't know. Miss Macpherson didn't say either. She just said that Annie and Tom were very sad and that she'd been glad that she had time to visit them because she hadn't after it happened as she had to get back to London – she called at Uncle Alfred's office, remember, and gave him that newspaper with Tom's story in it. Then she had to get another lot of children on a ship... she's been on a lot of ships, hasn't she?"

"When I'm big, I shall go on a ship", said John. "Maybe I'll be a sailor or... a pirate. Yo-ho-ho and a bottle of rum. Yo-ho-ho..." He began to stamp around the kitchen table waving an imaginary sword.

Harriet sighed. He was just too young to understand these things. She began to get the table ready for tea.

* * * *

On the Sunday before Christmas, Miss Bryden did borrow her brother's horses and sleigh as usual, but she and Annie only drove to Eden Mills and had dinner with Tom and the Hallidays. It was Susanna's idea. She thought that spending that particular day at Limehouse might turn the little tradition into a sad occasion for both Tom and Annie so, at the beginning of December, she wrote to Miss Bryden asking her and Annie to come to the Halliday farm instead. Besides, Susanna said, she'd love to have Miss Bryden visit her home and get to know her better. Much as she had appreciated Miss Bryden turning her surprise treat of that first Christmas in Canada into an annual event and Susanna's adaptation of it this year, Annie was concerned about all the driving. They had a lovely time together but decided that it would be wise to leave early because quite a lot of snow had fallen. While the sure-footed ponies skilfully pulled the sleigh over the packed down snow on the York Road on the way home, it was more difficult on the less travelled roads between the concessions. When they finally reached the Bryden farm, Miss Bryden's brother insisted on their staying in the sleigh while he drove down to the village with them because the snow was getting deep and the temperature was dropping and he didn't want them walking down. When he dropped them off at the store, Annie was glad to be able to get inside and stoke the banked up embers in the stove until the fresh logs she put in caught and blazed comfortably. She and Miss Bryden both stood in front of the stove until they thawed out, then Miss Bryden warmed up some apple cider and Annie hung their coats and blankets to dry.

"It's setting in for the night," said Miss Bryden, when they were seated and drinking the apple cider into which she'd sprinkled cinnamon and nutmeg. "We got home just in time, I think. They're a lovely family, the Hallidays, aren't they?"

"I like them a lot," Annie replied. "They've been wonderful to Tom with letting him go to high school and everything. Of course, Tom does work very hard on the farm, too, and the money for his railway fare and things would be his wages – if he didn't go to school, I mean."

"Don't worry, Annie," laughed Miss Bryden. "I certainly didn't mean to make you think that I didn't think Tom paid his way. I just meant that they're really nice people. From Dumfriesshire, they are. That's next door to Roxburghshire where the Brydens come from. 'Course I don't remember much about it – I was just a wee one when we came over. My ma missed Scotland dreadfully. She never did get used to the ways here. There was so much work for a woman to do in those days – the land here had only just been opened up then, long before the quarrying started and houses were built. They had to clear the trees up there themselves, just like Sam and Susanna cleared the land where they are. Ma, however, was not a strong young woman like Susanna and she had so many bairns, most of them dying within days of birth... Used to say I was the only one who lived was because I was a bonnie Scot born in the old country until, of course, my two brothers come along and lived to grow up, too. By then, she was too weak to see to them growing up, though..."

Annie knew that Miss Bryden's mother had been an invalid during the last few years of her life and had died, leaving Miss Bryden to bring up her little brothers. Later, when the lime kilns were built and the village began to develop, her father left the farm in the hands of his by then grown sons and took his daughter to live in the small house he purchased in the village. There, he turned the front parlour of the house into Bryden's Dry Goods and Staples. Over the next few years, the factories opened, lots were sub-divided and surveyed and homes were built for the workers. The railway came through and his business increased, along with the influx of workers to the village. The original front walls of the house were torn down and the store was enlarged to become quite a prosperous concern by the time he died.

"It's hard to imagine what it must have looked like without the quarries and the kilns and, of course, the railway," Annie said.

"Just one great rock it was, all the way from our farm down to the school – 'course the school wasn't there then. My ma taught me to read and write and I taught my brothers. It was a different world. Even when the common school did open, way down the road from where it is now, it was too far for the boys to go and they were almost full grown by then, anyway. Likely wouldn't have gone even if it didn't mean a four mile walk twice a day on top of being in the classroom from nine to four. There was always work to do around the farm and Pa taught them how to do that well enough that he could leave them to it when he went into the retail business. Pa was a proud and happy man when he died, God rest his soul. A successful farm business and a thriving store – he thought that was pretty good going for a man who'd arrived in Upper Canada, as it was called then, with nothing but what we carried with us. Well, I think that's enough reminiscing for now. We've missed teatime – and just as well that is after the big dinner we had – but I think I'll just warm us up some soup for our supper."

That night, before snuffing out her candle, Annie sat in bed and re-read the letter she had received the day before from Jennie Sparling. She and Jennie had written to each other for more than a year after they had both moved on from the Refuge but, eventually, Annie had stopped getting replies to her letters and had given up writing any more. So, after writing letters to both Jennie and Kate about Maggie's death and asking Miss Macpherson to see if she could find the girls and pass on the letters, she hadn't really expected to hear back from either of them. She knew that it often took poor Miss Macpherson all winter to deliver the letters and verbal messages she brought back to England with her from the boys and girls in Canada, so getting the letter from Jenny had been as good as getting a Christmas present.

Jennie said she was 'so sory' to hear about their dear friend Maggie and 'so sory' she hadn't written to Annie for so long. Jennie's writing, spelling and lack of punctuation made her muddled letter difficult to understand but, apparently, the aunt she had gone to live with when she left the Refuge had sent her off, as soon as she turned twelve, to be a scullery maid at a gentleman's house in Lewes. She had worked from half past five in the morning until after ten at night and had no time to do anything but sleep when not working. A year ago, when the previous kitchen maid left to get married, she'd been promoted to kitchen maid and now had every Tuesday afternoon off, in addition to every second Sunday. She would have written on a Sunday afternoon before now but thought Annie must have forgotten all about her after not hearing from her for such a long time.

Annie didn't know where Lewes was and decided to find it, when she had a moment, in her atlas. She imagined Jennie in an attic maid's room, which she probably shared with the nursery maid and the new scullery maid, toiling for several hours over this letter with borrowed pen and ink, working hard to remember her long unpractised writing skills. She would write to Jennie and tell her about the grave marker, her work as a full-time store clerk – the title Miss Bryden now attributed to her, playing the piano in a duet with Mary-Ann at the village Christmas concert last night, dinner at the Halliday's farm and the drive home in the snow. There was so much to tell her about…

CHAPTER SIXTEEN

"So how does Toronto compare with Guelph? Although, I suppose you haven't exactly been able to see much of the city with the hours they've had us put in so far…"

"You're right there," Tom laughed. "I only went to school in Guelph, though. Then it was back to work on my foster father's farm each day, and I was lucky enough to get a place at the model school in the next town, so the routine was the same. I'm no authority on towns and their amenities, I'm afraid."

He'd been partnered with the young man, whose name was Hartley Clifford, to prepare a presentation on what they had learned from the lecture on maintaining pupils' interest in school subjects which appeared to have no relationship to their own lives. Tom hoped he didn't appear nervous. Maybe Hartley would write him off as a country bumpkin now. Perhaps he should have claimed greater acquaintanceship with Guelph. Hartley was quite obviously city born and bred and his clothes were expensive, compared to Tom's well-worn woollen suit.

Since passing their admission examinations to the Toronto Normal School two weeks before, the sixtieth session students had been on the school premises from six in the morning until six in the evening every day except Sunday. There had been lectures, introductory talks from the various instructors, individual interviews and evenings spent, after a quick supper, reviewing everything learned during the day before falling into bed. Tom had found lodgings, licensed by the Normal School, on Sherbourne Street, a short walk from St. James Square school buildings. At an extra cost, he was provided with a bun and mug of coffee in the morning, and stew and bread for supper in the evening. Dinner and tea were available in the school refectory. He was glad now that the government changes to teacher training had meant teaching for the balance of the school year after obtaining his third class certificate at the Elora Model School to qualify for Normal School courses. Like all students who were from outside of the city, he received two dollars a week towards his board and lodging, but his savings would never have stretched over the two sessions at the Normal School needed to obtain his second class certificate, without the small salary he had received from teaching at Elora. He'd could always find a position filling in for some other third class certificate teacher wanting to upgrade, and do the second session later but he'd like to do them consecutively if possible.

"Must be nice to live in the country with quick access to the town," remarked Hartley, "which you must have had if you were able to go to a high school and work on the farm."

"There was a two and a half mile walk to the Grand Trunk station at Rockwood and Guelph is the next station but, yes, I was lucky."

"Starting lectures at half past six isn't a problem for you, then?"

"It makes a change from milking cows and cleaning out the barn," laughed Tom. "But, you're right about all the hours we've had to spend here. It would be nice to have time to explore Toronto. I strolled over to Old St. Andrews on Sunday morning. They're mostly what they call old kirk, at our church in Eden Mills, and said it was the best church to attend while I was here and I'm to bring back all the details of the new building. It just opened in March."

"Near the high school, I know. You don't sound like a Scot. Nor like my ma and pa who're from Yorkshire. More like a Londoner I'd've said, but I haven't known many Londoners."

"I am," Tom laughed. "I've had Scottish foster parents since I was twelve, though, and most of our neighbours are Scottish, too. My sister and I came out with a Scottish lady who's brought hundreds of orphans to Canada and, since a lot of her contacts are Scottish, many of us ended up in Scottish homes."

"Ánnie Macpherson?" Tom nodded, and Hartley continued. "I've heard of her. I wouldn't have taken you for a poverty-stricken orphan though – you're not exactly stereotypical."

"Our father was a schoolmaster. We learned to respect education long before we became orphans. Anyway, lots of Miss Macpherson's orphans have made their way into the professions. The families taking her children agree to ensure that they are educated according to their ability and I'm certainly not the only one who's been able to go to high school. They're good people – mostly," he added, thinking fleetingly of Maggie.

"Is your sister a teacher, too?"

"No. She went to live with a maiden lady who keeps a dry goods store. Annie – yes, my sister's named Annie, too – practically runs the place now. And she's only sixteen. We'd better stop jawing and get to work…"

"We have everything we need in the way of notes, don't we?" Hartley asked. Tom nodded, and he continued. "So, why don't you come for supper and we can work at my house instead of staying here."

They were at one of the long tables in the refectory after tea, surrounded by other students either finishing their tea or engaged in work they had been assigned, in some cases, both. Since most were from towns and villages across the province and, like Tom, boarding in small rooms with studies shared by two or three, the refectory was a more comfortable place to work on an assignment given to partners. Hartley, with his reference to 'my house' obviously was from a local family.

"Where do you live?" asked Tom.

"Yorkville – it's a little village north of the city. The street railway – the TSR – goes almost to the door and the fare's five cents each way – you can afford that and it'll be a better meal than your landlady's stew, won't it? So, is it a deal?"

"Your people won't mind?"

"With four sons and two daughters, my parents are always assured of at least one extra person for supper, usually more than one," said Hartley. "Let's get moving, though. There should be a streetcar on its way along King to Yonge Street as we speak, and we need to get over to Yonge before it gets up here."

It still felt strange to be in a city again, Tom thought, as he and Hartley hurried out onto Church Street and around the corner to Gerrard. He'd grown up in the city – a bigger city than this, yet he didn't feel as if he belonged here. His six years in the country had turned him into a farmboy!

The two young men reached Yonge Street and waved the horse-drawn streetcar to a stop. Hartley pointed out the streets and some of the buildings that they passed and explained how the swampy ground here had been drained early in the century to build the road. Beyond the immediate buildings, the less densely populated area to their left was mostly still commons. The estates of the wealthy Denison and Cruikshank families covered much of the area, although parts of the land had been sold off as large building lots. The university was along there, too. When they reached the intersection with Bloor Street, he pointed out Potter's Field, the original burying ground for the area. The caskets were being moved because the land was needed for homes and factories now – they had been in the process of re-interring them at the Necropolis for over twenty years, and were now in the process of re-burying the rest at the new Mount Pleasant Cemetery Hartley said, laughing. He didn't know if it was taking so long because there were so many bodies or because it was difficult to find workers to do such an awful job. The big inn opposite was the Red Lion, and had been there for seventy years and was popular with travellers as well as the local people. Its proximity might possibly account for the process of moving the graves being so slow. The idea had them both chuckling as the streetcar continued up the road to its terminus at the town hall.

While Hartley extolled on the wonders of the Yorkville Town Hall and pointed out the Severn Brewery further up Yonge Street, Tom watched the horses being unhitched and watered. He thought of the farm horses, grazing peacefully in the clean country air on the Halliday farm during their breaks from work. Thinking of them, he felt sorry for these hot and dusty animals who would all too shortly be hitched back up to the streetcar to take passengers down to the city – a distance comparable to the two and a half miles he was used to walking from Eden Mills to the Rockwood Grand Trunk Station every morning. He'd walk back down to his lodgings, he thought. It was silly wasting five cents on the streetcar, which had been hot and stuffy on the way up. The walk down Yonge Street in the still warm evening air would be healthier. It was all right for Hartley to ride all the time – he didn't have lodgings to pay for.

"This way," Hartley said, leading Tom down a lane branching off from the road beside the Town Hall. "Oh, look – there's Letty. She must have been at her friend's house for tea since she's carrying her school books." He cupped his hands around his mouth and shouted, "Letty!"

The girl, who had come out of one of the houses and was walking down the lane ahead of them, turned and waved, then stood and waited for them to catch up with her.

"Letty's my younger sister. She's starting her last year at the high school and wants to be a doctor. She's been influenced by my older sister's friend, Augusta, whose mother's practicing without a licence. She's qualified – studied in New York – but the College won't licence her because she's a woman."

"I don't see why women shouldn't be doctors," said Tom.

"That's not the point," Hartley told him. "The Toronto School of Medicine is allowing women in, but very few. They license them but they don't grant degrees, and the University won't take women, so it's all very complicated – and Dr. Stowe doesn't want anything to do with them… Hey, Letty, come and meet my new friend, Tom Denton."

"Hello Mr. Denton," Letty said, retracing her steps as they came nearer to her.

"Pleased to meet you, Miss Letty," Tom said.

"Let me guess," she said, laughing, "you're a Normal School student, too."

"For my sins," Tom agreed, pleased that he felt comfortable enough to sound quite blasé.

"Tom and I are working on an assignment, so I asked him to supper," put in her brother.

"I'll make sure my mother knows you have to work on an assignment," Letty said *sotto voce* to Tom, "my brother has problems with concentrating on what he's supposed to be doing and you'll never get to it unless Ma lays the law down."

Hartley, of course, overheard her as he was intended to do. "Start telling tales out of school and I just might not be so circumspect about the TWLC..." he said.

"No, no, beloved Hartley," cried Letty. "Anything but that..."

"What's the TWLC?" asked Tom.

"Letty's secret."

"It's not exactly a secret," explained Letty. "My friend Jane and I have been going to the Toronto Women's Literary Club meetings. It's a new club for women..."

"That's surely harmless enough."

"It's said to be a front for suffragettes," said Hartley. "And both Pa and Jane's father would say they're too young to get involved which, of course, they are..."

"It's not only about suffrage," Letty said, crossly. "Dr. Stowe is a brilliant woman. She talks about opening up opportunities for women generally – girls should have a right to go to high school, not just the lucky ones like us. And we should be able to go to university and have proper jobs like men. Anyway, Mr. Denton" she turned to Tom, "we don't mention the name or the initials around Pa – he thinks it's just a book club for young ladies which, in fact it is– Dr. Stowe founded it with Mrs. Sarah Anne Curzon, the poet."

"Oh, you can count on me – I won't say anything. I'm sure Hartley and I will be too busy to spend a lot of time chatting."

"Well," said Hartley, coming to a stop and waving his arm. "Here is the house that Pa built."

"Don't be silly, Hartley," said Letty, opening the gate. "Our father is a building contractor," she explained, seeing Tom's puzzled expression. "What does your father do, Mr. Denton?"

"My foster father is a farmer," said Tom. "I'm an orphan. My real father died when I was ten. He was a schoolmaster."

"Both are admirable professions," the girl said, almost as if she envied him. "I don't mean that there's anything wrong with being in the building trade. I suppose that building houses for people is as necessary as growing their food or providing their education…" Somehow she didn't sound convinced.

"Pa buys up land to subdivide and sell. He's building all the houses on the new streets in the west end of the village," Hartley said. "People are removing to Yorkville by droves and buying the lots over there. They want to be in the country. I know you must find that rather funny coming from the real country but it's very fashionable for the middle classes. This street is one of the original ones created when Mr. Bloor and Mr. Jarvis first divided the land into lots forty years ago. When Pa bought it the house was a single storey cottage, and he gradually enlarged it and put on the second storey and loft as the family grew larger. He did much of the early work himself but, as he began to get more and more involved in administering the building of houses for other people, he had to contract out the work on our house. Anyway, let's go in and get to work."

They went in and Letty disappeared upstairs, saying she'd see them at supper. Hartley explained that the ladies' voices coming from the drawing room belonged to the members of the Yorkville Ladies' Benevolent Association who were probably just leaving and, while they were doing so, they'd slip out to the kitchen to let Mrs. Hugden who, he said, helped Ma with the cooking and housekeeping, that there was a guest for supper. Then he'd introduce him to Ma after her friends had gone.

After all this was completed, the two young men settled in Hartley's room to work. Tom found himself doing all the writing while Hartley laid on his bed offering contributions from time to time. He didn't really mind. It was nicer than working in the study that he shared with three other young men at the boarding house. He missed Sam and Susanna and the endless chatter of Malcolm and Elspeth. He also found himself missing the shy presence of Jim, the young orphan boy who the Hallidays, in readiness for Tom's leaving them for the city, had taken in during the previous spring. Jim, who looked upon Tom as a mentor, had travelled the same route as Tom himself, from the London to Eden Mills, or "from Ragged London to the Garden of Eden" as Sam liked to joke, often adding that maybe all of Canada should be considered the Garden of Eden given the opportunities it held. Just two weeks ago, he'd been showing Jim how to bind the sheaves of barley as they came off the reaper. The Clifford's smart Yorkville house had little in common with the Halliday farmhouse, but it was nice to experience a family atmosphere again.

With the exception of the eldest daughter, Lydia, who had graduated from the Normal School and was now teaching in Cobourg and taking courses at Brookhurst Academy, the woman's college affiliated with Victoria College, all the Cliffords were present for supper. Hartley's mother insisted on calling it dinner – something that, to her children, was an ongoing joke. Even her husband laughed and said they may have come up in the world since arriving in the city as a simple carpenter and his bride, but back home in Yorkshire, dinner was what you ate at midday and that was good enough for him.

Hartley's oldest brother, James, worked with his father and the one in between Lydia and Hartley had lately graduated from the architectural drawing class at the Mechanics Institute. His name was George and he told Tom he was hoping to article at Langley, Langley and Burke where a spot would soon be coming available. The youngest, fourteen-year-old Percy, went to the high school with Letty. All this was explained to Tom after Mr. Clifford said grace, and Mrs Clifford served the soup. While they enjoyed the lamb cutlets that followed, he became involved in conversation with George, who was sitting beside him. He told him about Annie's friend Jimmy McGuire, who had managed to get apprenticed to the Guelph architect, Mr. John Hall and was working with him on redesigning the high school that Tom himself had attended. On his other side, Percy interrupted to tell him that he, too, wanted to be an architect but that he didn't have grand ambitions like George and would be happy to build houses for ordinary people like his father. Houses would be needed in Toronto because the city was set to grow very fast in the next few years, he said. At least, it would as long as Sir John A. won the election and put an end to the economic recession, which Mackenzie's government hadn't been able to do.

Percy and Letty, it turned out, were highly influenced by a teacher at the high school – the only man, apparently, who was allowed to teach the young ladies. He was campaigning for a Conservative government that promised to support the growth of manufacturing in the city by increasing tariffs on imports. There would be many jobs, families would come flocking to the city and they'd all need homes. There were people already talking about Yorkville becoming part of Toronto and the two world-wise high school students said that the city would grow all the way up to the third concession in a few years.

Tom found the lively conversation both fascinating and illuminating. He had not paid much attention to the upcoming election and was now receiving quite an education on the pros and cons of the platforms of the two parties. Sir John A's "Canada for Canadians" would bring back prosperity Letty said firmly, while James laughed and said that Mr. Mackenzie had the old humbug beat by a mile. Their father laughed, saying they could argue all they liked, but he was the one with the vote and, having started out in life as a simple carpenter himself, he felt more comfortable with the stonemason running the country than with the lawyer who'd already disgraced himself. Percy immediately defended Sir John A, saying that he'd been cleared of the charges of taking bribes in awarding the Pacific railway contract. It was amazing how aware Percy and Letty were of the political issues. Tom wondered if this was true of all young people in the city. Perhaps there had been boys at Guelph who were like them and he hadn't noticed because he just didn't have time – work on the farm, the journey back and forth to Guelph and lessons had filled his days. This was just as true of the year he'd spent training and teaching in

Elora which had involved yet more time travelling on trains each day. There must have been town boys who'd had interests beyond their lessons but he'd not had the time to get to know them. Of course, there had been no girls at his high school, while girls had been admitted to the Toronto Collegiate Institute for several years now. Young ladies really, he corrected himself, watching Letty's animation as she told her father that she and Percy were true Canadians who wanted to see the country grow and become powerful in the world – just like the old country.

"Well, love, that was the idea we had," he countered, laughing, "your Ma and me, when we decided to emigrate – bring up our sons in a new, developing country. I can't say I expected to have a daughter getting a taste for politics, though."

Letty appeared about to respond but stopped, glancing at Hartley who was seated next to her, and rose to collect the plates instead. Hartley had obviously been afraid she'd go too far if the topic was continued and warned her with a kick or nudge. Mrs. Clifford also rose from the table and carried the large casserole dish, from which they had helped themselves, to the sideboard. Letty deposited the pile of dirty plates there and returned with a tray of cheese and crackers while her mother brought a bowl of fruit over to the table.

"We don't normally have Niagara grapes with our cheese, Mr. Denton," Mrs. Clifford said, indicating for Tom to help himself. "One of the ladies who came to the meeting this afternoon brought a bunch for each of us. Have you ever had them before?"

Tom shook his head. He'd never heard of Niagara grapes.

"It's a grape that's being cultivated in Upper New York State," Hartley explained. "Ma's friend has a brother who's involved in the experiments there and he's shipped some to her the last couple of years. It's all very secretive and you have to swear never to try to plant the seed yourself." Tom must have continued to look perplexed because Hartley added, "It's a nice dessert grape but, of course, it's the wine that'll make their fortune in a few years."

"Winemaking in Canada?"

"Oh yes. There's already a winery right here in Toronto which started up last year, and there's another in Welland or Lincoln, or somewhere around there. These fellows have big plans for the Niagara grape and expect it to make North American wines famous. Meanwhile we get to be some of the first people to sample it."

"Something that couldn't happen in MacDonald's vision of Canada," pointed out George. "There'd be tariffs on everything coming across the border even if it was just families sending each other things."

Letty and Percy were both about to respond when Mrs. Clifford firmly said she was not prepared to listen to any more political arguments and maintained polite conversation about the first copies of the cook book to which she and her friends had contributed recipes. The book, apparently, was a unique idea of a Mrs. McMaster and was being sold to raise funds for her Hospital for Sick Children, something that especially appealed to Letty.

Walking down Yonge Street on his way home, having told Hartley that he needed the exercise after having so much to eat for supper, Tom reflected on all the things he had learned during his visit to the Cliffords' home. He hoped Hartley would repeat the invitation… not least because he'd really like to see Letty again.

* * * *

Letty Clifford thought the young man seemed interesting. He'd be good for Hartley. Her brother tended to be a slacker if there was not somebody around to help him keep his nose to the grindstone and Tom Denton was obviously a worker. It was more than that though. She must be honest with herself. She liked him. In fact, she liked him more than any other of her brothers' friends who were the only young men she knew, girls at the Toronto Collegiate Institute being taught in an entirely separate part of the building to the boys. The Rector did not believe that the girls he reluctantly admitted to his school should be taught with the boys – even the playground was fenced to keep them apart. It was only now that she, and the handful of girls who would be graduating with her, had some (albeit well chaperoned) classes with the boys and their male teachers, including the Rector himself to teach them mathematics.

Hartley was sure to bring Tom Denton home again while they were at the Normal School together. It was annoying that the strict rules for girls at school prevented them from leaving the grounds. The Normal School was, after all, only a stone's throw away from the high school and, since her brother was studying there, she should surely be allowed to meet him there, and whomever of his friends he chose to bring along. She pictured herself and her good friend, Jane, taking tea with Hartley and Tom in a public tearoom, not that she'd ever been to a public tearoom and wasn't quite sure how they looked beyond the tables and chairs, of course. Silly day dreamer, she chided herself, there was so much work ahead of her before she realized her dream of being a doctor that such fantasies were a hopeless waste of time. She had a distinct feeling, however, that she and Tom Denton would see more of each other in the days to come.

CHAPTER SEVENTEEN

Hartley did, indeed, invite Tom to supper on several more occasions during the two Normal School sessions they attended together before receiving their second class certificates. Between the two sessions, Tom went home to Eden Mills for Christmas and, by prior arrangement, brought Annie back to the city with him two days before the Normal School session began. They took the TSR up Yonge Street to Yorkville where she would stay overnight at the Cliffords' house, sleeping in the truckle bed in the bedroom Letty and sister shared.

Annie was a little diffident at first but soon blossomed in the company of Letty and her older sister Lydia, who was home for Christmas. Letty was, in fact, the instigator of the plan to bring Annie to the city. She had expressed interest in meeting Annie almost as soon as Tom told her about his sister who was younger than she was yet ran a village dry goods store almost by herself. Annie, of course, explained that Miss Bryden really just, very kindly, left things to Annie so that she could develop the skills that would ensure that she would always be able to earn her living. Annie, on her part, thought it was wonderful that Letty was able to go to high school and learn the things that boys learnt. The girls were soon chattering together as if they'd know each other all their lives, and Tom hoped that it was the beginning of a long friendship for his sister. He still felt badly that she had not been able to have the education that their father had hoped she would have, despite her telling him that education took different routes and that, in fact, Miss Bryden's accountant had told her that she knew almost as much about keeping accounts as the clerks in his office in Georgetown.

By the time Tom left to go to his lodgings, Annie was quite at home with the Cliffords. Annie and the young Cliffords, except George who was visiting a friend, accompanied Tom to the Town Hall to board the day's last streetcar, which he agreed to ride since it was beginning to snow quite heavily and he had his heavy bag to carry, having come straight up to Yorkville from Union Station. Hartley said he should stay the night with them but Tom knew that he needed to stake his claim to his old room before the landlady rented it to another student the next day.

The next morning, Tom walked up to Yorkville to meet Hartley, Letty and Annie and they spent the day showing his sister around the city before she caught the afternoon train to go home. There was now a late afternoon mail and passenger train, which would stop at Limehouse when mail or passengers were to put down there. They rode the TSR, on which sleighs now replaced streetcars down Yonge Street because of the night's snowfall, and walked to the harbour where they watched the ice yachting. Hartley, who had a little experience in the sport, explained the fundamentals. Then they went up to Gerrard Street and took Annie on a tour around the Normal School grounds including a visit to the Provincial Museum and the pavilion in the Horticultural Gardens, the gardens themselves being all but hidden under the snow. Afterwards, they had luncheon at a nearby tearoom that Tom and Hartley knew was frequented by many of the young lady students at the Normal School as a change from the school refectory and, therefore a suitable place to take Letty and Annie that wasn't too expensive, Letty's fantasy, unbeknown to the others, becoming for the most part realized.

Then, reaching Adelaide Street, as they walked back down Yonge Street, Hartley pointed out the Grand Opera House where, amazingly a spark could turn all the gaslights on at the same time. Letty told Annie about Mrs. Morrison, the manager there until last year, and said she thought it was wonderful that a woman should be the actor-manager of Canada's greatest theatre. She enthusiastically informed Annie that they'd live to see women in all sorts of men's occupations and maybe, not just voting but, electing women to parliament, too. Hartley shook his head at Tom as they listened to the conversation. Tom smiled, but he loved Letty's spirit and rather hoped Hartley would be the one to eat crow in the years to come, not that Hartley, with his affable nature, would mind at all.

They visited the shopping district on King Street, where the multi-storied emporiums with their huge variety of merchandise contrasted greatly with Bryden's Dry Goods and Staples. Annie purchased a scarf for Miss Bryden – to thank her for letting her have the time off, she said – and the others bought notebooks ready for school the next day. The street here was well cleared of snow in order to attract the many customers arriving by train, TSR and private sleighs. It was a short walk, after that, to Union Station where Annie boarded the train and they all waved goodbye.

Hartley and Letty took the TSR back to Yorkville and Tom made his way to the boarding house. He felt happy about bringing Annie to the city and was glad that there hadn't been too much snow. Annie had worried about that when Tom first suggested the trip, imagining the need to stay in Toronto, in the event of a storm, until the trains were running again. That first Christmas in Canada, when the relentless snowfall had covered the windows of Miss Bryden's store, always remained in her memory.

Christmas in Eden Mills, followed by the two days spent with his sister, made a pleasant interlude between the two sessions at the Normal School, then Tom was, once again, back to long days of study. Teaching the Model School boys was the highlight of his days. He was popular with the boys in all four levels and, since they liked him, they behaved well and Tom received high grades for his class-work for which the largest percentage of the mark was for the level of control maintained. The boys were mostly the sons of merchants and men who owned the businesses in the immediate area, and the younger ones were much like the boys and girls he had taught at the Elora Model School. The older ones, however, were more sophisticated, and Tom could well see the point of teachers being required to take the Normal School courses. He enjoyed teaching them. Unlike the boys in Elora, most expected to go to high school and then to normal school or university and, therefore had a completely different outlook on education.

At first he thought that this was because in the city, there were more opportunities for children to learn so much more about the world than country children, but soon found that it was because they came from families where it was expected that they go on to careers in commerce or professions. Many of their fathers were, themselves, graduates who now held important posts in business and government. Getting their children into the Toronto Model School was, in their parents' view, the first step to putting them on the right road for the future. He discussed it with one of the Model School teachers. Together, they came up with the theory that, if all children were taught more about the things they would need to know when they were older, they would be more amenable to attending. If they could see the use of what they were being taught, even those who attended only because the government said they had to, or whose parents only reluctantly sent them, would perhaps even want to attend for more that the minimum four months. Tom thought of children he'd taught in Elora. Boys, who could see no purpose in learning the multiplication tables, had become interested when Tom drew a picture of sheaves in a field and showed them that counting sheaves in one row and multiplying it by the total number of rows was a lot quicker than counting all the sheaves individually. The children in the Toronto Model School were growing up in the city, exposed to many different cultures, but children in rural Canada knew only village life and occupations centred on deriving a living from the land. He found himself eagerly looking forward to tailoring education to fit the circumstances of the children he would be teaching next year.

After the six days of examinations towards the end of the session, Tom was summoned for his pre-graduating interview with the principal. Since he would, most likely, be getting a Grade A second class certificate at graduation, he was encouraged to give some thought to returning to the Normal School for his first class certificate at a later date. Tom had not really given much thought to his future beyond acquiring the permanent teaching certificate now required by the new Department of Education for career teachers. He was more than a little surprised when Dr. Davies went on to say that he could quite easily follow in the footsteps of Mr. Scott, the headmaster of the Boys' Model School, and his brother-in-law, Mr. James L. Hughes, the previous headmaster who was now Chief Inspector of Toronto Public Schools. These were both young men, contemporaries at the Normal School, who had obtained their first class certificates and gone on to teach in the Model School and were now well on their way to claiming a place for themselves in Canadian education history.

"I can see I've surprised you," Dr. Davies smiled, "but I would seriously suggest you give some thought to applying for one of the several opportunities, advertised in The Globe, where the school trustees intent on keeping posts open for teachers attending Normal School and require teachers for the interim. Young people who have their second class certificates are the first to be considered for these places. If you took one of them instead of looking for a permanent position at this time, you can consider the advantages of furthering your qualifications while teaching."

Tom said that he was eager to get back to teaching but would certainly think about returning at a later date, once he had saved some money. First, he thought to himself, he must get back to the farm to help with the haying. He found himself homesick for the countryside after the year spent in the city and could scarcely wait to take the train back to the 'Garden of Eden' for the summer.

The remaining lectures advised students on how to go about applying for posts and conducting interviews with school board members. They were told to bear in mind that, while these local landowners, merchants and professionals were interviewing them as prospective teachers, it was also their opportunity to ensure that these men and, occasionally women too, respected the qualifications they had worked so hard to acquire and were prepared to compensate them accordingly.

Tom delayed his departure for a couple of days after the end of the Normal School session to attend Letty's high school graduation tea party. Letty had asked him to escort her. Mothers and, in some cases, fathers were present to celebrate their children's achievements, and prizes were handed out but, for the graduates, the dance was the highlight of the afternoon. Tom had been to village dances and could dance adequately but was rather doubtful about going to a dance in the city, even if it was only an afternoon high school event. However he found that he by no means discomforted his partner and they both enjoyed themselves. Letty had scored the highest marks in her class and would be going to Cobourg in September as a student at Brookhurst Academy, the ladies' institution affiliated to Victoria College. She looked forward to starting to work towards her elusive goal of one day being one of the first few women to achieve a medical degree, but, for now, was happy to bask in the triumph of the present… and dancing with Tom.

Letty, and Hartley too, came down to see him off when, at last, Tom left Union Station for the farm in Eden Mills that he still considered home. Both were hoping to be able to make the journey west sometime during the summer to visit with Tom and Annie but, as Tom explained, June and July were busy months on the farm and their visit must be put off until August. Meantime, they would correspond. As the whistle blew, Letty quickly kissed Tom on the cheek, begging Hartley not to tell their parents. Embarrassed, but pleased, Tom stepped up into the car and waved to them as the train moved out of the station, then stowed his grip on the rack and settled down to read the advertisements in The Globe. Hartley had accepted the junior teacher post offered to him by the board of directors at the new two-room schoolhouse his father's firm had built in the fast developing area west of Yorkville. Tom didn't envy his friend for having an influential father and had politely declined offers of help in acquiring a post in the city. He told Hartley what Dr. Davies had said about returning to the Normal School for a first class certificate and explained that he'd rather be in the country while he decided what he wanted to do. Hartley had teasingly suggested that he might have felt differently had Letty been staying in Yorkville. Tom wondered if this might be true but didn't admit to it. Letty had confided to him that she felt certain that her family expected her ambition to recede when she saw all her friends getting married and having children but that they were wrong – she was determined to become a doctor. Tom pointed out that both Dr. Stowe and Dr. Trout had married long before they became doctors. Letty had looked at him wonderingly for a moment, then laughed and said she'd take one thing at a time, and first came the scientific courses she had enrolled in at Brookhurst.

It was after this conversation that Tom had begun to give serious thought to Dr. Davies's proposal for his future. Taking the first class certificate and qualifying to teach in a model school where he could concurrently work towards a university degree would put him on the road to teaching in high school or becoming a school principal.

Reading *The Globe* as the train chugged into Parkdale, Tom spotted the advertisement that would solve his dilemma. It was at Norval-on-the Credit, a town on Grand Trunk line that he'd actually be passing through on his way home. The board members were requesting a junior teacher to assist the principal at the two-room schoolhouse while the incumbent attended the Normal School – at least that was what he assumed from the notice. He had visited the village on two or three occasions with Sam and Susanna and the children, when he was younger. He remembered jogging along the York Road in the farm cart and visiting Annie at the store on the way there or back. They had taken her with them once. It must have been a village fair or some kind of celebration. Once he started high school, there had been no time for such outings.

The Grand Trunk railway station there was quite some distance up a hill from the village itself so that little could be seen from the train. He did take more notice of the area when he arrived there, however, and read the advertisement again:

Teacher required to assist principal, as of September, during absence of incumbent.

Position includes teaching basic science and physics at Mechanics' Institute. Second Class certificate mandatory. Recent graduates welcome to apply.

Forward details to:

Mr. R. Noble,

Secretary,

Board of SS7 Esquesing,

Norval, Ontario.

Tom folded the newspaper and determined to write his application this evening while he visited his sister and put it in the post at Limehouse before he caught the early train on to Rockwood in the morning. Miss Bryden possibly knew who was on the school board. She might even know somebody who could put in a good word for him. And, if there was somebody on the board who was also a session member at the church known to a session member at his own church – well, then, there was another meaningful character reference. He was beginning to feel that the position was within his grasp. He could most likely board where the regular teacher lived and walk to the school. Even if the position was available only during the "incumbent's" first session at the Normal School, he'd be able to save enough to finance the year's course for a first class certificate and if the position was for the entire school year, he'd be almost wealthy. After all, he'd be earning a full salary, unlike the year before last at the Elora Model School when he'd managed to save enough to support himself in Toronto this year despite the minimal earnings paid to new third class certificate teachers, thanks in part, of course, to Sam who'd paid him labourer's wages last summer.

The train's whistle pierced his thoughts and he realised, with a start that they'd passed through Georgetown and were rounding the bend and traversing the planked road as they approached Limehouse. He rolled the newspaper and slid it into his pocket, and pulled his bag down from the rack. The train slowed to a stop and there was Annie on the platform, anxiously peering into each window as it passed her. She spotted him and, smiling happily, ran towards him and opened the door. He jumped down onto the platform, dropped the grip and hugged her.

* * * *

Harriet couldn't imagine living on the farm that Tom so vividly described in his letters. Annie's shop was a little easier but she knew it was not much like the shops on the Bow Road, it being what they called a country store with a stable, although they didn't actually keep a horse, and trees and shrubs and lots of space at the back for growing fruit and vegetables. The farm where Tom was working until he started being a teacher again was much harder to imagine, but then she had always lived in the city in a house that was part of a terrace. Uncle Alfred's house was at the end of the terrace but the road was narrow and the next terrace little more than twelve feet away and the little backyards only separated the houses by a stone's throw. Everything was close together in London. She really couldn't imagine living in the country among the trees and meadows. Both Tom and Annie had written about how the birds singing in the trees would wake them in the morning. The sparrows did sing in their back yard at Bow, but she had never actually been awakened by their singing. Maybe Canadian birds sang louder.

Perhaps one day she'd see Canada – she knew that Miss Macpherson sometimes took people out to visit children who were now grown up and married – brothers, sisters, mothers. One day when Tom and Annie were married and had homes of their own and after she had finished her pupil teacher years and attended the training college to be a certificated teacher, she would go and see Miss Macpherson about it. She could help look after the little children and teach some of the older ones about the land they were going to live in. She knew a lot more about it than anybody at school because of all the letters she received from the brother and sister she hadn't seen for so many years. It would be a long time before she could go, but she'd really like to see them again. It was different for John. He had only been a baby when their mother died so he had only ever known life with Uncle Alfred and Aunt Ella. She was old enough to remember Tom and Annie, especially Annie who had been her constant companion during their mother's illness. She remembered, too, the room in the slums down Poplar way where they had lived – not a happy memory, except for the images of Annie or Tom telling her bedtime stories while the other one worked on the matchboxes and Annie taking her shopping for their meagre supplies, leaving Tom to look after Ma and the baby for a bit. That was what she'd say, relieved to get out of the room for half an hour. One morning, Annie had taken her up to the matchbox factory but she had walked too slowly and they'd nearly made Tom late for school. Ma had been cross with Annie, which wasn't really very fair since it wasn't Annie who walked too slowly, and said she wasn't to take her again. Tom getting to school was the most important thing. Tom, she knew, felt badly about Ma always insisting on Annie arranging everything around him getting to school but Annie always smiled and said she didn't mind.

Harriet was in standard six this year and would be able to apply to be a probationer when she passed her exams. She was glad that Uncle Alfred believed in children going to school unlike the fathers of many of the children who had left school after standard five because their parents thought it was a waste of time and they should be contributing to the family's income instead. These were large families, of course, and their attitude was understandable. She knew she was lucky to live with an uncle and aunt who had no children of their own and could afford for their niece and nephew to go to school. Once she was a pupil teacher, she'd be able to hand most of her small wage to Aunt Ella to pay for her food, and she'd buy the material with the rest to make her clothes – even to be a probationer, she'd need more grown up dresses after all. Annie must wear very grown-up dresses serving her customers in the shop but, of course, Annie was almost grown up now. She most likely wore her hair up and was quite the young lady. Harriet wondered how she would look herself with her hair up like a lady… but Aunt Ella would say that thirteen was much too young.

CHAPTER EIGHTEEN

"…and, dearest Harriett," Annie wrote, *"I hope you and John will like the enclosed cabinet card photograph. Joe, one of Miss Bryden's nephews, drove me into Georgetown in the trap when he went to the new Mechanic's Institute there, so that I could meet Tom, who walked up from Norval after school. Tom discovered the photographer's studio when he had terrible toothache and his landlady sent him to the dentist. Yes, the photographer is also the dentist. Perhaps that should be the other way around. He was a dentist first and became so interested in the art of photography that he bought a camera and turned one of the rooms in his house into a studio. I know that barbers used to pull teeth out in the olden days before dentists had to have licences, but I'd never heard of a photographer being a dentist. However, it was great fun. When he heard that the photograph was for our little sister and brother who we hadn't seen for eight years, Mr Bennett the photographer-dentist, said he would make seven copies and only charge the amount advertised for six copies. Tom and I can now have one each and I am going to give one to Miss Bryden and one to my friend Jimmy. I expect Tom will give one to the Hallidays and one to Letty. I've told you about our friend, Letty, who wants to be a doctor, I'm sure. She has been told that she will be allowed to attend the School of Medicine lectures at Victoria College in Cobourg, the town where she has been attending a young ladies' academy…"*

She put down her pen and read the letter through from the beginning. She wrote to Harriett once a month and had done so ever since she arrived in Canada. In the early days, her letters had been delivered by Miss Macpherson or one of the other ladies from the House of Industry. As she grew older and was paid a small wage, she began to mail them herself so that the children had news of her regularly instead of receiving two or three or even a small bundle of letters each time one of the ladies arrived back in London. Now that her little brother John could read and write, she wrote separately to him although she put both letters in the same envelope to save on the cost of stamps. This letter was special though. This year Miss Bryden was, at last, going to make her journey back to the old country and Annie would be in charge of the store, by herself, for the whole summer. Miss Bryden would take the package with the photograph and letters from Annie and Tom to their brother and sister and post it when she reached Glasgow, drastically shortening the length of time it usually took for letters to travel from Limehouse, Ontario, Canada to Bow, north of Limehouse, Middlesex, England. Miss Bryden, herself, would then embark on the long railway journey from Glasgow to Kelso where she would stay with cousins she had not seen since she was a small child. Annie imagined herself visiting Harriet one day in the future when they were both old ladies like Miss Bryden and her cousins.

Jimmy had once said that when he had finished his apprenticeship and become established as an architect they would be married and visit both London and Londonderry on their honeymoon. Of course this was just a dream. Annie knew that it would take years for Jimmy to become established despite Mr.

Hall having said that he was 'definitely a talented young man and had the ability to create what people needed'. Quite apart from that, Jimmy had never actually asked her to marry him. He had just made the remark on one of his rare visits home when he'd been talking about buildings and cities, and how he'd like to see some of the architecture in London. She hadn't taken it very seriously because she didn't think she was really meant to. Afterwards she had wondered if she would like to be a wife and decided that she preferred working for Miss Bryden and did not want to leave Limehouse to live in Guelph where she knew nobody but Jimmy.

"Annie. Annie lass."

Miss Bryden calling up the stairs put an end to Annie's reverie. She wiped her pen, put it down and started down the stairs. Miss Bryden was standing beside an overflowing steamer trunk, wringing her hands.

"The family's here in the trap already, so I have to be off but Dugald says he wants to take the steamer trunk over to the station before he unharnesses Bess. He's dropping Mary and the boys at the hotel and coming back in a minute. Trouble is, I can't get the lid down enough to close it so, what I thought was, if I sit on it – me being the heavier one – you could fasten the straps…"

Annie laughed. "Just sit there and stop getting yourself into such a stew. You should get them to put some brandy in your tea at the hotel – you're not going to enjoy it if you don't calm down…"

Miss Bryden looked shocked. "Not on the Sabbath, lass."

"I'm just joking. Now sit down and let me fasten it. I hear the trap outside."

Miss Bryden's brothers came in as Annie finished pulling the straps through the hasps on the front of the trunk. Miss Bryden arose, still looking worried. Annie took her keys from her and safely locked her possessions away, then the two men each took a handle of the steamer trunk and carted it out to the trap. Miss Bryden's worried look turned to one of alarm.

"Oh my Lor'" she said.

"Come on now," Annie said, handing back the bunch of keys. "I'll get your bonnet and we'll go out and wait for them to come back. You're going to have a nice farewell – *bon voyage*, they call it in books, although I never actually heard anyone say that – a nice tea at the hotel, then we'll be off to evening service, have a cold collation for supper, then it's off to bed for an early night. You have a long day ahead of you tomorrow."

"Och, you're right, and there's no way I'll be able to sleep on that train, and it's such a long journey…"

Annie personally thought the motion of the train would send her to sleep in no time, but Miss Bryden swore that she would never be able to sleep in a train. She'd only ever been to Guelph on a train, and once to Toronto, but she just knew that the chugging and whistles would keep her awake all the way to Montreal, where she was boarding the ship for Glasgow.

Once the Brydens were all off to the hotel and Bess was happily munching the grass beyond the vegetable garden at the back of the store, Annie poured herself a mug of Miss Bryden's sweet apple cider and ran back up to her room to finish her letters. There was so much to tell Harriet and John. Tom was coming to stay with her while Miss Bryden was away, riding over to Eden Mills each morning on the pony Sam Halliday was lending him – they'd made the garden shed which, in fact, been a stable in Miss Bryden's father's day, into a temporary home for her. Tom would be coming tomorrow afternoon, which was the last day of school, then he would take the early train over to the farm in the morning. He was working there again for most of the summer and would be going to Toronto in August to enrol in more sessions at the Normal School and at the University, too. Sam was glad to have him back again and made the offer of the pony because he said that taking the train and walking to the farm from Rockwood was a waste of time when the pony would get Tom there and back far more quickly and in his own time. It was getting very warm now, she told Harriet, and there was a large crop of strawberries in the yard, which she must pick very soon now. She would be making the jam all by herself this year, although her friend Mary-Ann might be able to come and help her if her mother didn't need her to assist in their jam-making. She had nearly finished making her dress for Alison Armstrong's wedding. Alison was having four attendants, which nobody in the village had ever heard of before, but Miss Bryden had acquired the material for all five girls' dresses at a very reasonable price so it wasn't as wastefully lavish as it sounded. As she described this to Harriet, Annie thought again about the possibility of marrying Jimmy – the dress could easily serve as a wedding dress. Jimmy still had years of his apprenticeship to do so, even if he had been serious, it was silly to think about such things yet. Alison and Mary-Ann, while they had become her friends, were both several years older than she was and, naturally, would marry before she did. She must put the whole idea out of her head and get back to the letter.

When the long letter was finally finished, Annie folded it, along with the one to John, around the cabinet card photograph and placed everything including Tom's letters, given to her at the photographer's studio, in the envelope, which she had already addressed to her uncle's house in Bow. She took it downstairs and placed it on the hallstand ready to go in Miss Bryden's travelling bag in the morning. There was already a book by Mary Agnes Fleming there and an American serial magazine. Miss Bryden was expecting to do a lot of reading on her journey. The Brydens were back by this time and already re-harnessing Bess. Annie put on her bonnet and went out to walk along to the church with the boys while the older Brydens rode in the trap.

The next day passed in a whirl. Annie walked down to the station with the nervously chattering Miss Bryden and found a number of villagers on the platform waiting to wave the popular storekeeper goodbye, as well as to advise her on how to call porters to transport her luggage throughout the journey. She stood back as Miss Bryden's friends jostled to hug her goodbye, watching as the train arrived and the steamer trunk was loaded into the caboose. Then Mr. Pulford handed Miss Bryden up into the car and shut the door and everybody, including Annie waved madly as the train moved off with Miss Bryden still standing at the window waving back.

She walked back up to the store with some of her neighbours and they became the first customers of a very busy day, for people came in throughout the day to ask if Miss Bryden had got off all right on her long-awaited journey back to the old country. In the late afternoon, the errand boy from the station brought up the scheduled order of straw hats, news of which travelled through the village at lightning speed and brought a number of customers into the store who would not otherwise have come in. It was haymaking time and it seemed that almost everybody needed a new straw hat. Since most of the farm families, at this time of the year purchased on credit, this entailed careful account-keeping, and Annie was kept busy way beyond closing time. At last, she was able to set about closing up and had removed the cash from the drawer under the counter and locked it away in the strongbox. She was wiping down the counter when Tom arrived. He had walked most of the way from Norval, through Hungry Hollow, but a carter had given him a ride up from Stewartown to Henderson's Corners. From there he had walked along to the village with a couple of men coming home from work at the Williams Mill.

"I only brought what I needed," he told her, putting his pack down near the stairs, "and a belated birthday present for my favourite sister. I'll borrow Sam's pony trap tomorrow evening and go down and fetch the rest of my things before I come back here for supper. I'll wash the floor for you, if you like, and you can make the supper – I'm hungry after that long walk. Miss Bryden get off all right?"

"I've been asked that question a hundred times today," laughed Annie, going into the back room and through to the scullery. "Of course she got off all right. Although it was touch and go with her packing yesterday. Luckily, her brothers forced her to finish by insisting on taking the steamer trunk over to the station before they took her for tea at the hotel."

Tom followed her and pumped water into the pail then fetched a mop and went back into the store to wash the floor. Annie sliced bread, mutton and cheese, put pickled onions, beets and dilled cucumber into serving dishes and set the table for their supper. Then she ran out to the garden and picked some strawberries, which she brought in, washed and put into two dessert dishes. Tom finished washing the floor and took the pail down to the cesspool to empty before the two of them sat down to supper.

Tom left the table and went to get his pack while Annie whipped cream to go with the strawberries. He brought out several small packages of cakes and cookies that the children had given him as farewell gifts. There were also handmade cards wishing him well.

"Were you sad to be leaving them?" Annie asked, bringing the strawberries and cream to the table and sitting down again.

"It was hard after seeing how some of them progressed during the year and knowing that I'll be far away in Toronto when they come back to school after the summer. That's part of being a schoolteacher, I suppose. Even if you do stay at one school for several years, your pupils are always going to be moving on and, well, your job is over, isn't it?"

"It's never forgotten though, is it? I mean schoolteachers make a big impression on children, don't they? You don't know it when you're a child but, as you grow older, you see how much influence they had on the way you think and feel about things."

"True, I suppose," agreed Tom. "Have you forgotten that I said I had a birthday present for my favourite sister?" He held up a small box.

"No, of course not. You shouldn't say that, though. You only have two sisters, so it's unfair."

"Well, Harriet's hardly likely to hear about it. But, you're right. I'm sorry. Happy birthday, late though it is."

Annie took the box from him and opened it. She held up the seed pearl pendant on its silver chain.

"It's beautiful, Tom," she said, tears coming to her eyes. "But you shouldn't have spent so much money…"

"It's for your eighteenth birthday, Annie. A girl – that is, a young lady – should have something to keep for always on her eighteenth birthday. It's what mother and father would have wanted."

"Thank you, Tom." She stood up and kissed his cheek. "Can you do it up for me?"

Tom fastened the chain and sat down again. "Now let's sit down and eat our strawberries. We can have the shortbread squares with them. The little girl who helped her mother make them told me that her father said they are the best he's ever tasted. Have you thought any more about becoming a school-teacher, Annie? You're eighteen now and no longer need to stay here."

Annie smiled. "You're the teachers in the family, Tom – you and Harriet who, it seems, is very serious about it. As I keep telling you, I like being a store clerk. I really do. And, what would Miss Bryden do without me? I couldn't leave her. She let me get more education that she was obliged to do, and has taught me so much about ordering and how to deal with drummers and bartering, and with delinquent customers – so well that she can go away for two months and leave me in charge of her store! Besides, I care about her, just as you care about the Hallidays…"

"All right. I just want to make sure that you have the same opportunities as I've had because I know that's what Pa would have wanted. I can't do anything about Harriet and John but I know that Uncle Alfred will respect Pa's wishes – well, I'm sure he will with John, but Aunt Ella might have other plans for Harriet now that she'll be finished with the upper class… Anyway, if you're sure you don't want any further education, I won't mention it again."

"Tom," laughed Annie, "we continue our education all our lives, don't you see that. I mean, I was last in the schoolroom when I was fourteen – learning double-entry bookkeeping that summer, remember? But that wasn't the last time I received education. I receive that every day because I learn something new every day. Miss Bryden and I have been reading Thomas Hardy's novels of late in the evening. Joe and Doug borrow them from the Mechanic's Institute library for us. They're supposed to be improving their own minds by reading good literature but they say they don't have time. Harriet, by the way, has applied to be a probationer… with Aunt Ella's agreement. I had a letter last week."

Tom smiled and rose from the table, picking up some of the dishes as he did so. "That's wonderful. Come along. I'll help you with the dishes, then you can show me how well the garden's growing before it gets dark."

"No. You leave them alone. I'll look after them. There's a pan on the stove with the water already warm so it'll only take me a few minutes. Go along outside where it's cooler now. I'll be out in a little while and we'll water the vegetable plants."

Annie hummed to herself as she put the left over food away in the pantry and set about washing the dishes. It would be nice having her brother here for the summer. Of course, she wouldn't see much of him as he'd be leaving early in the morning and coming back probably after supper or, at least, to a late supper most nights. But, it would more than she'd seen of him than anytime since Dr. MacGhie had taken them to the Refuge in Spitalfields and he'd been placed with the boys and she with the girls.

CHAPTER NINETEEN

When Tom left for Toronto at the end of August, he was able to rent his old room on Sherbourne Street again. Jimmy McGuire had been designated to oversee the building of a new stone church at Rockwood and had agreed to live at his parent's farm for the next two weeks, going daily to the site. He would drop into the store and see Annie each morning and evening on his way to and from the station. Annie and Jimmy would be seeing more of each other than they had done since Annie's early years in Limehouse when Jimmy was still at Gibralter School with her. Tom knew that they had been good friends then and had remained so despite Jimmy being a weekly boarder while at high school in Oakville, then living in Guelph. Although Annie assured him that she had plenty of friends to look out for her, he was glad Jimmy would be around to see that everything was all right until Miss Bryden returned. Well into his architectural apprenticeship now, this was the first time Jimmy had experienced so much responsibility but, as he explained, he had worked exclusively with his boss on the commission. A busy architect like John Hall could hardly be expected to be in Rockwood every day so, since Jimmy's family lived nearby and he knew many of the tradesmen in the area, it would be convenient for everybody for Jimmy to take over entirely. Jimmy could scarcely believe his good fortune because, in addition to building the church, he'd be in position to find out about other possibilities to tender for work in the area.

The Normal School Session did not begin until the next week but Letty was home and she and Tom had arranged through their letters, which had remained constant during the year that she was in Cobourg and he in Norval and on through the summer, to spend a few days together before Letty left for Cobourg again. Brookhurst Academy had closed but Letty, with the help of the family of her sister Lydia's great friend Augusta Stowe, had been accepted among a handful of female students to take courses at Victoria College. These would enable her to eventually sit the matriculation examinations set by the College of Physicians and Surgeons, although it was not likely that the hospitals would allow women to intern in the foreseeable future. Like Augusta's mother, private practice would be the only option for both her and Augusta and any other woman who wanted to be doctor as obtaining a licence without the required internship could take years. Tom found it hard to believe that even studying to become a doctor should be so complicated but Letty told him that it was only because the Medical School didn't really want women students. She had spent the summer helping at the Toronto Free Dispensary and had been pleasantly surprised at how gracious the doctors there were in training her to assist the people for whom they were the only option for medical care. She'd been quite prepared for them to treat her as doctors everywhere were known to treat their uneducated nurses, and her family hadn't expected her to endure the experience for very long – perhaps, even, to give up the idea of being a doctor altogether. However, the experience had strengthened her resolve, and when Tom arrived in Yorkville, she talked so much about the work that he was reduced to nodding and smiling until Hartley, who had escorted his mother to a garden party, and the lady herself came home.

"My goodness, Tom," said Mrs. Clifford, "you're as brown as a berry. We townies look quite pale by comparison."

"Good afternoon, Mrs. Clifford," Tom replied, "I apologise for arriving a little early. I must have walked faster than I intended. Letty thought it would be all right to let me in since you were expected home any minute."

"Oh, you don't need to worry about that, Tom. Why, you're almost one of the family – at least, you were before you decided to hide yourself away in the country. You're as bad as Lydia. She likes her little country school down near Cobourg so much and they like her so well that she's been engaged for another year. Of course, it's just as well since Letty's going back there and can live with her big sister which puts our minds at rest. All this studying at a university with male students, it's very worrying for Mr. Clifford and me."

"There's nothing wrong with the country, Mother," said Letty. "You'd love the little village where Tom's sister lives – all the little villages between Toronto and Guelph, in fact. They're just the way Yorkville must have been when you first came here, before we were born."

"And before father started building houses," put in Hartley.

"Now don't you start criticizing your pa, my lad," Mrs. Clifford resorted to her native Yorkshire vernacular in defence of her husband. "We certainly wouldn't have been able to give you children the education you're all getting if he hadn't done so well in his business. Why, you might have been an errand boy or working in a factory if it weren't for your father's success. Now, I must go up and take my hat off, then see how thing's are going in the kitchen. I imagine Letty's asked you to stay for dinner, Tom?"

"Yes, Mrs. Clifford. If that's all right with you."

"Of course. Now why don't you young people go out into the garden until dinner's ready? Letty, you get some lemonade and take it out to the summerhouse."

Tom and Hartley went out into the garden behind the house and were soon followed by Letty, bearing a tray with glasses and a jug of lemonade. Tom thought fleetingly of the apple cider that was the drink of choice in Eden Mills and in Limehouse on a hot day.

"So you're back in the city for the year," said Hartley. "How were things at the Normal School when you went in to register?"

"Dr. Davies is back already making preparations for the year. Told me he was glad I was taking his advice and suggested I go into the university and get a prospectus to see if I can get started on a baccalaureate by fitting one or two of the junior level courses into my schedule. He seems to be convinced I should aim at becoming a board of education bureaucrat..."

"... and you want to teach country boys to become farmers," Hartley finished for him. "You're lucky you don't have our parents, isn't he Letty? Ma would be telling you to be a bureaucrat and Pa would want you educating farm boys. You'd have to duck out like me and just be an ordinary elementary schoolmaster which has its up-side, you know. If you hadn't had to save your salary and then make more money working on the farm to support yourself while you study some more, you'd have been able to explore the country with me. I have to show you what I bought in Montreal."

Hartley jumped up and ran into the house.

"He bought a camera," Letty told Tom. "He's driving us all crazy. At least, he was. He's run out of money now but, I expect once school starts and he's getting paid again, he'll be buying more plates. It's a new process. He'll tell you about it. How's Annie?"

"Annie sends her love. She says she'd like to come to the city again after Christmas like she did when I was here before. That's if your mother doesn't mind her staying here again. I imagine Victoria University will let you out for Christmas... Anyway, she was writing to you when I left so you should get her letter before you leave for Cobourg on Friday."

"Of course, we'll be 'let out' for Christmas. It'll be lovely if she comes back with you for a couple of days. She must be so grown up, though – being in charge of a store all by herself. I hope she doesn't find me childish."

"Don't be silly. She admires you for fighting your way into a man's world. So do I."

"I wish my father did. He still thinks I'll tire of it and give up. But I won't."

Hartley came back at that point, carrying a small wooden box and a photograph album.

"It's a new kind of camera," he said, holding the wooden box out for Tom to take. "They had just come in from England and I thought that, if I was going to see the country, I should record what I was seeing. You see, it doesn't have to be processed right away. The photograph is recorded on what they call a dry plate – glass covered with bromide and gelatine. The first lot I had came with the camera but there's a factory in Rochester, New York, that's shipping them to Toronto so they're reasonably priced. I don't have any at the moment. I'm going to learn to make my own and set myself up a dark room, but have to get back to work and earn some money first. Here's all the photographs I took in Quebec and Halifax, St. John in New Brunswick, and I went to Charlottetown, too."

Tom looked at the photographs and half wished he had gone with Hartley.

"Annie and I could have had you take a photograph of us. We went to the dentist in Georgetown, who has become a photographer, early in the summer, so that Miss Bryden could post it to our little sister and brother when she got to the old country."

"Hartley talked Father into paying for some plates and the processing so that he could take some family photographs," Letty told him. "Show those ones to Tom, Hartley."

Hartley went back into the house again. Tom took the cabinet card from his pocket and held it out to her. "I thought you might like a copy of the photograph Annie and I had taken to send to England. Although, I imagine, with Hartley's new hobby, you'll have lots of photographs to keep in your room in Cobourg."

Letty smiled. "That's not quite the same thing as a young gentleman friend giving me his picture," she said.

"Annie's in it, too."

"Well, Annie's my friend, too. We write to each other all the time, you know. She told me about the photograph back at the beginning of the summer. She said your other sister is trying to get your uncle to have a picture taken of them to send to you both. I would think it's less expensive over there. Hartley says London is the centre for advances in photography now, but he thinks this man in Rochester is going to provide competition in the future. Anyway, thank you for the photograph. Let's show it to Hartley."

"I'm a bit afraid to now that he's become such an expert. He'll probably tell me he could have done a better job."

Hartley brought out the album of family photographs he'd taken and admired the professional picture of Tom and Annie, saying that he was more interested in landscape photography and had only taken the portraits so that his father would be able to see that the camera was an acquisition worth having. Mrs Clifford sounded the gong she kept in the dining room to call everybody for meals just then, and the three of them went indoors.

Later, walking back to his lodgings, Tom reflected on how stimulating visits to the Clifford house were. Perhaps dinner conversations would have had the same effect in the house near Bow Common if his family had been lucky enough to remain together. Of course, Ma hadn't had Mrs. Clifford's desire for the gentility of dinner instead of supper in the evening but they would, most certainly, have had soup and freshly baked bread before going to bed, and discussed the events of the day. Pa would probably be the headmaster at one of the area schools by now… Tom told himself to stop dreaming and think about what was really happening instead. He hoped Annie was all right by herself in Limehouse. Wouldn't it be wonderful if he could telephone her? Mr. Clifford had purchased one of the new inventions for his office. They were already stringing the wire to add his telephone to the exchange, he had announced at dinner. Soon all businesses would have one – wouldn't be able to operate without one, he had said. The telephone directory, published last year, had fifty-six subscribers and there were lots more already. One day every street would be lined with telephone poles with wires leading to every house – at least, that's what people were saying. Many wondered if it might prove dangerous.

The next morning, Tom went to the university bursar's office to pick up a prospectus and sat on one of the benches in the gardens at the front of the building to read through it. Concentrating on the compulsory courses, he compared the class times with his Normal School schedule. Dr. Davies had said that all the junior level courses repeated a fair amount of the material that had earned him his first class academic certificate from high school and his second class grade A teacher's certificate and that his Normal School timetable could easily accommodate two courses. Thirteen were needed for a degree and a degree was needed to be a high school teacher. He was, apparently, eligible for a number of scholarships which would help with the cost of continuing to work on the courses required for an honours degree. A first class teacher's certificate would provide him with specialist credentials for teaching either science or mathematics, which in turn would give him regular free periods during school hours in which to attend university lectures. This, Dr. Davies assured him was the way it was done and many of his better students had become high school teachers this way. His other option was, once the Normal School session was over, to finance staying in the city and enrolling in more university courses by advertising himself as a tutor for boys who needed help with the high school entrance examination. There would be families looking for help in the New Year as the end of the school year came into sight and getting a high school place took precedence. He needn't make the decision yet but decided that he would take Dr. Davies's advice and start working on the degree and made his way back into the university bursar's office to enrol in the junior level Latin and mathematics courses. It would be sad to see so much of his carefully saved money spent so quickly but it put him on the road to finding bursaries to help finance his studies and prove to be worth the expense.

Returning to his lodgings, he wrote the letter he had promised to Annie, letting her know he had arrived safely, although what could happen to him on a train between Limehouse and Toronto he couldn't imagine, but that's the way sisters worry about nothing. He told her about enrolling at the university as well as at the Normal School this morning and that he would be meeting the Cliffords and riding out to the west end of the city on TSR to go to the Toronto Industrial Exhibition this afternoon and would post the letter on his way to meet them. He also told her he'd write and tell her all about the Exhibition this evening but, after that, she was to expect only short notes because he would be too busy to do more than attend lectures and study.

The letter he wrote that evening described the exhibits in the Crystal Palace. Hartley, he told Annie, had warned him that they were only going to the Crystal Palace and, if he wanted to look at 'cows and things', he'd have to make another trip out by himself. As if he hadn't spent enough time with 'cows and things' throughout the summer! Seriously, he continued, they really must arrange, perhaps next year, for Annie to come and visit the Exhibition – the TSR would be expanded to run right to the Exhibition by then, so it was said. Letty, too, would probably be writing to tell her all about their afternoon, so he'd just describe all the new inventions that were demonstrated and leave Letty to tell her about the ladies' things. He wrote several long paragraphs about phonographs and typewriters and what they were and how they worked; about cameras, including almost a page about Hartley's photography and about the electric light bulbs, which would one day light every home, until he found himself falling asleep at the desk. Hurriedly finishing the letter in the communal study, he went to his room, quickly undressed and was soon sound asleep.

* * * *

A few days later it was Letty's turn to board a train. Her journey was in the opposite direction to the one from which Tom had returned. She and her sister Lydia, who was still teaching at her Cobourg school, were taken by cab to Union Station in company with their mother who wanted to be with her daughters as long as possible. She continually bemoaned the fact that they both should spend the school year so far away and wondered why she, of all the ladies she knew, should have the ill-fortune of losing her daughters to, not marriage as everybody else did, but to the desire to have men's occupations. Why was she not blessed with daughters who followed feminine pursuits? Instead, one had rushed off here, there and everywhere all summer to meetings with those Stowe women and the other had volunteered to work in a dispensary full of ruffians. Now, both would be off out-of-town until Christmas. The sisters were relieved to finally wave goodbye to their mother and her complaints as the train chugged out of the station.

Letty could not help feeling excited as they journeyed towards Cobourg and Victoria College. There had been a few special lectures there last year, which the young ladies from Brookhurst Academy had been allowed to attend. This year, although the College of Physicians and Surgeons refused to register women as matriculated medical students, she would be a *bona fide* student alongside the men studying first year physiology, chemistry, botany and anatomy, although she had been told that she would not be able to attend certain lectures, instead would have to study by herself with *Grey's* and *Heath's Practical Anatomy*. Augusta's mother, who had finally been granted a licence this summer, having practised without one for many years, had persuaded the college principal, Mr. Nelles, to admit Letty to Victoria College to study medicine as he had her daughter Augusta last year. Working at the Free Dispensary during the summer, Letty had decided that it really didn't matter that the hospitals wouldn't allow female graduates to intern. She could do what other female medical graduates did and go to New York to intern and be licensed, but she would really prefer to give up on the idea of working in a hospital until, perhaps, Dr. Stowe's vision of a women's hospital came to fruition, and start a private practice, instead and be able to look after poor people who otherwise couldn't afford to see a doctor. Like Dr. Stowe, she would probably eventually get licensed that way.

"Poor Ma," said Lydia, breaking into Letty's thoughts. "She really doesn't understand the importance of the need for women to have the same opportunities as men in education and work. She'd much prefer us to help her with her various committees until 'Mr. Right' comes along."

"I think she's already decided that Tom's my Mr Right and she's very suspicious of the letters that you've been telling her are from a lady friend called Susan all summer," Letty replied. "She thinks the handwriting is too manly for a woman. I just said that Susan was a large person and very forthright so her handwriting sort of matched her personality. Since she's imaginary, I didn't think there was any harm in giving her some characteristics. I don't know why you don't just tell her that a charming Irishman wants to marry you, but you want to carry on at the school."

"You know why I can't tell her. She'd have the church booked the next day she's so eager to get me married off. You wait, she'll be the same way with you in a couple of years, and the only reason she'll wait that long is because she knows Tom can't afford a wife until he's finished his studies."

"Yes, and my degree will take a lot longer…"

"She won't see that as a barrier to marriage. You know that…"

"Well, I do. The way things are, it'll take long enough without getting further delayed – oh, of course Tom is a modern young man and won't expect me to give everything up and run a home. He wants me to get that medical degree as much as I do but, once he's finished having to juggle teaching and studying and is qualified for whatever level of teaching he decides to engage in, he'll need a permanent home. And that'll mean starting our marriage possibly far apart from each other because I most likely won't be able to live in that permanent home during college sessions. Far better to wait until the College grants me a degree and we'll know where we are. I know that getting licensed is not likely to follow as it would for a man, but I will be able to set up a dispensary and attend poor people wherever Tom happens to be teaching and, perhaps, even start a small practice of paying patients. So that's when we'll get married and Ma will just have to wait until then."

Lydia shook her head.

"Wouldn't it be wonderful," she said, "if women could carry on teaching after they married and could study medicine knowing for certain that they'd be able to continue those studies through to being licensed?"

"They will one day if Mrs. Stowe has her way," Letty shrugged, "but not necessarily in Mrs. Stowe's lifetime and certainly not in time for me to study without having to find ways and means to get accepted into the required courses. I'm really lucky to have Gussie to guide me through the work that they won't let me study with men this year. The advantage we have in medicine over teaching is that, since they don't actually recognize women as doctors, they can't stop us working when we marry the way the school boards do with teachers."

"Actually, now that I have five years of experience," Lydia said, "I'm thinking I may apply to one of the academies if there are any vacancies next year. They allow you to continue working after marriage, unless you have a baby, of course. I'd rather not teach in a private school because I believe that education is for every child not just those who can afford it, but if it's the only way…"

"It's through private schools that you meet the people who have the influence to change things so it's hardly a bad thing," Letty pointed out. "And that's how Mrs. Stowe managed to teach and earn the money to raise Gussie and her brothers when Mr. Stowe was ill in the sanatorium. It enabled her to save the money to go to New York, too, and study medicine. Of course Nelles Academy is a public school now—"

"And still turning out influential people," laughed Lydia. "Just teaching in Cobourg creates a reputation for teachers because it's where Dr. Ryerson developed education for all children, but I know what you mean. I can, perhaps, do more for the women's movement by marrying and teaching at young ladies' academy then refusing to marry so that I can stay where I am. Believe me, little sister, I am giving it a lot of thought."

"Good," said Letty. "Ma can announce your engagement then?"

"Don't you dare tell her. And don't say anything to Colm when he meets us at the station."

"Of course I won't. I won't have time to stand around chatting anyway. I want to get to Mrs. Grant's, get unpacked and then up to the college to check my registrations. Gussie says they may accidentally-on-purpose leave you off the list – even if you're not allowed in the lecture hall, you need to be on the list or you could end up without the credit. It's hard being a woman…"

CHAPTER TWENTY

"It's good to see you again, Jimmy," Tom said shaking Jimmy McQuire's hand.

The two hadn't met since the year Tom had returned to the Toronto Normal School to take his first class teacher's certificate course. Although they had never had the chance to know each other well, their mutual interest in the well-being of Tom's sister Annie had brought them into contact with each other at several irregular intervals over the years. Now, Tom had the opportunity to finally move away from teaching and studying in Toronto. During the past three years he had acquired both his first class teacher's certificate and a baccalaureate from the University of Toronto, taking short term posts in city schools to finance his studies. He was going to acquire some high school teaching experience at the school he had attended himself in Guelph, where a Ministry of Education grant would afford the opportunity to work with his one-time headmaster in the first stages of integrating agricultural sciences into the school syllabus for public school senior, continuation class students and high school students as well as during teacher preparation in the normal schools. Mr. Tytler, having been the headmaster in Guelph since before Tom's years at the school and held teacher and headmaster positions in several other western Ontario towns before that, naturally understood the need for education in agriculture and farming for rural school populations. Tom's observations during his conversations with Toronto Model School teachers, during his practice time as a second class certificate student at the Normal School, had not gone unheeded. With the subject having now become a focus point in the Ontario Legislature, somebody had connected Tom's remarks with William Tytler's long-held views and the fact that Tom had gone to high school in Guelph and suggested Tom being assigned to assist the well-respected Guelph educator in assessing the ways and means of implementation. For Tom, it would mean teaching regular science and mathematics classes at the school and sitting in on lectures, as well as getting involved in practical work at the nearby Ontario Agricultural College and Experimental Farm. For the summer, he had lodgings at the college while he reviewed the diploma course that was currently in progress there. Many students, of necessity, dropped out at this time of the year when their families required their help as first planting, then haying got underway and the newly appointed college president was quite happy to accommodate him.

"So you're all settled in at the agricultural college, then?" Jimmy didn't wait for an answer. "I thought you must be once I got your note. Hope you don't think I always eat at the top hotels in town."

"Sorry," laughed Tom. "Mr Tytler brought me here the day before last to introduce me to the other men involved in the project. It's the only eating house I know."

"The man has good taste, I'll give you. I've only been a couple of time with clients – only recently at that. A journeyman architect's salary doesn't stretch to such things in the normal course of events. Let's go in – they prefer the term 'dining room', by the way."

The two young men made their way through the lobby to the dining room and were soon seated and enjoying their meal. Tom explained the project he'd been engaged to develop.

"So you teach part of the time and evaluate the ways and means of teaching agriculture the rest of the time?" Jimmy asked.

"The problem is, you see…" and Tom fell to explaining the problems involved in keeping boys in attendance at rural schools. "Here, in Wellington County, the Agricultural College is the answer for many farmers. They can see the use of their sons attending although, even there, half of them don't graduate because they're needed on the family farms just at exam time. But, the point is that the boys get an education that'll be useful to them as farmers whereas going to high school is considered a waste of time to most farmers. What is really needed is for the courses being taught there to be made not only part of the high school syllabus but also taught in the upper standards at elementary school because, as both you and I know, not many children in rural areas even have the opportunity to go to high school. And such courses need to be included in teacher training programs, too."

"I imagine the new president is all in favour. They say he wants to affiliate with the university in Toronto and offer degree courses and…"

"So that's general knowledge, then?"

"Well, probably not with the population generally. My boss is on the school board, among other things – a good buddy of your friend Mr. Tytler, in fact. The Mercury editor, James Innes, used to be, too – before he went to parliament. Remember him? He published that sixteen-year-old boy's essay way back when…"

"I didn't know about your boss. You're right, though. Mr. Mills is very ambitious – he wants to get the university affiliation, but he also sees how so much of the content of the present diploma courses can become part of the public school curriculum. He's one of the chief instigators in getting the Ministry of Education to look at the situation. Oh yes,I did know about Mr. Innes. He was at our meeting here – I'm to write some articles for the paper later on."

"So you're going to be here for a while then?" Jimmy asked. "Annie didn't tell me much in her letter – just said you had a job in Guelph and that she was giving you my address, and my office address, so that you could get in touch when you got here."

"The school board has engaged me in combination with the Ministry of Education contract. It sounds complicated but, basically, it just means that I need to be effective in both areas to keep the job and, since it's a dream job for me, I intend to be. It's going to take a minimum two or three years to complete, possibly more. So, Guelph is going to be home for me for a bit. I don't know it very well though. They think that because I went to high school here, I do. Actually all I did was get off the Grand Trunk and walk to the school each morning and the same thing in reverse in the afternoon for four years. I was a farm boy – a model of the boy I'm now trying to create a suitable education for."

Jimmy laughed. "Well, I can help you there. I've been working here for five years now and there's not much I don't know about the town."

"I'll be taking you up on that – I only ever knew the roads between the station and the high school and up to Wyndham Street to St. George's Square, and Exhibition Park, of course. I have a room right at the college for the summer while most of the students aren't in residence but I'll need to find permanent quarters when the new school year begins with a new intake of first year students."

"You could do what I do and board at one of the hotels. It's the Guelph way – in fact, they may even have a preferred hotel at the high school for where their teachers live, although I imagine it would likely be one without a liquor licence! That's technically a boarding house but they're still known as hotels. You see, the town became full of hotels because the farmers needed somewhere to stay when they came to market but now, with the railways, it's a day trip for a lot of them so there are lots of empty hotel rooms and the owners are really happy to get long term boarders. It's very convenient. Especially for me, since I have to go out of town a fair bit to superintend jobs so, if I rented rooms in a boarding-house, I'd be paying for many nights when I don't get to use the bed. This way, I travel light and can leave anything I don't need either at the farm or at the office, then move back into the hotel when I come back to town. Then, of course, it's a lot easier for meals - often when we're working on preliminary drawings, we work right through supper time and into the night so we eat right there in the office.

Living in a hotel, I'm not bound by a boarding house keeper's schedule and paying for meals I'm not there for. Don't get me wrong – I'd prefer a home, but this is best for now. There are lots of good boarding houses, too. Proper ones that didn't used to be hotels, I mean,"

"I've mostly been in school- or school board-approved boarding houses for the last few years and, of course, the last few years working on the degree has meant being confined to Toronto so it's nice to have somebody to point me in the right direction."

"If you like, since you don't really know Guelph, I could show you around on Sunday," Jimmy suggested. "I was going to go home to Limehouse for the day but I was there last week so they're not necessarily expecting me."

"That would be appreciated, believe me. I'll have friends visiting me so I can hardly bury myself at the college for the summer, although it looks as if I'll be kept busy auditing the summer term courses. But I need to learn something about the town if only *not* to look as if I've been buried."

Jimmy laughed. "Annie already told me how you're hoping Guelph will impress your young lady enough for her to think about starting her clinic here when she finally gets that medical degree and can hang out her shingle. In fact, it would be a capital idea - Guelph is a city now and, since incorporation it's grown tremendously. You're going to be very surprised – probably already are, after seeing all new buildings just around here – the one we're in for a start. The new school buildings, by the way on Catholic Hill – you must have noticed the boys' school, at least as you came over, are our designs. One of my jobs just now is to superintend the builders – not that there's much I can do if I found anything wrong now… except get fired… Don't worry, I know how to keep an eye on things without annoying them. Here, we should move into the public lounge for our coffee."

"It sounds like there's a lot of responsibility," Tom said, as they made themselves comfortable in the lounge beside a window overlooking the street. "Being an architect, I mean."

"Journeyman," Jimmy corrected him. "Not really – here, we're still we're architect-builders and have to know how to construct a building from digging a hole to–" he looked up for inspiration– "to installing the drapery rods. It's not like your friend George in Toronto where the architect works on design then lords it over the builders. I'm not saying your friend does that – probably doesn't seeing as his father started out as a – what did you tell me, a carpenter?"

Tom nodded and picked up the coffee cup that the waiter had poured from the table beside him.

"But often the big Toronto architect firms that win commissions here really annoy the tradesmen, even bring in men from the city which, of course, annoys them even more. They're much more comfortable working with local designers."

"You never thought of working in the city yourself?"

"Me? No way." Jimmy sipped his coffee. "I'm a country boy. Guelph's getting too big for me, if you want to know the truth. Once I can start winning my own commissions, I'm setting up in a town that's still small. Maybe Acton or Georgetown – Rockwood, maybe. I'm happy where I am right now, but this is not where I want to have a home and family."

Tom looked out of the window across the dusty and darkening street to the Golden Lion Dry Goods Store. People were still shopping but he had quite a walk back to the college and, not being entirely familiar with the streets yet, did not want to get lost in the dark. He finished his coffee and turned to Jimmy.

"I'd better get on my way before it gets too dark. Which way do you go?"

"Opposite direction, I'm afraid. I'll walk down as far as the bridge with you. To be perfectly honest, I'd quite likely get lost over there myself. There'll be lights to guide you once you get to the college grounds I should think."

"Oh yes. We were later returning there last night so the gaslights were on but we drove so walking over this evening was the first time I've done it. I don't think there's any danger of wandering off the Dundas Road though – as long as there's some light still." Tom raised his arm to call for the bill. "You know what would really be the answer for men like us not yet at the stage in life of being able to afford a horse and carriage?"

"I know what you're going to say," said Jimmy. "Every fellow I know says the same thing and it won't be long. There's a company in Burlington manufacturing bicycles and one – maybe more than one - of the machinery manufacturers here in Guelph will soon enough follow suit. And you know something else? It won't be the horse and carriage we aspire to for much longer. Somebody will soon come up with a practical way of using steam or electric power – or, maybe, this new petrol engine - to move the carriage by itself."

Tom smiled. "It's a good few years away yet. I think I'll aim at having a horse and carriage – my doctor wife-to-be will surely need transportation long before those horseless carriages take over the roads."

"So you really are set on enticing Miss Letty to settle in Guelph."

* * * *

It wasn't until the last week of August that Letty, accompanied by Hartley, came to visit Tom in Guelph. She had spent the summer working at the Free Dispensary, just as she had done for previous three summers. It was the only way she could get experience that compared to some extent with the hospital internship that, as a woman, was denied to her. The doctors there, busy with their practices and, in summer, the need to take their families on vacation, trusted her – after all, they had trained her themselves – and tended to leave her to direct the nurses, midwives and dispensers on her own for much of the time. At first, she had been afraid these subordinates would resent her. Instead, they admired her determination to obtain a medical degree and were happy to share information on their own specialties with her when she explained the overall requirement of the individual cases. They were all quite sad when she said goodbye to them, having been told that this was the last summer she would be working there. By next summer, she would have her degree and be ready, even if not granted a licence, to start her a practice. The doctors had clubbed together and presented her with a very expensive leather doctor's bag which they said would last her a lifetime. She promised to visit them all when she was back in the city and said she'd definitely volunteer again later when she was established.

She had, however, been thinking more and more of Tom's suggestion that they get married after her graduation next year, and start her practice in Guelph. She had been alarmed at the fact that Tom was talking about something that would last for several years when he had first written to her about being offered the contract to work with on the Ministry of Education's project to develop agricultural education programs for the province's elementary and high schools and teacher training institutes. She was glad for him, knowing that it was an appointment after his own heart – he'd talked about the need for agricultural education in rural schools ever since she had first known him – but, somehow she hadn't imagined them beginning their married life so far away from her family. Of course it made sense – Guelph, after all, was where the Agricultural College was and, naturally that would be where the project would centre. She wondered if it meant their marriage being put off indefinitely but, being in the middle of exams at the time, had determinedly put it out of her mind until it was time to return to Toronto for the summer. Tom had made the suggestion the first evening they had spent together. His own convocation at University College was the next afternoon and his sister would be arriving by train early in the morning. Annie was, of course, the only member of his real family, but his foster parents were taking time out from the planting season to bring their children to the city for the occasion and Letty's own family was providing a celebration tea afterwards. Letty decided that, while she didn't want to disappoint Tom on the evening before his big day, gently said that there was far too much to consider before she could give him an answer. It was different for him. He had learned, of necessity, to adapt to living in different places since childhood but Yorkville had always been the at the centre of her life and, despite taking what everybody thought was a brave step in studying for an unconventional career, she had never really thought about living somewhere far away from her family.

The fact that Annie was coming to the city and going home again on the same day did indicate that train travel in modern times made distances seem less than they used to do, and Tom was not slow in pointing this out. While Letty had not actually been to Guelph, she had travelled as far as Rockwood with Tom to visit the Halliday farm and knew that the town was only the next station west on the Grand Trunk Railway so the distance wasn't really such a consideration as her acceptance as a doctor was. Toronto surely, for a female doctor, was the place to be. The Women's Medical College would finally open for the next school year on Sumach Street. She'd continue to have the support of the Stowes and the suffragette movement. The doctors volunteering at the Free Dispensary would refer those patients they felt were better served by a woman to her.

Letty had thought about the problem off and on throughout the summer. Tom's letters were full of the advantages living in Guelph had over living in Toronto. The experimental farm, a part of the Agricultural College, was in the countryside just across the river from the town. While there were smoke-belching factories, access was quick and easy to the countryside that, indeed, surrounded the town on all sides. It was probably much like Cobourg where she enjoyed living during term time. By contrast to these towns, Yorkville had actually amalgamated with Toronto earlier this year due to the growth of its population in recent years and could hardly be described as the village in the country that it was during her childhood. Yes, she did accept that Guelph appeared to be a nice place to live, but would it be a nice place for a female doctor?

Travelling with Hartley was fun. He had made the trip to see Tom twice during the summer and busily pointed out everything of interest along the way, quite forgetting that Letty had been as far as Rockwood before. Of course her brother was an old hand now at travelling. He spent every summer visiting different places all over the country armed with his cameras and even photographed places that were being called tourist destinations on contract for a railway agent. He was even talking about giving up teaching altogether to concentrate on being what he called an artistic photographer.

The train finally slowed as it travelled over the river and into the Guelph station, and they took their bags down from the rack as it came to a standstill. Hartley helped Letty onto the platform as Tom came running towards them. He hugged each of them and took Letty's bag.

"There's a cab waiting for us," he said adding, as he noticed Hartley's raised eyebrows, "now that I'll be keeping all my earnings, I can afford such things now and again. Besides there's no TSR equivalent here you know! There's what's called the hotel bus – a carriage that meets the trains and takes people to the different hotels – but I thought a cab would better suit my city friends."

"I should hope so, indeed," Hartley rejoined. "Knowing you, I had expected to walk – we'll make a gentleman out of you yet!"

"Stop it, you two," Letty laughed. "Let's get to wherever it is so that we can have some tea and catch up on what we've all been doing."

"Here we are," Tom said as they reached the station fore-court. "It's just a short ride. As I explained in my letter, I still have my room at the College and these are the rooms I'm moving into ready for school – they're halfway between the school and the college so they're ideal. The landlady's had a bed put into what will be my study for you Hartley and Letty will have the bedroom. The windows in both rooms look out over the river. And, as for tea, I've already arranged for the landlady to have it ready for us. It's not a service she usually provides since her boarders are not normally home as this time of the day but a young lady visitor is an unusual occurrence and she thinks it's fitting."

"Little does she knows that it's a suffragist she'll have on her hands…" laughed Hartley.

"Don't be silly, Hartley," said Letty. "she's hardly likely to know what a suffragist is. He's referring to the fact that the TWLG is now officially the Canadian Women's Suffrage Association," she explained to Tom. "We're still ladies. Ladies who get things done – in a little over a month the Women's Medical College will be a fact."

They arrived outside a large house surrounded by a shaded garden across the street from the fields and farm buildings along the banks of the Speed River. Letty looked all around her and relaxed. She had been afraid she wouldn't like it but immediately decided that it would be nice to spend the next few days here.

"The College is over that way," Tom said pointing to the south and a little eastwards. "And the high school is north west of where we started out at the station, so I'll have about a twenty minute walk to whichever one I have to go. Half an hour if I'm going from one to the other since there's a more direct route to the bridge, which is along that way. You can't see much of it this time of the years with the trees in leaf."

Letty looked at him and smiled. "This is really nice, Tom," she said.

CHAPTER TWENTY-ONE

"I'm applying to go to the Stockwell Training College," Harriett wrote. *"It's British and Foreign Schools but Miss Rostick says that doesn't matter now that we have the school boards, and admission depends on the exams not on which kind of school you're doing pupil-teaching at. Best of all they don't charge fees like Battersea – just the entrance fee because their sponsors pay for what the London School Board grant doesn't cover. I don't mean that Uncle Arthur won't pay the fees, it's just that I'd rather he didn't have to so that he'll have the money for John's apprenticeship which I'll tell you about later. And I don't want you and Tom to, either. I have enough for the entrance fee at Stockwell and enough for my board during the exams in July – they take nearly a week and you have to pay for that. Other pupil-teachers from my school have gone there and speak highly of it so I'll even have other girls to travel home with on Sundays by train."*

Annie put Harriett's letter down when the bell rang and the store door opened. The freezing cold had been keeping people at home over the past couple of weeks but, sooner or later, they had to come out to shop.

"Good morning, Alison," she said, slipping the letter into her pocket as her friend stamped snow from her boots on the big mat placed inside the door for the purpose during the winter months. "Don't let the cold in with you! Did you know the overseas post finally came through? I have a letter from my sister in London and Miss Bryden has one from Scotland."

"That's good. Did you hear about the express train that was stuck in the snow this morning. Half the men in the village were helping to dig it out – a pretty good way to get warm, don't you think? I don't think I've ever known it be so cold for such a long time ever in my life! I wouldn't have attempted to walk over here except that I'm right out of tea and Bob said if we have to drink tea made from thrice-used tea leaves again, he'll divorce me."

Annie laughed. "Well, we'd better fix that. How's little Bobby?"

"Oh, he's fine now," Alison told her as she came over to the dry goods counter. "Still coughing a bit, but full of beans. He wanted to come with me but I didn't think that was a good idea. Bob's ma has come round to look after him and the baby. Said she'd come down here for me instead but I didn't think that was a good idea. Thought I'd like to get out for a bit any-way and have a bit of a chat, never mind the cold. I have my own list and hers – just hope it'll all fit in the basket."

She put her large basket on the counter and went over to the stove and sat down on one of the stools there, holding her hands towards it to get the chill out of them. Annie joined her there.

"Like some mulled cider?" she asked. "We're keeping it on the stove here so that our customers can warm themselves through before they venture out again." She picked up the ket-tle o warm mulled cider and poured some into a mug to hand to Alison. "They say there's never been such a cold February.

Hand me your lists and I'll get everything while you're warming up."

"What does your sister say about the winter weather in London?"

"I don't think she's even noticed it. She's full of her plans to apply to a teacher training college. Teachers are trained differently over there. She's been what's called a pupil-teacher for three years now but she has to go to college for three years to get a certificate. Tom only had to learn for six months at the model school in Elora before he was eligible for the normal school – he actually worked out the rest of the school year to earn some money before he went – but he graduated from high school first whereas over there they start the pupil-teacher program at fourteen or fifteen instead of going to high school. Funny, isn't it? Here she is all grown up and she was four and a half years old when I last saw her. Tom and I taught her to count. We made matchboxes and she'd count them out into bundles of twelve."

"Be nice for you to see each other again."

"Maybe we will one day. It sounds as if she'll be pretty busy for the next few years though just like Tom was when he did the sessions at the normal school in Toronto, then all those courses he took at the university. It's nice to see him so well established in Guelph as a teacher at the high school and a Ministry of Education advisor at the same time so that he has the money to help Letty – his wife, you met her, remember? – to get her practice and, most of all, her free dispensary established."

"I hear Jimmy's firm got commissioned to build some big government building in Guelph. He seems to be doing well, too. Maybe, he'll soon have enough money for the two of you to get married and you can go to England on a wedding trip and see your sister."

Annie smiled but didn't say anything. Alison was always trying to get her married off. She carefully wrote up both Alison's and her mother-in-law's accounts, then packed the basket. Just as she finished, Miss Bryden came in from the back room where she had been reading her own letter.

"My cousin's telling me how tired they are of the rain and fog!" she exclaimed. "I wonder how she'd manage in this freezing weather we're having here. I've never known such icy cold. Hello Alison, I see you're thawing yourself out there."

"Morning, Miss Bryden. Your mulled cider hits the spot. I'm fine now. Wish I didn't have to go back out, though. Annie and me – we've been talking about how well those young men are doing in Guelph. The high school teacher and the architect, there."

"Och, that reminds me," Miss Bryden said, slapping her hand on the counter. "Last evening at the Ladies' Fellowship (and not too many made it to the church, let me tell you, so cold it was), Kathleen McGuire was asking me to put aside five yards of the maroon worsted. She wants to make new curtains for her parlour and thinks that'll keep the cold out. Yes, Annie's lucky to have such a successful brother as well as a successful gentleman friend."

"I would hardly have called Jimmy McGuire a gentleman – no offence Annie, but Jimmy and that William, from the Graham's farm, were little hellions back when I was a monitor at school trying to keep them in order when the teacher was busy with the little children."

"Jimmy was a monitor himself when I came here, so your good work must have been an example to him. William, too, come to that," Annie said. "They were both kind to me when the other children weren't very happy about having 'a street arab' dumped in their midst. Not that I *was* a street arab. Tom and I did plan to run away if our uncle attempted to put us in an orphanage so, I suppose we could have been, but a good friend of Miss Macpherson's came to our rescue and took us to her. Of course, the children weren't to know that but, anyway, Jimmy and William were in senior fourth that winter and looked out for me."

"I know. Miss Bryden's right. Jimmy was always a hard worker. He wasn't always kept busy at that stage so he and William would get up to mischief when they'd finished their work. I'd left before the new teacher started but he was much better for the older boys."

"Now that we've got all that out of the way," said Miss Bryden, "what does your sister have to say, Annie?"

"Oh, I haven't finished reading it…"

"I came in and interrupted her," said Alison. "And here's another interruption," she added as the door opened and the bell rang again.

"Yoo hoo," cried Betsy Kruger, stamping her feet. "Stamp you feet now, Henry. Get the snow off. You too, George Junior." This done, she herded the two boys towards the stove. "Some children got badly frost-bitten on their way to school yesterday so they've closed the school until the weather gets better. I thought to would be safe to bring them this far. Unwrap your scarves while we're in here, boys, or you won't feel the benefit when we go back out. I left Sukie looking after Baby

– she didn't want to come out in the cold anyway. William walked over with us so Henry had a ride on his shoulders most of the way. He said to say hello – can't stop as he's on is way to the Wright's farm to help shore up the side of the barn that caved in from the wind storm, 'though I expect it's more to see Nancy, truth be known. Looks to me like they're going to be the next around here to make the trip to the altar. Lucky she's got all those brothers to work their farm, as I don't think my pa would relish losing William after him working for us all these years. Ooh, I do go on, don't I?"

"Have some mulled cider, Betsy," said Annie, moving over to the stove again, "we've got it set up here by the stove for all our customers coming in from the cold. They say there's never been another February as cold as this." She poured the cider into a mug and handed it to her. "Here you are, boys. Henry. George. Now be careful not to spill it."

"We were just talking about William," said Alison. "About how he and Jimmy McGuire used to play around on me when I was their monitor. You remember – you were in Fourth the same time as me."

"Junior Fourth – I didn't do Senior Fourth and didn't get to be a monitor, thank goodness. So how's Jimmy doing, Annie? Last I heard Jimmy's gov'nor was bidding on some big government building they're building in Guelph. That would be something to keep him there for a while wouldn't it? He used to always talk about coming back here to work once he was qualified – how long does it take to be an architect? He must have been there in Guelph seven – no, eight years or more by now. He'll never lead you to the altar at this rate, Annie."

"You can hardly expect the lad to pass up the kind of opportunities he gets in Guelph now, can you?" Miss Bryden said a little sharply. "Where's he going to design government buildings in Limehouse?"

"Well," said Betsy, "I was thinking more Georgetown, say."

"It's still not like Guelph. Guelph's a city now and likely next most important place to Toronto," Annie said. "But, you're right, Betsy. He does want to come back here eventually. He says both Acton and Georgetown are getting big enough now to produce enough business for the area to have an architect of its own. But I think I have some say in when and if I'm led to the altar."

"Annie is still deciding if she wants to be married or to be an old maid like me," said Miss Bryden. "Don't you laugh now, my dears. There's something to be said for not having to wait on a man, to have time to yourself…"

"My goodness," squealed Alison. "Who knew ! We have a suffragist in our midst…"

"What's that?" asked Betsy.

"Don't you read the papers, Betsy? Suffragists are ladies who want to have the sort of jobs like men have and to be able to vote…"

"And not get married?"

"Oh, they get married," said Annie. "My friend, Letty – my brother's wife – knows lots of suffragists. She used to go to their meetings when she lived in Toronto. Her sister gives talks on it at meetings all over the province. Anyway, they're both married. It's got nothing to do with it. There's men who support their cause. People get the wrong idea and think they're against men. They just want to be in control of their lives and have a say in government."

"She had to go and live in Guelph though, didn't she? You told me that," said Alison. "So she wasn't in control…"

"Tom did persuade her – yes, but her friends – the ones with the Women's Medical College –said it was her opportunity to be the first woman doctor in Guelph, so it wasn't just because of Tom. It was very hard for Letty to get all the education she needed in the first place so she had to be a fighter, not the kind of woman to be controlled. Now that she's got her practice going, Tom's the one who's going to have to stay in the area and won't be able to take other opportunities if they come up."

"I didn't know that your Tom's wife was a doctor. I know you have a brother and I remember last year – more than a year, now, I s'pose – when you went to Toronto for his wedding. Isn't that something? A lady doctor. It would be nice to have a lady doctor I would think but I don't know that my George would let me go to one… What kind of people go to her there in Guelph? How do they know about her?"

"Well, you have to know influential people, don't you for anything like that. Tom's been working with the Agricultural College there, as well as being a teacher at the high school, so he knows some important people and then, there are people associated with her friends, both medical and her family in Toronto. And Jimmy helped, too, because he was able to introduce her to the doctors at the Homewood Retreat which he helped to design a couple of years ago. So she actually has an office there where she sees the women for their physical maladies. The women who go there, for treatment of their nervous dispositions, are pretty well off, you know – well, you'd have to be, wouldn't you? Letty says the income from them finances her free dispensary for the poor. She worked at a free dispensary in Toronto in the summer all the time she was in medical school so she's very experienced at that which I think is wonderful, don't you?"

Betsy shrugged. "Still and all, I don't know if it's very seemly. Ladies doing men's work, I mean. Women are supposed to be housewives. I don't know what my George would think if I upped and decided to be something a man's supposed to be…" She shook her head. "I'd better get my shopping and be on my way home in time to make his dinner. You finish up your cider, boys. Here, where did I put that list…"

Later, after she'd gone, Annie and Alison laughed at her simplicity but agreed that, there being so many women like Betsy, the road for women to achieve the education and standing of men was going to be a long and hard struggle.

* * * *

It was mid-afternoon before Annie was able to return to reading Harriet's letter. Miss Bryden had been picked up by Agnes McFarlane who was driving the McFarlane family's sleigh over to the church where the Ladies' Sewing Circle met each week and, while a constant stream of customers kept Annie busy for the first part of the afternoon, this had, at last, begun to dwindle. She poured herself a mug of mulled cider and took it over to the drapery counter. She withdrew the letter from her pocket thinking about how she always enjoyed hearing from her sister. Harriet, ever since becoming competent in reading and writing, had been regular in corresponding with her so that

Annie felt she knew her almost as well as she would have done had they remained together. With their brother John, of course, it was different. He had, after all, been only a baby when she last saw him so that, for him, both she and Tom were strangers. Harriet always kept them informed of his progress and, in this letter – after telling Annie all about her plans to go to the teachers training college, she had news of John. Their little brother was going to be a solicitor, she wrote. He would be articled to one of the Uncle Alfred's solicitors when he finished at Coopers Grammar School next year and, in the meantime, he was to be an errand boy after school and during the school holidays. He had to go from school to the Bow Road office each afternoon, instead of coming home for tea as he used to, and deliver any messages and take the letters to the post office and things like that. Being articled, Harriet explained, was the same thing as an apprenticeship and it would be for five years at the least.

Annie smiled as she thought of the baby who she had fed using a bottle given to her by the local midwife after their mother stopped having any milk due to her weak condition. Some years ago Harriet had sent her a cabinet photograph of John and herself with their uncle and aunt but, it was the baby John whose image came to mind when she thought of her little brother. He would be fourteen in a few weeks and next year old enough to become an apprentice solicitor. He had been fourteen months old when she last saw him.

Harriet's letter became more serious after that. They had asked about the cost, she said, when their uncle told them of the solicitor's decision and he explained how that was the main reason why he had only taken in the two of them after their mother died. He would never have had enough money to support four children and set them all on their way to a secure future. For two children he could manage it. That was why he had taken the younger two to live with him and let the older ones go to Canada.

Annie had no idea how much the apprenticeship would cost but imagined it would be pretty expensive since you didn't hear of too many working class boys becoming solicitors. Uncle Alfred, himself, was only a clerk – a very well respected one, she'd heard, but not an actual solicitor. He was probably right in the decision he had made that dreadful day all those years ago. She was glad really. Her own life with Miss Bryden had turned out for the best and Tom was happy with his. The only thing they both regretted really was being parted from their young sister and brother. She thought of Alison's quip about a honeymoon in England. Perhaps she would, one day, marry Jimmy and go to London for a wedding-trip. Tom said Jimmy was well-respected in Guelph as a result of working for John Hall, so he was always busy. It was funny that Tom should have ended up working in Guelph after all those years studying in Toronto. She was glad he had though. Guelph was much nearer than Toronto and far easier to visit on a Sunday afternoon. She had decided on her last visit to Toronto, which had been on the occasion last year of Tom and Letty's wedding, that she was definitely a country girl. The city had no appeal for her.

She had gone with the Hallidays, with whom she had actually felt quite the experienced city girl. Neither Sam nor Susanna had visited Toronto since the day, more than twenty years before when they travelled by train from Quebec City to the hundred acres of unseen and uncultivated land they had purchased in Eramosa Township. Elspeth, at the impressionable age of thirteen, had been entranced but Malcolm, now a student at the Guelph Agricultural College, thought Guelph was a much nicer town. Annie felt that she agreed with him but hoped that marrying Jimmy wouldn't mean having to live there. She'd much rather stay here. She shook her head, laughing at her own imaginings – Jimmy had never really officially asked her to marry him, after all…

CHAPTER TWENTY-TWO

Jimmy McGuire knew that he was a very fortunate young man. As the youngest member of an Irish immigrant family, the only one born a Canadian, he had been allowed to go to school every day, and on to high school. There, when Jimmy was in his senior year and wondering how to obtain an apprenticeship in engineering or designing – he wasn't quite sure what he wanted to do, but knew he wanted to be involved in building things – Bernie, one of his older brothers, was promoted to being a foreman at the Gowdy and Moore kilns at that time. This led to Bernie coming to mention his young brother during a conversation with Mr. Gowdy, who made arrangements for Jimmy to meet the architect who had designed his house in Guelph. John Hall had begun his adult life as a carpenter but soon aspired to design buildings. The son of an Irish immigrant himself, he doubtless saw in Jimmy, his own younger self and offered him an apprenticeship, explaining that, after impressing the school board members with the design of a number of houses and re-construction of several notable buildings in Guelph, he had been commissioned to build an elementary school in the east end of the town and to expand the existing high school. There would be lots of work for a keen and willing apprentice – mostly copying drawings, but that was how you learned best. Jimmy was definitely keen and willing. That was eight years ago.

In Guelph, they had designed and overseen the construction of schools, houses, the big organ factory on Carden Street and other commercial buildings, and they'd worked on the beautiful Presbyterian church in Galt with its 182 foot spire. He'd taken Mechanics Institute courses, been able to work with other architects with whom John Hall was collaborating, and had continued working, both as a journeyman as well as after becoming fully qualified, with his former apprentice master until his untimely death three months ago. Now, after finishing the outstanding jobs and finding a place for their apprentice, he must start out on his own. Mrs. Hall had insisted her lawyer pay him an extra three month's salary in addition to paying his salary for the work involved in winding up the business. He had all the money he needed to set himself up – and to survive until getting paid for his first commission, without even drawing on the life savings deposited with the post office and earmarked for the day when he and Annie would get married and take a trip back to their homeland, not that Annie yet knew of these plans.

Today, Jimmy had acquired that first commission. His having been apprenticed to John Hall and knowing the local tradesmen had been the deciding factors in his favour as the architect required to draw up plans and oversee the building of a new residence for one of the tannery owners in Acton. While the budget, compared to the jobs he had worked on with John Hall was small, it was a start to running his own business. Looking around the town, before making his presentation, he had not failed to note all the recently built new homes and stores. Acton was definitely growing, he thought as he retraced his steps along Mill Street, and there would be lots of business for him if he could make an impression with this first commission. Over the last few years, he had mostly ridden through the town on the GTR on his way to and from Guelph during visits home to Limehouse and it was quite some time since he had walked along the streets of the town. He had been unaware of the many changes.

He was longing to get on his way back to Limehouse and tell Annie and his parents the good news but, first he must find premises to rent here in the town. If he could only find affordable rooms, he could go and pick up the drawing board and other equipment Mrs. Hall had said was his to keep, and get started on his new life tomorrow. He stepped into the newspaper office.

* * * *

An hour later he was striding down the concession road and through Glen Lawson on his way back to Limehouse, the key to two rooms in a house around the corner from the town hall in his pocket. The owner, a widow, lived in the basement and rented the rest of the house to what she called her "business clients", an insurance company rented the top storey and half of the ground floor was an office and living quarters to a solicitor. The other half was vacant, owing to the doctor who had been renting the rooms going into partnership with another doctor and moving to larger premises. Jimmy could quite easily turn what had been the doctor's office into a bed-sitting room and the waiting room into a studio. He could hardly wait to move in. Dropping into the newspaper office had been the right move – the issue, in which the advertisement for the rooms appeared, had only just rolled off the press and had not yet been distributed. He'd gone back and given the clerk instructions for his advertisement in the Business Listing to begin with the next issue of the paper, noting that an architect he knew in Guelph was advertising. People would be surprised when they found an architect opening an office right in the town of Acton. The clerk had told him the editor was bound to include a paragraph about him in the column he wrote about events in the town so he gave him some details on the work he had done with John Hall and ordered some business cards from the paper's printing department.

It seemed to take no time at all to walk the five miles from Acton to Limehouse and he was soon opening the door of Bryden's Dry Goods and Staples. Annie looked up with a quick smile before picking up the shears to cut the cloth she had just measured for a customer. He wondered if she could read the good news he was bursting to tell her just by looking at his face. Miss Bryden, sitting beside the cash drawer, was saying goodbye to old Joe Morton who had finally brought himself a new straw hat, evidently leaving the disreputable old one to be disposed of by Annie.

"How's it look?" the old man asked Jimmy, who stepped back and held the door open for him.

"Very fine. You'll have all the ladies following you home," Jimmy assured him.

"That'll be the day."

Jimmy closed the door again and went over to Miss Bryden.

"I won't ask," she said. "Not that I have to – it's written all over your face. But Annie deserves to be first to be told – she's been on tenterhooks for you all day. Here Jessie Oldacre, you bring that three yards of calico here and I'll bundle it and put it on your bill."

Annie's customer did as she was told and Annie pushed the bolt of cloth back into its slot on the shelf as Jimmy went over to the drapery and haberdashery corner of the store.

"You got the job and you've found a place to set up in," she said, turning back to him. "Oh, I'm so glad for you."

"They gave me the go ahead, so I went round to the newspaper office to find out what premises were being advertised and found one. The paper had only just been printed so I went round right away, ahead of anybody else, and paid a month's rent. I can move in right away. It needs a good clean first, though."

"Your ma and I will take care of that this very evening if you like…"

"No, no, no. You're invited to a celebration supper tonight. Cleaning and moving will wait until tomorrow. I'm sure Miss Bryden will let you have some time off tomorrow, 'tho…"

"'Tho nothing. I want to help get it ready and Miss Bryden already said that, once you find place, she'll manage on her own for a day, while I help you get set up so we'll tell her that day is tomorrow. She's had a gift set aside for you for some time now," Annie added, lowering her voice. "Don't let on I told you."

"I'm just going to make the tea, you two," Miss Bryden called from the back of the store, "you can stay for a cup, can't you Jimmy? It's still cool enough for a pot of tea yet, despite old Joe

Morton going all out with buying a new summer hat." She went through to the back room without waiting for an answer.

"Take it Jimmy's staying home now – no more gallivanting off to Guelph," said Jessie Oldacre, the lady with the calico, as she opened the door to leave.

"Yes, he has a commission in Acton and is setting up his office there," Annie told her proudly.

"Well, congratulations young man. Won't be long before we're hearing wedding bells an' all, now."

Annie blushed. "We're in no hurry to do that just yet," she said. "It's more important that Jimmy get lots of business first, then makes time to build us a fine house."

"Gallivanting," Jimmy repeated when she had left. "I hope she doesn't really think I spent these eight years in Guelph just gallivanting…"

"Of course, she doesn't. It's just her little joke. You know how proud of you the whole village is! You are going to stay and have tea with us, aren't you? I know your ma's waiting to hear what happened but it won't take long."

"Ma'll be wanting me to bring you along with me. She wasn't expecting me to find those premises so quickly. No more than I was. It was a most welcome surprise. So, I'm going to have tea with you and Miss Bryden, then run over to tell Mr. Pulford of my good luck. He deserves to be one of the first to know, following my progress all these years as he has. And young Freddie's the latest boy to have my old job there after school, so he can take the news to Bernie's house and I expect they'll all come over to Ma's this evening. But I haven't seen William since I came home so I'll just have time to run over to the Graham farm as long as I don't stay too long at the station…"

"You should have stopped there on your way down the road – you went right by the laneway."

"I wanted to get here first. It won't take long for me to run back up there."

"It's a mile up there and a mile back. You should have gone in when you passed by."

"I wanted to tell you first."

Annie smiled and pressed his hand. "That's nice but you didn't have to walk an extra two miles just for me."

"'Course I did. You're the most important person in the world to me."

Annie blushed again. "I think the tea's probably ready. Let's go and see." The door of the store opened just then, and two children came in. "You go ahead and tell Miss Bryden the Wilson girls just came in so I'll be in when I've got their list filled." She crossed to the children. "How was school today, Mary?"

Jimmy went through to the back room as the two children told Annie about what they had been doing at school.

"Tea's brewing, Jimmy," said Miss Bryden. "Sit yourself down at the table. There's good Scotch pancakes to eat with your tea, today." She sat down herself, buttered a drop scone and pushed the plate across the table, indicating for him to sit there. "So, you're going to smarten up Acton, are you?" she said buttering another one of the scones for herself.

"Be nice if I could," Jimmy replied, laughing. "Be a bit of a challenge to design tanneries and manufactories that look smart, though. I'll be happy to have a few houses to build at first. Once I can prove myself, I'll get considered for bigger jobs. Well, I hope so, anyway."

"There's talk they'll be building new draw kilns over at Dolly Varden, you know. That'll mean more men'll be needed. So, maybe they're planning to build more houses to rent to them, like they did when they first started the quarry there, and Mr. Gowdy knows all about you, doesn't he?"

"I don't think he'll remember me. It was a long time ago now that he arranged for me to meet Mr. Hall. He came to Mr. Hall's funeral, but I don't think he noticed me. There were an awful lot of people there – it seemed as if half the city turned out. Anyway, I think it's Mr. William who's running things in Limehouse now. His father is involved in so many of businesses in Guelph now, and is what they call a rising politician, too."

"He knows about you, boy. Don't you worry," laughed Miss Bryden. "Whole village is proud of you getting to be an architect and building the big houses and factories in Guelph. They'll make sure young Mr. William remembers you when he needs them houses built."

"I hope you're right. I can see what Bernie says – he'll know something about it for certain."

"Think a lot of Bernie, the Gowdys do. You want your tea topped up?"

"I haven't had a chance to drink any yet what with you keeping me busy talking, Miss Bryden. Maybe I'll take a sip or two and then you can warm it up." Jimmy sipped his tea and held out the cup to be filled. "Thank you."

"I was just telling Jimmy about the new draw kilns going in at Dolly Varden, Annie," said Miss Bryden as Annie came and joined them. "With professional premises set up in Acton there, he'll get the job of building houses for the extra workers now, don't you think? So, I hope you're planning on getting up early in the morning, Annie, to get up there with mops and pails to get that place ready. You haven't told us where it is yet, Jimmy."

"It's on Bower Street, just around the corner from the new Town Hall, opposite the glove factory."

"Well, the bolt of velvet I've been saving for this occasion will definitely make up into draperies that'll do your windows proud right there by the Town Hall. Now, don't you argue–" she stood up for emphasis "–your Ma and me, we've had it planned for some time now. "Course we didn't know you'd be settling in Acton, but we always figured on making your offices look sophisticated. Come along just this morning, she did, and picked it up so she could get a start on the sewing the rings on the tops. Now she'll be able to get the measurements for the length."

"Well, I'm really grateful. Can't wait to get home now and see how she's doing. You'll certainly have me looking professional between you."

"Bower Street, huh?" Miss Bryden went on. "Well, it's a pity you weren't there a bit sooner, lad. They wouldn't have needed those architects from Toronto and the builders from Brampton, indeed, to build that Town Hall."

Jimmy laughed. "I don't think I'm ready to work on buildings of that scale, yet. Not by myself, anyway."

"You have lots of experience, though, working with Mr. Hall on big city buildings," put in Annie. "Miss Bryden's right about there not being a need for the authorities to go to Toronto…"

"We still don't know why those Mallory people got the job." Miss Bryden interrupted. "They had very few commissions in the area. There was influence at work there, you mark my words. When the young lad won the design competition, there was no reason for not taking it to – well, your Mr. Hall, for instance. He wouldn't have cost any more than people coming from Toronto would he?"

"We worked with the Mallorys in Galt, Miss Bryden" Jimmy said. "They're perfectly deserving architects. Mr. Hall mostly only competed for specialized assignments and smaller commissions on projects outside the Guelph area – the sort of size like the Rockwood and Elora jobs that he entrusted to me, when I became experienced enough, or to Henry, his previous apprentice who was on salary with him the first couple of years I was there. The Town Hall is a handsome building. So is the glove factory that they built."

"I still say there was influence involved there," snorted Miss Bryden.

"There's influence involved everywhere. It was Mr Gowdy got me apprenticed to Mr. Hall in the first place. The Gowdys were influential in getting Mr Hall himself started way before that. Having been apprenticed to Mr Hall is what got me the job in Acton. One day, maybe, I'll be influential in helping other men get started."

"Of course you will," said Annie staunchly. "This is just the beginning. You're going to design buildings that will still be here in Halton County, and Wellington County too, in the next century and the people will say, "That's a Jimmy McQuire house... or church, or school –"

"James, I think, sounds more professional," put in Miss Bryden, rather sternly.

"Yes, James. Although it's hard to think of you as a James..."

"No more than it is to think of you as an Ann," Jimmy said, laughing. "Well, there goes the bell – it was nice to have such a long tea-time without you having to run into the store, Ann. No" – he shook his head – "you're definitely an Annie…"

"And I'd better get in there. I'll be ready when you've done all your visiting."

Annie went into the store, and Miss Bryden began clearing the tea things away.

"Thank you for giving me tea, Miss Bryden. I'll be back to fetch Annie at six o'clock when you close the store."

"Off you go, lad, and tell that young nephew of yours that I'm waiting on the ladies' and children's cotton hosiery I ordered from the Brampton mill. It was supposed to be on the morning train so let's hope they just missed it and it's on the afternoon one."

"I will."

Jimmy left the store and walked down to the station. It was good to be back in Limehouse. Since finishing his apprenticeship and being paid a salary, he had mostly lived in hotel rooms. It had made him feel pleased with himself at first – the young man about town – but the novelty had soon worn off. He had spent too many years in family homes to really be a young man about town – first, with his own family, then with the family where he had boarded for high school in Oakville and more recently his apprenticeship master's home. Of course, he'd still be living alone in Acton, but Limehouse was a little more than an hour's walk away and, as soon as he had proved himself and was able to compete and win more commissions, he'd build a house of his own and he and Annie would get married. If Miss Bryden was right and he did get to build the new workers' houses at the Dolly Varden quarry, they'd be able to get married even sooner than he'd expected.

Yes, he thought, it's time for a formal engagement. He'd propose this evening and they'd announce it to his family, along with the news of the commission and the renting of the premises in Acton. Everybody would be happy with the news, he knew. Perhaps he and Annie would have time to go over to Guelph and give Tom and Letty the news on Sunday. It had been nice having Tom working there, then the two of them since their marriage, almost as neighbours. While they had not had a lot of time for socializing, he and Tom had become firm friends, and he admired Letty for her fight to become a doctor in the hostile male world of medicine. In the time since she had started her practice and opened the free dispensary, she had become so busy that she already needed a partner. When he'd told him about his appointment for the interview in Acton, Tom had laughingly said that, even if he got the job there, he would have to come back to Guelph to add purpose-built premises to their house, if Letty did take on a partner, as there wouldn't be enough room in the house for a himself, two doctors with a large dispensary and waiting room. One must surely make full use of a friend whose qualifications included assisting in the design of two large hospitals!

Thinking about that, Jimmy decided that Glen Lawson would be the ideal place to build their house – his and Annie's. The Acton Grand Trunk station was just up the hill and it was a comfortable walk the other way to Limehouse. Annie was certain to want to continue working at the store until they had a family, possibly even afterwards. Miss Bryden would love being an adopted grandmother. She was always complaining about her nephews not getting married and starting a new generation of Brydens. Yes, Glen Lawson was the ideal place, and he would soon be able to find out if one of the land-owners was interested in sub-dividing a lot. Quite apart from the expansion of the quarry up the hill at Dolly Varden, there was talk of somebody being interested in rebuilding the burnt out Glen Lawson mill. And several factories had located in the south part of Acton over the last few years. Yes, there could be projects within his scope coming up that would realise the capital he needed to get the next stage of his life started.

He crossed the railway tracks to the station platform, remembering the day he'd met the scared little orphan there and taken her up to Bryden's Dry Goods and Staples. She'd been so upset at being separated from her brother and was trying so hard not to show it. His admiration had been won there and then, he thought. Later, he'd learned more about her life in London's tough East End and all that had happened to her and her family before her tenth birthday which, she told him, had been such fun to celebrate on the ship after everybody had recovered from sea-sickness. She explained how she had shared her birthday with Maggie, who had later died so tragically over at Everton, because Maggie had no idea when she had been born and had never had a birthday.

At the station, Jimmy told the station master his news.

"I suppose you and Annie'll be making plans to get wed now then?" commented Mr. Pulford.

"It'll be a while yet," he replied. "I need to get a lot more work before I can start working on my own house but you're the first to know that I'm expecting to make our betrothal official this evening."

"That's no surprise. I knew you two were made for each other back that day she arrived here. Couple of children who were going places – knew that from the start, I did."

Jimmy laughed. "They say you don't miss much, Mr. Pulford. Where's young Freddie? I wanted him to deliver a message to his father."

"I sent him down to the paint factory with a shipment but I'll tell him to tell the family your news."

"About the commission and the premises I've rented – not, about Annie and me. I need to talk to her first."

"Count on me. I don't think she'll be too surprised though. Half her customers have probably asked her about it at one time or another."

"I suppose so." Jimmy conceded. "I have to get up to the Graham's farm to see William so I'd appreciate you giving Freddie the message. 'Bye for now."

He left the station and walked briskly eastwards again towards the Graham Farm. He whistled as he strode along. It was good to be alive in this age of opportunity.